
★

The appearance of the body was puzzling. Although the clothes were worn and old, the fingernails on the hand lying in the anthill were clean and looked like they'd been manicured. The hands looked soft, not the hands of a field-worker or heavy laborer. The watch—Cartier—would have looked right at home on the elegant wrist. The man's dark curly hair was recently barbered, trimmed close to the scalp. There was discoloration and some swelling under his right eye, which didn't seem to have anything to do with the car tracks.

I was puzzling over the inconsistent details—careful grooming and expensive watch; cheap, worn clothing—when I heard two cars pull to a stop, the slam of a door, footsteps on gravel. "Down here," I called.

Hen and Dwight crunched down the slope.

"Don't tell me Tanner's really managed to do some damage," Hen drawled, hitching his belt.

★

"Definite down-home flavor, low-key humor, and comfortable prose..."

—*Library Journal*

"A delightful and entertaining read."

—*I Love A Mystery*

Linda Berry

DEATH AND THE HUBCAP

WORLDWIDE®

TORONTO • NEW YORK • LONDON
AMSTERDAM • PARIS • SYDNEY • HAMBURG
STOCKHOLM • ATHENS • TOKYO • MILAN
MADRID • WARSAW • BUDAPEST • AUCKLAND

DEATH AND THE HUBCAP

A Worldwide Mystery/January 2002

First published by Write Way Publishing, Inc.

ISBN 0-373-26409-7

Dedication

Many friends have encouraged and supported my writing, especially my critique group from the Denver Woman's Press Club, my cousin Johnny Shuman whose storytelling and experience with police work in south Georgia have been a priceless inspiration and resource, and Jerry Berry without whom I cannot imagine even myself, much less the people and events of Ogeechee.

Those who deserve special thanks for helping me comb out errors are Jo Anne Haynes, Pat Barnett, my sister Jackie Swensson, and again, Jerry Berry. Thanks, y'all.

While I hope my story will have the ring of truth and believability, the real truth is that all the people and events are fiction. I've heard of real people who make sculptures from automobile parts, and I've heard of real people who get around using only a hubcap and imagination, but the people in Ogeechee who do those things, like all the others in the town, are products of my imagination.

ONE

IT HAD BEEN a slow-moving Saturday morning. Henry Huckabee, Ogeechee's Chief of Police, was slouching against the doorframe between the dispatch room and the file room, where I, Trudy Roundtree, was sitting at the typewriter working on incident reports from the day before. Hen was watching me work. Maybe he wasn't trying to get on my nerves, but odds are he was, so I was trying to ignore him.

Hen added me to the police force a couple of years back because our grandmother (Jessie Roundtree) and his mother (my Aunt Lulu) leaned on him to give me a job so I wouldn't move back to Atlanta. They reasoned that all I'd had in Atlanta was heartbreak in a variety of sizes and colors, and they were looking out for my best interests as they saw them. Hen grudgingly went along, but he cuts me no slack and makes the job as safe and tedious as possible, no doubt hoping I'll decide I'm bored in Ogeechee, even with a job, and will get myself off his payroll and his conscience. As the only male in the immediate family circle, he's old-fashioned enough to feel like he ought to be the protector of the women. As the chief of police and my boss, he's supposed to put me—a police officer—in contact with people who might not have my best interests at heart. I'll admit, but not to him, that I know he has a problem reconciling the two roles. Understanding his dilemma doesn't make it easy for me to put up with. Besides being his cousin, I'm the only female on the force, so I have to take a double dose of aggravation. So far, the only satisfying course of action I've found is to do my best to make sure he suffers at least as much as I do.

Hen's attention was distracted from me when Dawn, the dispatcher, took a call. I was relieved, but only briefly. The next thing I knew, Hen was looking my way again and wearing a smirk on his face that boded ill for me.

"To serve and protect, Trudy, to serve and protect," he said. The normal crime rate in Ogeechee being what it is (low), Hen's fond of lecturing on the importance of the service aspect of the job over the crime-fighting aspect, so this comment didn't alarm me. It was the smirk that did that. Luckily for me, not all the genes that make Hen such a pain in the...well, a pain...are sex linked, so I sometimes manage to hold my own.

"That's what I signed up for, Your Excellency," I said, as perkily as I could manage. Sometimes if I'm irritating enough I can deflect him from whatever evil purpose he has in mind. This time what he had in store for me was so satisfying he was undistractable.

"It's Tanner Whitcomb," Hen said, and his smirk threatened to become a full-fledged grin. "Says he's run over somebody."

For you to understand why the chief of police would be slouching and smirking over a report that somebody has been run over, instead of, for instance, calling an ambulance and hightailing over to the scene, you'll have to know more about Tanner Whitcomb.

Tanner grew up in Ogeechee just like Hen and I did, and everybody knows him, or at least knows who he is. Most people probably wouldn't recognize him up close, though, because he's usually seen from a distance, walking along the side of the road out on the edge of town, picking up aluminum cans to recycle to augment his meager monthly check from the county—what Dwight Wilkes, who hired on with Hen when he retired from being a prison guard, calls Tanner's "crazy check." Tanner walks; that's all he does, although if you don't want to get him stirred up, you don't let on that's what you think he's doing. As far as he's concerned, he's driving, and that accounts for the hubcap he's always holding out in front and turning like a steering wheel. If you get close enough you can usually hear engine noises coming from his throat, complemented by high and low whines when he's pulling a hill and has to downshift. When insulted or inconvenienced by other motorists, he pounds the center of his hubcap and honks or gives the highway salute.

Some people like to stir Tanner up, tease him, and some of those people are employed by the Ogeechee Police Department. That's one of the reasons—but only one of the reasons, as I have already tried to suggest—that Hen likes for me to respond to calls about Tanner. When Dwight goes out to help Tanner change a flat (which has happened), it doesn't always add to the peace of the municipality. Being a guard at a maximum-security lock-up made Dwight well trained, if not overtrained, for most of the business that comes our way. It also made him mean and cynical. I don't doubt he had natural talent along those lines, but his work experience surely helped.

Me? I have never felt so low about myself that I had to stomp on somebody else just so I could be sure I was standing taller—especially if that somebody else was somebody like Tanner—and my grandma raised me not to be rude just for the sake of it. The situation was a little tricky the first time Hen sent me on a Tanner call to the grocery store parking lot, where Tanner said his battery was dead and would I give him a jump.

"Where's the battery?" I asked.

"Women!" Tanner said. "Don't know thing one about cars!" At first I thought Hen or Dwight had put him up to it, but later I found out that sexism is as much a part of Tanner as his body odor and the wine bottle in his pocket. I won't say it doesn't bother me, but at least I know how to deal with it, and I consider the source. I figure Tanner has an excuse Hen and Dwight don't have. At least Hen doesn't.

Even in my most insecure moments, I'd be secure enough to know a reasonable person couldn't expect me to know where the battery is on an imaginary car, so I made an on-the-spot decision that has helped me in all my subsequent encounters with Tanner: I handle him the same way I handle Hen's six-year-old daughter, Delcie. I play along.

"I'm not familiar with this particular model, Tanner," I said. "You're going to have to show me where to put these cables."

"I'll do it myself," he said scornfully. "Gimme the cables."

Fine. I fished the jumper cables out of my trunk and watched with real interest as Tanner attached one end to my front license plate and the other end to the hip pocket of his faded brown jumpsuit, fussing the whole time about what was the world coming to when women are in uniform and carrying guns and don't even know how to jump start an engine. Grocery shoppers on the way in and out of the store eyed Tanner and me. Most managed not to come too close to us. Nobody offered to help.

Finally Tanner had all the adjustments made and told me to rev 'er up. Okay. I stepped back into my car and revved 'er up. Apparently it worked, because he went on his way without so much as a thank-you-ma'am. The cable pulled loose from his battery as he drove away, mercifully sparing me from having to chase him down and pull him over to get it back. When Hen asked me about it later, in front of Dwight, naturally, I said I thought maybe Tanner ought to have all his fluids checked because he seemed to be about a quart low on everything but alcohol.

All of which goes to explain why it was with a mild sense of being witty that, upon being told that Tanner had run over somebody, I asked, "Anybody hurt?"

Hen looked at Dawn and she answered. "I don't know, really. A woman named Bessie Overstreet called in. She said Tanner flagged her down and told her to go get the police because he'd run over somebody and we better come look. She said he was upset."

"I can see where he would be," I said.

"You better run on out there and see what it's about. You can save those reports for later." Hen might have thought he was doing me a favor, knowing how I hate doing the reports. Little as I like Tanner, I'd rather serve and protect even him than sit in the office on a beautiful morning and write reports.

But I didn't want to appear eager. I managed a sigh and a pseudo-wistful glance at the computer. "Well, okay then. Where'd this accident occur? Where do I run out to?"

"Miz Overstreet said she was coming back from Glennville, so out that way," Dawn said. She was answering my question, but she was looking at Hen for clues about how she was supposed to be taking this. She was having trouble knowing how seriously we were taking this call, but she idolizes Hen and lives in fear that she'll disappoint him so she was being careful. Hen's smirk had by now frankly given way to a grin, but that didn't seem to be helping Dawn.

"In town?" I asked.

"Find out," Hen said. We have a constant tug of war with Rufus Badcock, the county sheriff, over jurisdiction. Naturally, I wouldn't have minded being able to hand Tanner's problem over to him. Just as naturally, Hen would want to stick me with it if he could.

"I'm on my way," I said, and left Hen grinning and Dawn unenlightened about the source of the humor. She's a natural-born straight man—simple, sweet, and literal-minded. She started working for Hen right out of high school. I started working on her lamentable case of hero worship as soon as I took my job, but I've still got a long way to go.

Leaving the station, I followed Court Street to Main Street, turned south, toward Glennville, and started looking for Tanner, thinking how nice it was to be out of the office and away from Hen, even if I was headed for Tanner.

It was a beautiful morning, the kind of day that reminds me how much I love south Georgia. Pines are the dominant tree around here, so we don't have drastic changes of season like you get farther north, with vivid color just before everything drops its leaves for the winter. It was mid-September but it wasn't even cool, and the trees that do shed hadn't gotten around to giving it any thought. It didn't take me long to find Tanner, sitting on the ground with his back to the road and leaning against a guardrail on a bridge, on the east side of the road, inside the town limits.

I slowed to a crawl when I got close, crossed the road,

and pulled off onto the gravelly shoulder. Now I could
see that Tanner was curled forward over his hubcap. His
overalls were covered with fresh dirt, as though he'd spent
some time wallowing around on the ground, and his newish Falcons cap was also dirty and askew. A half-empty
wine bottle with a label showing a palm tree leaning over
in a hurricane lay in the dirt beside him. He didn't move,
even though he must have heard me coming. I walked
around to face him.

"Hey, Tanner."

When he looked up at me, his expression was a mixture
of belligerence and fear.

"You!" he said, his glance darting away from me in
disgust and toward the shadows under the bridge.

"Uh-huh. Me. What's the matter?"

"Women!" he said, and the idea of his innate superi-
ority seemed to perk him up. "I told that woman."

"Miz Overstreet said you told her you ran over somebody." His whole body began to shake. I took a step back
from the rich combination of odors—old sweat, wine,
grease—that wafted my way. "I guess you'd better tell
me about it. Who did you run over?"

"Don't know."

"Well, what makes you think you ran over somebody?" This was delicate ground. I tried to sound busi-
nesslike and respectful, and I tried not to think of how
much Hen and Dwight would enjoy my predicament.
"Did you...did you feel a bump?" His glance slid away
from me again. There was no doubt that something had
upset him.

I nudged the wine bottle with my shoe. "You been
drinking and driving?" Of course, technically, he could
not have been drinking and driving, but I've never been
able to count on finding the point where Tanner's fantasy

intersects with reality. Not knowing if he's been taking his medication as directed makes it even trickier. Anyway, on that morning it was clear he'd been drinking. Whether he'd hit the bottle before or after the "accident," and whether it would make him less coherent or more agreeable, remained to be seen.

His eyes narrowed as he considered the pros and cons of the situation. Clearly, he wasn't sure how serious a drunk driving charge would be. He went for simplicity. "No," he said finally, "that bottle ain't mine." But he licked his lips at the sight of the sloshing wine.

"Okay, then. Let's start over. How do you know you hit somebody?" No response. "I wouldn't worry about it, then," I told him. "Maybe you didn't really hurt whoever it was."

"He's lying there dead, ain't he?"

"Is he? Where? I don't see him." I made a big show of looking around, inviting Tanner to look with me at the wide ditch along the shoulder of the slightly elevated road, the pines and dense tangle of underbrush on the far side of the ditch, the gentle grassy slope down to the river under the bridge and up again on the other side. I was getting a little wistful for my untyped reports.

"Tanner, you've got to help me a little." I crouched beside him, but not too close, pulled out my notebook and pen, and tried to be patient. If there's one thing I know about children and slow thinkers, it is that they can't be hurried. As Hen might say in one of his folksy moods, you can pull a fishing line through water, but you can't push it. Finally, Tanner looked up at me. He looked at my notebook and my pen. He looked back at me steadily for a few seconds, then he darted a glance toward the shadows under the bridge. About the fourth or fifth time he did that, I began to get it.

Following his glance down the slope where free-spirited motorists have worn an access road down to the riverbank under the bridge, I saw something in the deep shadow at the base of a piling. Now we were getting somewhere. Whatever that was—a goat? driftwood? a stray dog?—had to be what had upset Tanner. I went to take a closer look. With every step I took, it became more obvious that the shape that had appeared to be a pile of trash or an animal partially covered by leaves was neither. As I got closer and my eyes adjusted to the shadow, the shape began to look more and more like a person. A rock became the bottom of a shoe. The shoe was on a foot. It was attached to a leg. It wasn't moving.

Ogeechee is near enough to the state prison it's not unheard of for us to have wayward tourists on unauthorized leave, so it doesn't hurt to be a little cautious. ''You just wait there while I take a look,'' I called back to Tanner, not that he'd shown any inclination to follow me. With my weapon drawn, I approached what was undoubtedly somebody lying very very still in the sand by the piling. It took no more than a glance for me to know there was no need to be worried about danger from this man, though. The fixed, dark, staring eyes—with a coating of sand that had not been blinked away—told me there would be no pulse. His dangerous days, if he had ever had any, were over.

He lay on his back with the right arm close to his side, the left arm outflung, the hand resting in an ant hill. The ants might originally have resented this intrusion but had adapted and were matter-of-factly going on with their lives, some detouring, the single-minded ones going in as straight a line as possible right over the café-au-lait-colored wrist. Tire tracks ran the length of his body, from right leg to left shoulder, just missing his jaw. Sand and grit clung to his clothing. His faded jeans and cotton sports shirt looked neat and clean except for that track. Where they weren't rumpled from the kneading and crushing action of the vehicle as it ran over the body, the clothes showed signs of having been pressed. The athletic shoes were worn, but the socks looked newish and clean. Touching nothing, I went back to my cruiser and called for help.

"Six twenty-four, Ogeechee. Looks like I've got a ten fifty-seven out here," I said into the radio, using the code we like to think will keep any riffraff who can afford a police radio from knowing everything that's going on in town.

"He really did kill somebody?" Dawn gasped.

"No, Dawn. I'll bet my pitiful little old paycheck he didn't. Will you tell His High-and-Mightyness and get things goin'?"

"Right," she said, but couldn't resist adding, "Trudy, you shouldn't talk about him like that."

"Right," I said. I surely do have a lot of work to do on her.

Knowing the scene was about to become cluttered with emergency and investigative teams, and guessing the confusion would not add to Tanner's ability to be coherent, I figured I had about five minutes to see what I could find out from him about what had happened.

"Tanner! Come down here!"

"Don't want to."

"Do it anyway."

After a few seconds I heard the rumbling and growling that told me Tanner was getting in gear. An eerie whine told me he was doing it under protest. He stopped well back from the body.

"Are you sure you don't know who that is?"

He clutched his hubcap and shook his head violently, his pale eyes fixed on mine, his lank, dirty, gray-blond hair flopping this way and that.

"Did you even look at him?"

He shook his head again. "I think he musta been drunk," he volunteered. Well, it was something.

"Why do you say that?"

"Couldn'ta missed seeing me."

It began to dawn on me that Tanner was even further out of the loop than usual. He really didn't know what had happened. "When did you first see him?" I asked.

"I come down here lookin' for cans. I was backin' out. Made a wide turn and hit him. What's he doing over there's what I wanta know."

I tried to translate what he said into something that made sense, then translate my thoughts into a language Tanner would respond to. "So you're telling me you clipped him when you were backing up for a turn?" I hazarded.

"That's what I said."

"Okay. I just need to get it straight. And what then?"

"I got that woman to call the po-lice, and they sent you." His sneer showed he was recovering a little.

"So you didn't look at him. Then how did you know you ran over him?" The question seemed to unnerve him. He started cursing again and folded his hands under his armpits, the hubcap in his right hand practically wrapped around his back. This protective gesture didn't work out quite like he'd planned because it called my attention to the gold watch on his dirty wrist.

"Nice watch." He stuck his wrist farther under his armpit. "You been robbin' a dead man, Tanner?"

"No."

"You kill him for his watch?"

"It was an accident. I told you. He ain't got no use for it, has he?" Tanner was getting worked up again.

"You give me that watch and go wait up by the road, away from the crime scene so you don't mess anything up 'til we find out what happened."

"It ain't your watch."

"No, it ain't, but it ain't yours either and I'm taking custody of it. You want to add robbery to the charges?"

With a hate-filled look at me, he removed the watch and handed it over. I was glad he didn't ask me what charges I had in mind. Not vehicular homicide and not driving under the influence. Not hit and run, since even if it turned out that he might technically be said to have hit, he hadn't run.

"You take anything else?" He turned his back to me and shook his head. "You stay out of my way, then. When Hen gets here he'll want to talk to you."

"Huckabee shoulda come in the first place," he said. As I turned my attention back to the scene, I could hear sputters and whining as Tanner pulled up onto the shoulder. He crossed the ditch and began to idle in the shade of a pine tree.

The appearance of the body was puzzling. Although the clothes were worn and old, the fingernails on the hand lying in the anthill were clean and looked like they'd been manicured since mine had. The hands looked soft, not the hands of a field worker or heavy laborer. The watch— Cartier—would have looked right at home on the elegant wrist, and it was still ticking away. No help there on the time of death. *Takes a licking and keeps on ticking,* I thought, but that was a different brand, and this situation wouldn't make a very good commercial, anyway. The man's dark curly hair was recently barbered, trimmed close to the scalp. There was discoloration and some swelling under his right eye, which didn't seem to have anything to do with the car tracks.

I was puzzling over the inconsistent details—careful grooming and expensive watch; cheap, worn clothing—when I heard two cars pull to a stop, the slam of a door, footsteps on gravel. "Down here," I called.

Hen and Dwight crunched down the slope.

"Don't tell me Tanner's really managed to do some damage," Hen drawled, hitching his belt.

"No, not on the evidence, but somebody did. I've never figured out exactly what Tanner is capable of, but I'd be surprised if he could produce tire tracks." I stood aside so they could get a look. "Funny place for him to be, since he's obviously not a teenager looking for a little privacy, but the sandy car tracks on the body look like a match for the soil right here, so I'm guessing this is where he was killed. I don't think he's local and whoever killed him didn't rob him. Funny place for an accident, though. He was wearing this." I held up the watch I'd taken from Tanner.

Hen gave me that amused, surprised look he puts on when I'm unguarded enough to give the impression that I care enough what he thinks to be trying to impress him. That look always brings out the worst in me. I looked him up and down. "He's shorter than you by a couple of inches at least, maybe about five-ten or -eleven, and he took better care of himself than you do, too. Maybe one fifty to your two twenty."

That wasn't fair, but I had to do something to wipe that look off Hen's face. He works out and probably doesn't weigh more than a solid two hundred pounds, which is okay on a six-footer. He claims six-one, and I don't challenge him on that directly since I'm five-six and claim to weigh one twenty. Some things are just off limits.

We made what observations we could while we waited for the ambulance and the Georgia Bureau of Investigations mobile forensics van, which has to come from Statesboro, close to fifty miles away. When it arrived, the crime scene technicians whipped into action, looking for whatever there was to be learned from the scene. As the day wore on they took plenty of pictures showing how the body lay in relation to the piling and the rutted road, with close-ups of some of the tire tracks.

While the technicians were doing their stuff, Dwight and Hen went at Tanner again, but even they weren't able to get any more out of him except that he swore he had flagged down Mrs. Overstreet right after he ran over the man, which couldn't have been more than twenty minutes before I got to the scene. I didn't need an autopsy to tell me the man had been dead a good while longer than that.

I had an inspiration. "Hey, Dwight," I said, pointing to the wine bottle. "Maybe you better get the lab to take that in and test it for fingerprints. Tanner says it isn't his."

Dwight looked at me as if I'd lost my mind; Hen looked thoughtful; Tanner tried to look shrewd.

"Good idea," Hen said.

"Maybe it is mine," Tanner said, eyeing the wine.

"Well, then, maybe we'd better give you a roadside sobriety test," I said.

"That balloon thing?"

"Oh, yeah, and that walking thing."

Hen shot me a disgusted look that almost evened the score for his earlier amusement, but he rose to the challenge. "Yeah, Tanner. We may have to give you a ticket for having an open bottle of an alcoholic beverage in the vehicle, at least,'' he suggested.

Tanner apparently decided that the prestige of having a DUI appealed to him. He stuck his arms out from his sides, and began a wobbly heel-to-toe walk along the edge of the road.

Hen and I left Dwight and Tanner to amuse each other and went back down the slope to watch and make our own notes and diagrams of the scene. When the photographers were finished, the carefully gloved investigators placed the body on a sheet. They painstakingly examined everything they found near the body and placed it on the sheet. There wasn't all that much, if you don't count sand and ants.

One of the crew held up a scrap of cloth I'd noticed earlier lying partly under one of the dead man's shoes. It wasn't a rag, as I'd first thought, but a rumpled square, dirty but not old, about fifteen inches on a side, with a small design in one corner.

"That wouldn't be a monogram, would it?" I asked.

The technician grinned at me. "Like maybe the driver made everything easy for you and dropped a hanky for you with his initials on it? No such luck. Looks like a picture of a bird. Maybe an owl." Yes, an owl. I nodded. He dropped it onto the sheet.

The driver's license in the ostrich-leather wallet in the man's rear pocket identified him as Lester DeLoach and gave an address in Atlanta. The wallet and license joined the other items beside him on the sheet.

Finally the on-site investigation was wrapped up—literally. The technicians wrapped the sheet around the body and the collection of potentially useful objects, zipped the whole grisly package into a plastic bag, and slid it into the ambulance, which headed off to the mortuary.

What had started out as a low-key Saturday of catching up on paperwork had spun into something much more like what I used to think police work was about. Back when Hen was briefing me on the job—and trying to talk me out of it without being so obvious about it that I'd catch on—he claimed Ogeechee's crime situation was more like the country lanes of Mayberry RFD than the mean streets of New York City. Now that I've been at it for a while, I have to agree. That's not to say we don't have crime. We have people, so we have crime. Something about original sin, I guess. Still, our crime situation is small-town enough that I hadn't automatically assumed murder when I responded to Tanner's call. Even the presence of this body under the bridge didn't have to be murder. It could have been an accident, but I didn't think so. This was a strange place for anybody to be on foot. Whoever had run this man down had to have known it. Was it a drug deal gone wrong? That wouldn't be unheard of, even in sleepy Ogeechee.

Neither the man's name nor his address meant anything to me, but there was something familiar about him. Even without the Atlanta address on the driver's license, I'd have bet a summer's worth of Georgia peaches that the dead man didn't belong in Ogeechee. On the other hand, I'd have bet a June's worth of sweet corn that I knew him from somewhere. The big question was why Lester DeLoach had come down from Atlanta to end up under a bridge in Ogeechee with tread marks on his shirt and sand on his eyeballs.

TWO

BY THE TIME I got back to the station, leaving Hen and Dwight to decide what to charge Tanner with, it was into the afternoon. "Phil Pittman's been trying to get you," Dawn told me.

I punched in his number. "Hey, Phil."

"Hey, Trudy. You want to run away with me again? Next weekend? I've got a press release here somewhere. Just a minute."

Phil's the chief of Ogeechee's volunteer fire brigade; the editor, publisher, and main reporter for *The Ogeechee Beacon,* our weekly insight into affairs of note in the county; and, somewhat to my surprise, a friend. A good friend. More than a friend? How much more? I'm still trying to figure that out. Phil's a little older than I am, and we managed to grow up more or less alongside each other without it making much difference to either one of us. Now we're becoming friends, partly because there aren't very many single people of our generation in town. Most people who grow up here either light out for greener pastures as soon as they can or stick around to cultivate the family pastures and marry somebody with the same idea.

I pretty much fit the first category—the ones who leave—except that I came back to town about three years ago. I went to Atlanta as a bride, hung on after a hunting accident made me a widow, recovered a bit, then endured a brief disappointing romance before falling into the kind of depression that made me yearn for the womb that Grandma and Ogeechee represented. I'm not all that far into my thirties but for a while I was feeling—and acting—like an old, old lady. My job on the police force, which I took mainly to irritate Hen, turned out to be something I liked, and I started coming back to life.

Phil falls into the second category—the ones who stay in Ogeechee, marry, and settle down—except that he never did get married. Phil takes most of the photographs for the *Beacon*. On his own time he indulges in more serious, artistic photography, kind of an antidote to the line-'em-up-and-shoot-'em pictures that document various civic events for the paper. We renewed our acquaintance by working together on a fire that involved a dead body. It turned out to be a murder case, and circumstances beyond Hen's control put me in charge of investigating— and solving—the case. Phil and I celebrated by taking in a photography exhibit in what the OPD, for a number of sufficient reasons, calls Hot-lanta. We had such a good time on that trip that we did it again. And again. It's been a priceless contribution to my mental health. Much as I love Ogeechee, those years in Atlanta showed me there's a lot to appreciate in the world outside our town limits.

I know our trips raise eyebrows—two single people going off together!—but I figure it probably does as much for the mental health of Ogeechee's older generation as it does for mine, since it gives them something to talk about besides comparing everybody's medication. Even Aunt Lulu hasn't had the nerve to ask me right out if we're up to hanky-panky, which would be the closest anybody will come to asking to our faces if we stay in two rooms or only one.

Hearing Phil's voice on the phone now completed some complicated crosswired circuit in my brain and I had a vivid recollection of a trip we'd made several weeks earlier. We took off without any definite plans beyond the general idea of dressing up a little and getting a whiff of the air up there. We don't have a movie theatre in Ogeechee, so I was looking forward to an orgy of films; I knew I could leave it up to Phil to ferret out something more socially redeeming, such as an art gallery.

Part of the fun of our getaways is that, unlike in Ogeechee, nobody knows us. That means we're free to reinvent ourselves each time and explore new ideas without having to explain ourselves to people who think they already know everything there is to know about us. Hen, for instance, would never understand why anybody would want to spend good money to stay in a hotel when he could sleep in his own bed and eat his own wife's (or mother's) cooking, let alone waste time looking at stuff in an art gallery. Art galleries? I figure they're great places to observe people, more interesting than the zoo to someone in my line of work. As far as I can tell, Phil likes the art.

On that particular trip, we went up on a Friday afternoon and got there in time to have the Blue Plate Special at the Buckhead Diner. (We keep passing on the Kudzu Cafe because I'm not sure I'm ready for what I might find on the menu. Kudzu soup? I've heard a theory that the only way to keep that invasive vine from snaking its way all over the South and smothering it to death is for everybody to start eating it.)

After we ate, Phil humored me by going to see an old movie about a woman who joined the army and had to shave her head and take all kinds of guff while she was trying to prove herself. I admired her toughness. I have my own kind of toughness, like everybody else, but I sometimes think I'd be better off if I had a more highly developed aggressive instinct. Too much Sunday School in my upbringing warped me, I guess. Some of what she went through reminded me of my position on the OPD, although that's gotten a little better since I solved that fire/murder investigation and Hen decided I'm not just a bubble-headed nuisance amusing myself by playing cops and robbers to pass time until I figure out what I really want to do.

We idled through the day on Saturday, taking our time and enjoying the various outdoor sculptures along the downtown section of Peachtree Street. The gallery we had gone up to visit turned out to be a disappointment. All the paintings had an element that I found unsettling, unwholesome somehow—a doll without its head, a dead snake almost hidden in a still life. We didn't spend much time there, but down the street we happened on another place that was having an opening reception for exhibits by what seemed to me to be a pair of wildly mismatched artists.

The Upstart Gallery was one of those places so small and bare you know it has to be very expensive because they sure can't be paying the rent with volume sales. Except for the sprinkling of people and the well-supplied buffet table, there was nothing in the place but gleaming hardwood floors, low blocks of polished stone supporting sculptures that looked like they were made out of old car parts, and walls covered in palest gray linen serving as a background for romanticized oil paintings. One painting showed children playing with a puppy in the dirt in front of a tobacco barn about to be overtaken by kudzu. That kind of thing. Phil humors me by going to cheesy movies; I try to humor him by learning how to analyze the art and discuss it intelligently. I've still got a lot to learn, but I'm trying. My immediate impression at this exhibit was that the rough sculptures and the meticulous brushwork on the pastel paintings clashed with each other; the styles seemed to fight instead of complementing each other.

Even the titles came from different worlds. The rough, relatively crude shapes of the sculptures carried titles that proved that I may not know much about art, but I recognize a junk car when I see it. Where the paintings were labeled with titles that struck me as sappy, like "Wagging into a New World," the sculptures were "'59 Ford," and "'63 Chevy." I liked that, since it gave the art-loving public (me, for instance) credit for being able to figure out that the '59 Ford had metamorphosed into a huge dragonfly and the '63 Chevy was a Venus fly-trap big enough to swallow a rooster. Now there was an artist with down-home roots and a sense of humor as well as a way with a welding torch! It was only on the price tags that the two artists had anything in common. Big numbers.

The more time we spent looking at the pieces, between trips to the sushi and skewered fruit at the buffet table, the more I began to appreciate the way the differences in texture and shape and color in the two art forms set each other off. I still preferred the car parts, but I began to see something in the paintings. Maybe there's hope for me as an art appreciator.

I was polishing up a comment or two designed to show Phil how perceptive I was, and running my tongue over my teeth to make sure there wasn't any seaweed stuck there, when I saw Brad Phipps across the room. Brad is one of the reasons I came back home to Ogeechee (the brief, disappointing romance); I was glad to note that the only emotion I could identify when I saw him was vague amusement and generalized good will. Our tepid romance lasted less than six months and came to an end about the same time I lost my job and decided to go back home to Ogeechee. We had parted on good terms. Still, I thought my response to his appearance was very mature. I was even, in a very detached kind of way, able to notice that the well-groomed yuppie WASP good looks that had seemed safely attractive to me in the first place were holding up well.

Brad was talking to an absolutely stunning woman. If she was his current love interest, he had obviously grown up some in the three years since I'd left him pouting because he couldn't understand my objections to spending all our dates with his mother. This woman was miles beyond the Brad I had known. Not only did she look much too exotic for him, she just plain radiated attitude. Her head was covered with an elaborately wrapped orange, black, and yellow cotton scarf. A wide-sleeved round-necked tunic of the same fabric, over loose-legged black slacks, ended just below her knees. She stood, feet wide apart, hands on hips, on platform sandals that looked like they were made of rope and added three inches to her height, which still didn't amount to much. Shoulder-dusting earrings and a chunky necklace that looked like some kind of folk art completed the picture.

As I watched, her head tilted back and she looked up at Brad through slitted eyes. She smiled lazily, revealing a charming dimple and dazzling white teeth. From where I stood, it was a challenging pose, and Brad wasn't up to it. He averted his eyes from the wattage of her merciless glare and that's when he saw me. His face registered relief. Relief? I deduced that I represented a socially acceptable avenue of escape from whatever it was the woman was on him about.

Brad started toward us, guiding the beautiful woman

along with a hand between her shoulder blades, an intimate gesture. Her movements held a sinuous grace, somewhere between cat and serpent. She was fascinating.

"Try to look at me adoringly," I muttered to Phil.

"Huh?" Phil said through a mouthful of sticky rice.

"Trudy Roundtree!" Brad said. "Couldn't stay away from the big city after all!"

"Brad Phipps!" I said, trying to match his tone and trying to sound like somebody who was surprised to see him instead of somebody who'd been watching him for several minutes. "What a coincidence," I said. "And no, just slumming. Brad Phipps, meet my friend Phil Pittman."

Any doubts I might have had about my composure were erased when I managed that tongue twister without bobbling it. Phil did me proud. He couldn't decide whether to lick his fingers clean or try to wipe them on the flimsy paper napkins, so he awkwardly did a little of both and gave a half-wave and grin in acknowledgment, instead of shaking hands.

"Brad," he said, nodding.

"Phil," Brad said, smiling. Then, "Trudy, and…Phil, was it? Let me introduce you to Coreen Collins.

"Not only is Coreen one of the gallery's owners—"

"The important one," she interrupted, smiling.

Brad stopped cold. It took him a second to remember where his sentence had been going. "You're talking to one of the guests of honor."

"No kidding? One of the artists? I've been admiring your brushwork," Phil said.

"No, you haven't," Coreen Collins said.

"Oh, yes…" Phil was protesting when he saw me shaking my head. Phil has this tendency to look at the art in a gallery instead of the signatures and little infomercials they stick all over the place, so he hadn't connected C. Collins with the car parts. I'd connected the names but was having trouble trying to imagine this exotic animal as someone who'd be willing to get her hands dirty, much less hold a welder's torch or rummage around a junkyard for just the right piece of scrap.

"The brushwork you were admiring would be Andrew's," Brad said, clearly amused. He pointed across the room to where a burly man was putting a piece of California roll into his mouth. Andrew (Andrew Lamotte, I knew, since I do read infomercials) would easily have dwarfed Hen, and although he was balding, what hair he had was pulled into a blondish ponytail. If he hadn't just been identified as a specialist in oil painting, I'd have pegged him for a biker, going by the black jeans and T-shirt and the tattooed snake winding its way around his forearm.

"But there are plenty of things to admire about Coreen," Brad continued, calling our attention away from Andrew.

Years of being a journalist, even in quiet little Ogeechee, have taught Phil to take anything in his stride. He recovered quickly and tried to bury his social mistake under a professional cover. "How in the world did you ever find this particular medium?" His gesture took in the samples of Coreen's, not Andrew's, work.

She smiled again and shrugged, setting her enormous earrings in motion. I had been so dazzled by her that it wasn't until then that I noticed that her earrings and necklace were made out of car parts, too. They were on a much smaller scale than the sculptures, but undeniably car parts, little springs and clips and coils. The pendants on the necklace were spark plugs.

"I grew up out in the country next to a salvage yard,"

she said. "There wasn't much to do out there, so I started fooling around"—she paused after she said "fooling around," definitely overdoing the lilt, in my opinion, before she added—"with the welding." Phil and Brad seemed to think that was witty. What I thought was, *She's used that line more than once before, the phony.*

"This looks like pretty heavy work," Phil persisted. "Do you have a lot of help?"

She shrugged again, no doubt a charming gesture. "Cranes and winches and junkyard boys. I get as much help as I need."

Phil grinned at her foolishly, apparently unable to think of another penetrating question.

"South of here?" I asked, trying to place the lilt.

"Not far from Claxton," she said.

"The fruitcake capital of the world," Phil said, to show he was keeping up.

I gave him a look of disgust before I made my own witty contribution to the conversation. "Claxton? No kidding? We're from Ogeechee."

Coreen looked surprised. She stopped waggling her earrings at Phil and looked at me. "Ogeechee? Well, for… Uh… Oh, excuse me! I better go get Tariq in motion."

"Tariq's Coreen's husband," Brad said. "The other owner."

"At the moment, anyway, Sugar," Coreen said. She managed to pat both men on the arm and smile at me as she made tracks—gracefully in spite of those shoes—across the room to where an elegant man was talking quietly with a redhead in skin-tight jeans and a halter top. The redhead moved away as Coreen approached.

"Very convenient for an artist, owning a gallery," Phil said.

"They make a lovely couple," I said. I was trying to sound snide, but it was the honest truth. Compared with Coreen, Tariq was conventionally dressed, in tan slacks and a shirt that looked like silk and must have been dyed to match. The pair might have been carved from the same piece of some rare tropical wood and polished—definitely polished—to a warm rich dark brown. They were ideally cast as characters in the art world, where beauty is appreciated. In contrast, Phil and I would surely be cast as tourists. Phil has a boyish face sprinkled with freckles and a habit of fiddling with his glasses. He was wearing a navy blue golf shirt and gray slacks. I sucked in my stomach but was still aware that in my flat leather sandals and navy blue (yes, me, too) cotton knit dress, and nondescript short brown hair, I wouldn't stop traffic. Coreen would

Tariq clapped his hands for attention. When he spoke I thought how well his voice matched the rest of him—rich, cultured, polished. "I want to thank you all"—not *quite* "y'all"—"for honoring us with your presence this evenin'. Since you are our friends, I know you'll be happy to hear that Andrew and Coreen and this exhibit are going to have a nice little spread in the Sunday *Constitution*." There was a murmur and spattering of applause, which he waved away, adding graciously, "If there are other reporters here, we'll be de-lighted to grant interviews. Just set it up with Brad. Brad, wave your hand."

Brad obediently waved his hand.

"The rest of you, now, you go back to oohing and ahhing. Let me know if you want to work out an easy payment plan." Tariq raised his glass in a gesture that was both toast and benediction, smiled at his audience, and turned to whisper into his wife's ear. She listened briefly, then spoke, emphasizing her words with a sharp nod that set her earrings to chattering. Then, like an African queen holding court, she turned her attention to the people clustering around, casually taking up a pose with one of the sculptures, a lily the size of a cookstove. Her husband, meanwhile, cruised the room, stopping to say something to Andrew that Andrew apparently didn't want to hear. Andrew turned his back on Tariq, who merely straightened his shirt collar and drifted after the redhead.

"If she's really from Claxton, we could do a story for the *Beacon*," Phil said.

I shot him a look. "And when did Claxton move into our county?"

"Or maybe I could just make you a necklace out of film canisters," Phil said, recovering quickly. One of the things I like about Phil is that he's quick-witted.

All that had been weeks ago. Now, mysterious noises coming through the telephone—which Phil had obviously put down on his desk while he rummaged around for the press release—jerked my mind back to the present. As that trip, that occasion, replayed on my mental screen I knew why the body under the bridge looked familiar. The difference in clothing as well as the different context had thrown me off. The different name hadn't helped, either.

I waited impatiently for Phil to come back to the telephone, then I had to listen while he read me his press release about a gallery opening that actually did sound interesting, an artist who specializes in masks. I like the gimmicky stuff.

"Better not plan on it," I said with real regret. "I might be busy."

"Anything I ought to know about?" he asked, neatly leaving it to me to decide whether he was being personally or professionally delicate.

"I'm going to stick my neck out here and leak something to the press." Since the *Beacon* is a weekly, this is not exactly a reckless thing to do. Nothing would make its way into print in the next few days. With luck, we might even have things figured out in time for the next issue.

"Leak away."

I imagined him picking up the pad and pencil that were never out of reach as I said, "Looks like Tanner Whitcomb ran over somebody."

"Have you arrested him? Did he put up a fight? Is the CIA involved? FBI? GBI? When's the press conference? Will he be out on bail? Was it self-defense?" Did I imagine a rustle as he put the pad and pencil back down?

"Seriously, Phil, Tanner has found a body and somebody did run over it. I'd better not make any other plans 'til we get it cleared up."

"Hen thinks you're so valuable he won't let you off?" That was a low blow. Phil knows very well how hard Hen tries to get me out of his hair whenever a real investigation comes along.

"The subject hasn't exactly come up," I told him, "And it's not going to come up. I've got an angle of my own already."

"Uh-oh. Does Hen know?"

"Not yet."

"You goin' to tell me?"

I didn't much like the grin I could hear in his voice, but I didn't snap at him because I wanted something. "I don't want to make it too easy for you," I said, "but a good reporter would go over to Calloway's"—that's the mortuary where the body would be waiting until the wagon picked it up to take it to Atlanta where it would yield up its secrets—"and take a look at the victim."

"Really?"

"And then he'd call me back."

"Okey-dokey. I'm on my way."

"And Phil," I tried to sound like I was changing the subject. "You don't happen to have the phone number for the Upstart Gallery handy do you?"

"The Upstart Gallery? That place in Atlanta where we saw the fenders and bumpers? I think it's right here in my file. Why? You thinking of hiring Coreen to come make art out of some of your junk?"

I know my place needs neatening up, and I've been meaning to get to it, but that stung. Besides, I couldn't help but notice that, although Phil was pretending to be a little vague about the gallery, he had no trouble coming up with the artist's name. So I said, "I wanted to get in touch with Brad."

"Oh," he said. And then, without even asking "Brad who?" he gave me the number. Men!

THREE

I WAS GLAD Hen was still out at the bridge swapping stories with the GBI guys. My hunch would have been hard to explain to anybody, let alone a chauvinistic, paternalistic self-appointed protector of my delicate femininity who had trouble giving me credit for having a brain. I'd wait until I knew if this trail would take me anywhere before I invited him to explore it with me.

The telephone rang and rang at the Upstart Gallery. Finally, there was a click, and a voice I thought was Tariq's informed me that business hours were ten to five Monday through Saturday, noon until five on Sunday, and I could call again during those times or leave a message and he'd get right back to me. Unless I was mistaken about the body under the bridge, he wasn't going to be getting back to anybody. Since I was calling during their business hours, I wondered who was supposed to be minding the store and if whoever it was knew about Tariq, if it was Tariq. I left my phone number and a request for a call. It occurred to me I should have tried to sound like somebody who might want to buy a grasshopper made out of the bumper from a '69 Dodge, but I didn't call again.

Say I was right and the dead man was Tariq. What would he be doing in Ogeechee, alive or dead? Then I remembered Coreen Collins, Tariq's wife, saying she was from Claxton. Claxton's just down the road. Maybe they had come to spend a weekend with the family. Knowing full well that "Claxton" could encompass any amount of countryside around, I reached for the Claxton phone book and started calling Collinses. Naturally, it would be a name that shows up a lot around here. Even without including things like Collins Carpet, Collins Elementary School, and Collins, City of, I had more than twenty Collinses to check out in the places reasonably near Claxton.

"Coreen?" I asked for the tenth time, and for the eighth time I heard some variation of, "You've got the wrong number. We don't have a Coreen." I got one "What are you bothering me for?"; one "You sound like a nice person. Have you been washed in the blood of the Lamb?"; three answering machines, and five no answers before it occurred to me that if Lester DeLoach could become somebody called Tariq, Coreen might have chosen the name Collins because she liked the way it sounded with Coreen. If her name was even Coreen. I tried the gallery again and still got no answer. Then I had another bright idea. Brad. Even that wasn't as easy as it should have been. When I knew him, he lived with his mother, so naturally that's the only telephone number I had for him.

"Who is this?" she asked in that pseudo-Vivien Leigh *Gone With the Wind* voice of hers. "Ah can't quite place the voice, but it does sound the tiniest bit famil-yah."

I started to say, "I'm an encyclopedia salesman," but remembered in time that the woman had no imagination and no sense of humor. "Yes, ma'am," I said, barely resisting the impulse to disguise my voice and try to bluff it out. "This is Trudy Roundtree. Is Brad there?"

"Well, ah do decla-ah! Trudy Roundtree! That little girl from out of town. It's been quite a spell since Ah've heard

your voice." Try as I might, my sensitive ear could detect
no regret in word or tone over the fact.

"Yes, ma'am," I said again, using all my self control.
"It surely has."

"Ah guess you hadn't heard he doesn't live here anymore."

"We've been out of touch," I said, stifling an impulse
to cheer.

"Well, pooh! I know that!"

"Yes, ma'am," I said through clenched teeth. "Can
you help me get in touch with him?"

"Oh, fiddle-dee-dee, Trudy!" If I'd been in her presence, I'm sure she'd have tapped me with her fan. "I
believe he'd have given you his number if he'd wanted
you to have it," she suggested. Uh-huh. Like she thinks
he's hiding out from me.

"Oh, we blotted each other's names right out of our
little black books years ago," I said soothingly. I could
feel my drawl lengthening to match her. "This isn't personal at all. It's in the nature of a business call and it's
kind of important that I find him."

"You didn't take up art, did you? I'd never have expected *you* to do *that!*"

"Oh, no." Her inflection made me wonder what alter-
native horrors she had expected of me. "No, ma'am, but
I am interested in talking to him about something I saw
down at the Upstart Gallery."

"The gallery? Well, why didn't you say so, then, instead of wasting my time?" Without allowing me to waste
any more of her time, she reeled off numbers—home, office, beeper, cell phone, for crying out loud. I told her I'd
be able to manage without e-mail, fax, or social security
numbers, and I left my cell phone number and the OPD
number with her, wondering why Brad could possibly

think he'd be in such demand that he needed so many lines of access. I was fanning myself with the piece of paper I'd scribbled the numbers on when Hen walked in.

"That mobile lab is a wonder," he said. "They whipped our man Lester DeLoach's name through their computer and came up with an interesting background."

"Oh?" I said, figuring I'd wait and see what he already knew before trotting out my ideas. If I'd talked to Scarlett O'Phipps for nothing I'd find a way to get even with somebody.

"Looks like a little bit of fraud here, a little bit of petty thievery there, and one imaginative episode of foisting unordered but nevertheless personalized and therefore priceless and unreturnable Bibles on bereaved families. That was way back, though. Looks like Lester learned something over the years and he's gotten smoother and moved into more profitable work."

"Upscale, but playing it down," I suggested, thinking of the expensive watch and the worn clothing.

"Um-hmm," Hen agreed, his eyes still on Tariq's fact-sheet.

"Any of his smooth new profitable enterprises connected with the art world?"

For the first time, Hen looked up at me. He fixed me with his icy blue stare and waited. I have that same icy blue stare when I want to muster it up, so I'm more immune than most, but eventually I gave in.

"I'm waiting for confirmation on this, but if he's who I think he is—was—he was running a hoity-toity art gallery in Atlanta, the one where Phil and I saw that stuff made out of old car parts and priced like brand-new cars."

"Where y'all went and stood around eating different kinds of bait? That the place?"

"The very place."

"Besides the cheap horse doo-vers, there wasn't anything to make you think the man was up to no good?" Hen likes to act like a home-grown hayseed. He thinks it makes him more approachable, less intimidating, than if he went around in his off-hours wearing a three-piece suit with his Phi Beta Kappa key on a gold chain stretched across his belly. He's right. I've watched the act have exactly the effect he wants—it makes people who know him think he's cute and people who don't know him underestimate him. He just loves that. Sometimes, like now, he puts it on out of habit, to keep in practice, and for humorous effect. He knows it doesn't work with me. I never underestimate him and I try like the dickens not ever to let on I think he's cute.

"Everything looked perfectly *comme-il-faut* to me," I told him. I took a French class once and I figured he deserved that in return for the horse doo-vers. I waggled the piece of paper with Brad's phone numbers on it. "I've been trying to reach somebody who knows—knew—him and see if I can find out what he was doing down here. His wife's supposed to be from Claxton, so maybe that explains it. That sheet you're looking at have the name Tariq on it?"

He frowned and studied the sheet then shook his head. "What's a Tariq?"

"It's the name he used when he bought the bait," I said.

"Do tell."

"And Brad Phipps seemed to know him and his wife. Matter of fact, it's his wife who does that automobile sculpture we told you about. Anyway, I'm trying to reach Brad and see if he can tell me anything useful."

"Brad Phipps. Where do I know that name?"

I waited. He milked it.

"Oh, yes. It's coming to me. Yes. That's the mama's boy you were messin' around with before you came to your senses and came to work for me." He grinned. The ego of the man who could say that, since we both know he hired me because his mother told him to!

"He doesn't live with his mother anymore," I said and was instantly annoyed to realize I sounded defensive about it. Sometimes I'm sorry I ever tell Hen anything.

Hen grinned to show his satisfaction at getting a rise out of me. "Well, you talk to ol' Brad. Meanwhile, I've got the Atlanta people onto it, getting in touch with the next of kin, maybe that's this sculptress—or is that sexist? Am I supposed to say *sculptor* now, even if it is a woman?" Since the question was designed to show me how unreasonable I am on the subject of women's rights, he didn't wait for an answer but went right on with the briefing. "Ol' Rufus was sniffing around after you left the scene. I think he was sending one of his men back to borrow the high school's football chain to measure and make sure the body wasn't over the line outside our jurisdiction. I told him we'd let him know if we wanted anything."

Rufus Badcock knows as well as Hen and I know that he has no business with a city investigation unless we ask for his help, but he just can't help giving the impression that he knows he's got better people and better resources and we'll be grateful for the help. We might be willing to admit the better resources, but it's really bad manners for him not to wait until he's invited to the party. He and Hen go back a long way. The very fact that none of Hen's countless stories about police work and every other subject under the sun go into much detail about Badcock is suspicious. I know they don't like each other and there just plain has to be a story there. If it's a story Hen won't tell, it must be a doozy.

"You keep on workin' that angle, see if your Tariq is our Lester DeLoach. Right now I'm goin' back over there and talk to Tanner again. He just might be able to think of something to tell me."

With that official sanction of my activity, Hen started for the door.

"You might want to search Tanner as long as you're there," I called after him. "It occurs to me he could have taken something besides the watch. I'd have searched him myself, but knowing Tanner's opinion of women, I didn't want to touch him without witnesses, to make sure he didn't sue us for sexual harassment."

"You mean you didn't want to touch him, period." I could hear Hen laughing even after the door closed behind him.

I turned back to the telephone, but still had no luck reaching Brad. I wasn't especially surprised not to get an answer at his work number. It was Saturday afternoon, after all. But I left a message there and on his machine at home, asking him to call me. I had no idea what directions he might have gone without my evil influence, so he might have been anywhere—exploring the Batcave at Six Flags, getting a full-body massage out on the Buford Highway, climbing up Stone Mountain. The incongruous image of Coreen in her African garb and her lilting voice accompanying him in those activities kept intruding. I had just warmed up a cup of coffee in the microwave and was about to start dialing more Collinses when Brad called.

"Hey, Trudy. Mama said you wanted to talk to me. How you doin'?"

I grinned at the thought that his mama, after all, got to him before the messages I'd left on his two phones.

Maybe he hadn't changed all that much. "Yes, I appreciate your getting back to me so soon. You been out jogging?" I asked, saying the least likely thing that came into my head.

"Uh. No. Uh, Mama said she thought maybe you were interested in some art." His tone suggested he'd just as easily imagine the University of Georgia dumping that pampered bulldog Uga at the Dumb Friends League, but it also suggested he couldn't afford to ignore any potential business lead, however unlikely.

"I'm not sure what I said to her, Brad. You know how she always could rattle me. Do I gather you're selling art these days? Not still with that P.R. agency?"

"I've gone out on my own."

"Does that mean you're out of work?"

"Trudy, Trudy, Trudy," he said sorrowfully. "Freelancing isn't being out of work. I have a number of clients."

"Artists? Galleries?"

"Well, yes, some of them."

"Good. I was hoping you could put me in touch with Coreen."

"Coreen?" He might never have heard the name.

"The junk-car artist at the Upstart Gallery. I'm sure you remember. Coreen. Collins, wasn't it?"

"Oh. Yes. But you don't need to talk to Coreen herself. If you're interested in a particular piece of hers, I can help you."

"Actually, Brad, this is connected with my work, not hers."

"Your work? You know, we must not have gotten around to talkin' about what you're doin' these days."

"Is that right?" Couldn't fit it in around ogling Coreen, you mean. "Well, matter of fact, what I'm doin' these days is bein' a police officer. What did you say? Sounded like 'urk.'"

"Uh. Urk. How's Coreen mixed up with the police? Not somethin' to do with the gallery?"

"I'm not at liberty to take you into my confidence at this time," I said, loving the way that sounded.

"But your business, you said."

Yep. I had said that. "I just want to talk to her. Have you seen her today, or her husband?"

"Today? No, not today. But what..."

"I ran across..." I flinched as I said it and tried again. "I saw somebody this morning I thought was Tariq, and I thought I remembered Coreen saying she was from Claxton. Do you know if she has relatives there?"

"Never heard her mention anybody."

"Got any idea why he—or she—would be down here?"

"Why would I? They don't tell me all their business." An evasive answer if I ever heard one, and I've heard many more than one.

"Could you make a guess?"

"No. Wouldn't want to do that. You'd better talk to them. Unless you're after a nice piece of art. I could help you with that."

Trying to get anything out of Brad was turning out to be as futile as trying to get six-year-old Delcie to eat chitlins. He obviously didn't intend to be helpful. Finally he gave me a phone number for Coreen, which I recognized as the gallery number. After a little more nudging, he admitted he had another number for her. He gave that to me, her home number. I let him go and punched in the number Brad had just given me. No answer there, either.

I was pondering my next move when Phil called back. Like me, he'd been thrown off at first by the dramatic change in style, but he agreed with me that the dead man at the funeral home was the man we knew as Tariq.

"What next?" he asked.

"For you, I reckon it's trying to sell enough ads for the paper to break even next week," I said. "For me, it's trying to find Coreen and see if I can learn what Tariq was doing here. Hen's got Atlanta working on it, but I figured if he was down here, she might be here, too. I've been calling Collinses without any luck."

"Was his name Collins, too?"

"Who knows? His driver's license called him Lester DeLoach."

"Why not try DeLoaches? At least it'll be a shorter list."

Right. Like the joke about the man who was looking for his quarter under the street light, not because he'd lost it there, but because the light was better. Still, it was a thought. I punched the button that disconnected Phil, reached for the phone book again, and started calling DeLoaches.

FOUR

SWITCHING FROM Collinses to DeLoaches was almost immediately more productive. After only one no-answer, I connected with a George DeLoach, who said he used to have a cousin named Lester.

"Used to?"

"Well, maybe I still do, but I haven't heard from him in so long I don't remember when."

"Is there anybody who might have been in touch with him lately?"

"Who'd you say you was?"

Knowing what I knew about Lester-Tariq, I figured George DeLoach might be worried about L-T's behavior reflecting on the family, so I tried to disarm him. "I'm not a bill collector and I'm not trying to sell him insurance," I said. "I'm Officer Trudy Roundtree with the Ogeechee Police Department, but he's not in any trouble." Not unless you call being flattened by a motor vehicle being in trouble. "We have an accident victim by that name and I'm trying to get in touch with his family." I hoped that was vague enough to reassure George.

"Well, you found some of his family I guess, but we can't help with no bills. What kind of accident?"

"An automobile accident. Can you tell me how to reach his wife?"

"Lester was married? Whaddyuh know! Lord, it has been a while since I seen him."

"Can you think of anybody at all who might know where he is?"

"Well, there's Grandma DeLoach, but she don't know nothin'."

"Can you tell me how to get in touch with her?"

"She's at that home, that place over in Vidalia where they put the old people."

"Do you have the number there?"

"No. Why'd I call over there?"

"Is there anybody else you can think of, anybody who cares about him?"

"Well, maybe Uncle Oscar. He's Grandma's brother, would make him what? Lester and me's great uncle? Somethin'. Yeah, Uncle Oscar used to keep up with Lester. Maybe he's the one you want."

"That would be Oscar DeLoach?"

"Not DeLoach. Jackson. Oscar Jackson."

"Do you have his number?"

"No, never needed it, but if you're looking for the number, you have to look under the business. That's where he lives. Used to, anyway."

It sounded like George was a little bored with the conversation, but I couldn't let him go yet. This was my one warm lead. "What business is that?"

"Calls it salvage, but it's a junkyard, a junky old junkyard. Uncle Oscar and Granddaddy were in it 'til Granddaddy died. It went downhill after that. It was Granddaddy was good at the business end, Uncle Oscar was good gettin' things done."

"What's it called?"

"What?"

"The business."

"J and D, for Jackson and DeLoach, Salvage. It's over in Mendes."

"Okay, then. I'll try to reach your uncle Oscar. Thanks for your help."

"That's all right. Lester hurt, you say?"

It isn't our departmental policy to give people bad news over the telephone, but judging from George's attitude up to then I didn't think he'd be torn up too much, so I told him, "Yes."

"Yeah, well, Uncle Oscar's the one you want to talk to. He'd want to know. He used to think a lot of Lester."

I found a listing for J&D Salvage and Towing and headed out to break the bad news about Lester to a possibly caring family member, and maybe find out something useful while I was at it. The address in the phone book was Highway 169, which wasn't much help as a street address, but Mendes is small even by Ogeechee standards, so I went south, figuring I could find it, and I did.

The sign advertising J&D SALVAGE AND TOWING swung at an angle from a rusty pole, swung at an angle because one of the two chains that should have held it level had given up. Comparing it to the state of decay of some of the stuff out back of my house, and how long it had taken to get into that condition, I judged the sign hadn't been repainted since before the Carters took up peanut farming.

I pulled off the highway onto gravel in front of a Quonset hut surrounded by a dirt yard. Ramshackle is the most positive word I can think of to describe the place. Behind and around the Quonset, a chain-link fence outlined the area where a lot of old automobiles had come to end their days rusting quietly back into the yellow-streaked dirt. At one edge of the driveway, a couple of muscle cars and a

pickup truck, all elderly but not as far gone as those behind the fence, were in a row facing the road, "4 SALE"
signs optimistically propped in their front windows.

Through a window pane almost entirely obscured by
dirt and the back of some kind of display case, I could
see someone peering out. The ragged screen door swung
open ahead of a stout walking stick followed by a big
black man. He was old and he walked with the help of
that stick, but he was imposing. Big arms, big body a little
stooped. The hand gripping the walking stick was knobby
and scarred. I diagnosed arthritis.

"Mr. Jackson?"

"Um hum," he rumbled. "Somethin' I can do for the
po-lice?" He stopped leaning on the stick long enough to
use it to point at my badge.

"I'm hoping you can help me," I told him. "I'm here
about a Lester DeLoach."

"A Lester DeLoach? You know a whole passel of Lester DeLoaches and you here about one of 'em?"

"Actually, no." I couldn't tell if he was a dry wit or
an antagonist, or both, so I played it straight. "You have
a nephew named Lester DeLoach?"

"A nephew. Now that's right. I have a nephew named
Lester DeLoach." He just stood there, leaning on that big
stick.

"I have some bad news for you then, Mr. Jackson."

"Some bad news for me." I wasn't getting much in
the way of response, but at least it was obvious he was
paying attention to what I was saying.

"He sic you on me?"

"No. He's had an accident."

"He in the hospital? I'll pay his bill. He didn't have to
send the po-lice about that."

"No. Not the hospital."

"What bad news then? He's not in trouble with the law." He seemed pretty sure of that, which put him one up on me. I wasn't sure of much of anything in this conversation. I gestured back toward my car, hoping the OPD logo would help him focus.

"I'm from Ogeechee, and we have a body that carried identification saying his name was Lester DeLoach. I'm trying to find his next of kin, to let them know. Do you think that could be your nephew?"

"A body, you say?"

"Yes, sir."

"May be it's another Lester DeLoach." He stood up straighter and looked at—or through—my car.

"May be. You're right. I hope it isn't your nephew. Maybe it isn't. This Lester DeLoach lived up in Atlanta. He went by the name of Tariq."

"Tariq, yes. Sounds like my Lester. But he died?"

"Yes. I'm sorry."

"I don't understand what you tellin' me. Why would he die?"

"It looks like somebody ran over him."

"Run over him?" His gaze was now trying to burn its way through me. "Now, that don't sound like my Lester."

"What do you mean? He wasn't the kind of person to get run over?"

"I didn't run over him. What you here for?"

"Nobody's saying you ran over him. But the thing is, Mr. Jackson, somebody did run over a Lester DeLoach and he's dead, and whoever ran over him knew it and didn't get him any help. That makes it a crime. We've got people working right now on the physical evidence—the tire tracks and things like that—so we'll be able to prove who it was, once we find him. Or her." Much as I fuss at Hen about his sexist attitudes, I catch myself making assumptions sometimes, too. "The thing is, we have to find whoever did it. But the first thing is to be sure whose death it is we're investigating."

He nodded, taking that in. "You got a picture of your Lester DeLoach?"

"I could get one."

"I got a picture of my Lester. Come lessee if it's the same one. Lots of DeLoaches around here. Could be more than one Lester."

It would be surprising if there was more than one Lester DeLoach who had moved to Atlanta and changed his name to Tariq, but I didn't see any point in rushing the old man's acceptance of his nephew's death.

He led the way back into the gloom of the Quonset he'd emerged from, through a grease-stained waiting room with cracking red vinyl-and-chrome chairs and outdated calendars advertising phallic cars and come-hither women, through a vast shop where five or six cars—it was hard to tell how many complete cars the pieces might have made—were in various stages of repair or disrepair, past a huge hook with a car engine hanging from it, past a worktable littered with metal and a welding set-up, and out into the now-dazzling sunshine. The old man walked steadily, making his way along a zig-zag path between the cars. We seemed to be headed toward a row of towering pecan trees at the back of the lot.

I still had no reading on Oscar Jackson at all. On the whole, he seemed to be rational, if eccentric. He had seemed to have a lot of trouble understanding why I'd come, and not all his comments made sense to me, at least at first, but I could put that down to shock. Were we really going somewhere to find a picture of his nephew—his grandnephew—or was the idea to lead me to the pecan trees at the back of the lot and beat me to death with that stick? I lagged a little farther behind the stick and rested my hand on my gun.

We came to a halt in front of one of the larger derelicts, an ancient school bus, the yellow and black over-painted a long time ago with a pale blue. I could make out enough of the peeling black letters on the side to see that it had once belonged to the Frog Pond Baptist Church. Oscar Jackson hefted himself into the bus and stood near the driver's seat, beckoning to me.

Cautiously, I stepped up and came stock still with amazement. Everything else I'd seen at J&D Salvage and Towing showed age and neglect, so I was unprepared for the cozy living quarters I saw here. The seats had been taken out of the school bus and a bed fitted across the back end. An Oriental-style rug in cream and red and bright blue covered most of the floor space. The two recliners and a floor lamp with a built-in table looked relatively new, clearly not salvage, and they'd been chosen because the velvety blue of the chairs looked good against the rug. The red of the walls was the red from the rug. With no need to be concerned about privacy, he'd left the windows uncovered and the shade from the pecan trees shed a lovely dappled light. The effect was tidy, charming, peaceful. You'd never confuse this room with a spread out of *Southern Living,* but it was more attractive than a lot of store-bought pre-furnished mobile homes I've seen, and it wasn't just the contrast with the rest of J&D Salvage and Towing that made it look nice. I could see electrical and phone wires but I didn't know him well enough to ask about plumbing. Maybe he used the facilities in the Quonset.

On top of a low chest was a TV set and a scattering of brassy dime-store picture frames. Oscar Jackson picked up one of the frames and held it toward me, interrupting my study of his home.

"That boy your Lester DeLoach?" he asked.

The picture was not of the slick, expensive Tariq I'd seen in Atlanta, and it wasn't the pitiful crushed man in worn work clothes I'd seen more recently, but it was the same face, younger by maybe ten or fifteen years.

"I'm sorry," I said, handing it back to him.

He sank into one of the chairs, clutching the picture, and motioned with his stick for me to do the same.

"It's always hard to bring news like this, Mr. Jackson. I'm sorry I can't just leave you alone, but I do need to see if you can help me find out what happened." He nodded. "He lived up in Atlanta, but he was found in Ogeechee. Do you know what he was doing down here? Had he been to see you?"

He looked at me then, and I got the impression that he was still dazed but thinking. Now that we were sure we were talking about the same Lester DeLoach he seemed to be tracking a little better. "You said somebody run over him?"

"That's right. We don't know much yet. That's why I'm talking to you, to find out what I can. Were you close to him? Do you know of any reason anybody would run over him on purpose?"

"I just don't understand that," he said and then he fell silent, staring at the photograph, seeming to forget I was there.

"Do you know what Ta— Lester was doing down here?" I asked again.

"He came to see me, all right. He came to see me, but I don't know how he got run over. He walked out of here."

"Was anybody with him when he left?"

He shook his head. "Wouldn't nobody let him leave with 'em. They left him."

"He'd been here with somebody? Who? Who left him?"

"Coreen, that wife of his."

"Who else? You said 'they.'"

"That man they brought with 'em."

"Do you know his name?"

"I know they told me, but I don't think of it now."

"They just came for a visit? The three of them?"

"No."

"What, then?"

"Business."

"What business?"

"My business. Our business."

At this rate, it was going to be much more than twenty questions, and I wasn't sure I was learning anything anyway. But I kept on. "You said they wouldn't let him leave with them. Why?"

"Got mad with him, that's why."

"Why? Why did they get mad with him?"

"He walked out of here. That's what you want to know, isn't it? He walked away. Didn't nobody run over him here."

"But why? Why did he walk out of here? Do you know where he was going? There's nothing close for him to be walking to."

His answers had been coming more and more reluctantly. Now they stopped altogether. He narrowed his eyes and gripped his walking stick and shook his head.

I stood up and fished one of my cards out of my pocket. "I'll let that go for now, but you can expect to talk to me again. In the meantime, if you think of anything you'd like to let us in on, you can call me."

He took the card and nodded, but I wouldn't have bet he'd heard a word I said. As I stepped out of the bus back into the different world of the salvage yard, I could hear him muttering, "Run over, now! How'd he get run over?"

I picked my way along the path back to my car, late afternoon sun glinting on the many facets of the glass in the fractured windshields all around me. A tumble of bumpers near the back of the Quonset was like the bleaching bones of enormous beasts. Preoccupied as I was with Tariq, the pile reminded me of Coreen's sculptures. It took only a little imagination to see that with an ear here, and a couple of tusks there, the pile would become an elephant's head.

I was standing there, mentally supplying missing parts for my elephant, when I was startled by a sound behind me. Oscar Jackson had followed me after all. "You might better get on," he said. "I'll close up now." His stick edged me away from the elephant head and toward the door.

FIVE

It had been a long day, taking me from Tanner and Tariq all the way out to Mendes and Oscar Jackson, and I was glad to get home, but of course I took it all home with me. I'd be among the first to admit that my place is junky. Still, it irritated me that when I turned off the highway and came into sight of my home—my ancestral home—the image of J&D Salvage and Towing flashed into my mind. The street peters out at my property, with magnolias in front of the house and pine woods behind it and on the far side. The grounds are generous, so for convenience the driveway goes all the way around the house. I stopped in the street where I could get a good look at the place, noticing details as I would if, say, I was interviewing somebody at a possible crime scene.

Under that detached—okay, let's face it, brutal—scrutiny, it was obviously in need of some attention. Like J&D Salvage and Towing, the ambiance here had not developed by design or overnight. It just grew. When Grandma was alive everybody felt like this was the family homestead. She wanted us to feel that way, that it wasn't so much *her* house as *our* house. My earliest memories are of my parents and me, Hen's parents and him, and Aunt Alma and her kids at Grandma's. She liked having wagons and tricycles and sand toys, and later, bicycles and croquet and badminton sets around the place so we'd all enjoy being there, in case being with her wouldn't be enough. She was the kind of woman who didn't leave anything to chance if she could help it.

With the two acres of lawn and a lot more acres of pine woods behind it, there was plenty of room to store or park whatever people didn't have room for at their own smaller places. Besides, it was easier to find a spot for a broken lawnmower, for instance, than to figure out how to get rid of it, and anyway, you might be able to fix it one of these days. With plenty of space, that kind of thing was never a problem. Over the years stuff accumulated. Some of it— like the wood-and-cane wheelchair—went all the way back to when Grandma was a girl growing up there.

It's all still there, including the half-wild cats that make their home under the house and range freely into the woods and the decaying outbuildings, because I haven't been motivated to do anything about it.

Grandma died almost two years ago, right after Thanksgiving, and it's taking all of us a while to get used to two big changes: Grandma is gone and the place is mine, just mine, not the whole family's. I'm still feeling my way into ownership and thinking about how to do things. When I make my occasional comment about cleaning up, Aunt Lulu says I ought to get an antique dealer in. I appreciate that advice from her, because it shows progress in the family attitude that it really is my property to deal with. On the other hand, regardless of whether any of this stuff is antique instead of junque, can I get rid of it without losing part of myself? I don't think my lack of motivation has to do with denying she's gone or wanting to keep a shrine or anything like that, but it certainly could be rooted in a reluctance to admit any changes in all the love and security that Grandma represented in my life.

I know I need to do something. Sooner or later, you

have to face up to the responsibilities of ownership. I have a growing conviction that I need to fumigate, for instance, to try to get rid of some fleas and roaches and termites, but I haven't figured out how to do that with all those cats under the house. And it's definitely time to paint, but it's not a job I feel like tackling myself, and the steep roof and all those Victorian curlicues are going to call for a lot of painterly attention. I haven't had the energy, or the courage, to try to find somebody who can and will do either job at a price I can afford.

Anyway, I think what worries me is this: How much can I fix the place up without ruining all that I love about it?

Maybe the secret is to keep from going about it in a hurry. If that's the case, I have nothing to worry about. I could start by getting the underbrush and overgrowth trimmed and cleared out and hauled off. Then maybe it would be obvious what needs to be done next. If I get as far as hiring a truck, I could probably part with some of the most decayed relics at the same time. Heck, yes! I'd hire somebody with a big truck to help me haul off a lot of the trashy stuff that's accumulated, and then I'd re-group. I don't need to have a comprehensive plan at the beginning. One job at a time. One day at a time.

Idling there in the street while I looked at my own private junkyard, Oscar Jackson's junkyard and the junk-car sculptures came together in my mind. My first thought was that I'd have to clean the place up more than a little if a piece of sculpture of any kind, much less one made out of old car parts, was to stand out as art instead of just blending into the general mess. My second thought, which seemed blatantly obvious as soon as it occurred to me, was that the not-quite elephant head I'd noticed on my way out of J&D Salvage and Towing was probably exactly what it looked like—a piece of sculpture in progress. Could that be where Coreen worked? Her name hadn't sounded warm in Oscar Jackson's mouth, but I realize that doesn't necessarily mean anything in a business arrangement. Maybe, in spite of the elegant gallery and the big price tags, nobody was buying those imaginative sculptures. From what I could see of his standard of living, they weren't paying the old man much for the use of his workshop and materials. Still, when Oscar assumed— why?—that Lester-Tariq was in the hospital, he'd offered to pay the bill. Blood is thicker than water.

The sight of a cat skulking away from the house with something small dangling limply from her mouth pulled my mind back to the present. I drove on around the house and parked by the back steps, looking with a new eye at the ancient crumbling concrete birdbath and the old iron cookstove that Grandma had moved out there and slapped a door across to provide a garden workspace. Valuable antiques? Sculpture? Could be. I considered the idea of becoming a patron of the arts and declaring that my junk was art. Put a label on that rusty lawn chair under the fig tree—Art Deco '53? No, I guess not. No way I could get away with that. Nobody in Ogeechee would believe I knew anything about art, and Ogeechee being what it is, I'd have a hard time convincing people that it was art even if I had spent a lot of money for it. Wherever the Upstart Gallery was finding people to buy that stuff, it was people who had a lot more nerve and money than I do. Still, the idea of an alligator made out of chrome bumpers peeking out from between the azalea bushes over by the garage did have some appeal.

Hunger finally interrupted my flirtation with the arts, and I went inside. I had made it as far as the freezer on the back porch and was rummaging for something I could stick directly into the microwave, when the phone rang.

"Solved your hit and run yet?" Phil asked.

"We call it a vehicular homicide, and does your question mean you don't think it was Tanner?"

"I wouldn't want to make premature judgments, running ahead of the police investigation and all, but if I had to vote right now, that's how I'd vote."

"Except in rare cases, we don't settle these things by democratic process, Phil. We prefer to have trained professionals perform scientific analysis of physical evidence that inexorably leads us to the perpetrators of the crime."

"Well, naturally. I understand that. But if you can't get that and need a backup plan, I'll be ready to vote. You investigate and keep me posted, that's all I ask. But the reason I called, one of Daddy's cronies brought over a mess of catfish a little while ago and it seems like a shame to freeze 'em, so Molly said she'd make hushpuppies if I'd fry fish. You want to come help us eat 'em?"

Now, I know I've been making fun of Brad because all our dates used to involve his mother, but right then eating fresh fried catfish with Phil and his sister and his daddy sounded like exactly what I wanted to do. It was bound to be a more restorative way to spend the evening than thawing out some leftovers and spending the evening pondering the relationship between Tariq, Coreen, Oscar Jackson, and junk-car sculptures. Not to mention coming up with some way to turn my own junk into art. I could get back to my problems later. Fiddle-dee-dee. Tomorrow is another day.

"I'll bring dessert," I said. During my rummaging in the freezer, I had noticed a package labeled Blueberry Crumble, in Aunt Lulu's handwriting, so I knew I could do my share at a potluck supper with honor and without any effort.

SIX

I TOOK THE TIME to peel out of my uniform, shower, and slide into jeans and a T-shirt, but it was still not more than half an hour before I got out to the Pittmans', just a mile or so west of town. I parked behind an unfamiliar car in their driveway and made my way around to the back of the house, where I knew I'd find the fish-frying set-up.

Phil was dredging catfish at one end of the cook-station, a board supported by two sawhorses. A gas-powered cooker at the other end was already fired up and heating the grease.

Mr. Pittman and Lou-Ella Purvis, who is the secretary down at First Baptist, were sitting at a checkerboard on a card table in the shade of a sycamore. I was happy to see Mr. Pittman's walker leaning against the tree, a sign he was having a good day. On a bad day he'd be sitting in his wheelchair instead of the nylon mesh lawn chair.

Molly was putting plastic spring-clips around the edges of a tablecloth on the picnic table, assisted by a man I didn't recognize. Since I'm a crack police detective, no matter what Hen wants to believe, I immediately connected the man with the unfamiliar car in the driveway.

"Oh, here's Trudy," Molly said, when she caught sight of me. "You can start the fish, Phil." She started toward me, gesturing for the man to follow. Phil waved a mealy fillet in my direction. Mr. Pittman and Mrs. Purvis looked up, nodded, and smiled briefly before turning their attention back to the checkerboard. There must be more to that game than I've ever been able to see.

"Trudy, I want you to meet Craig Bland. Craig, this is Trudy Roundtree," Molly said, beaming from one to the other of us like a kindergarten teacher who hopes two new kids will make friends.

"Are you the onion Blands?" I asked, the onion Blands being known far and wide for the sweetness of their Vidalias and various onion-related products.

Craig shook his head. "Don't I wish. No, I'm the school teacher Blands, at the new high school. Different branch entirely."

"We got acquainted when I covered that Career Fair for the *Beacon*," Molly volunteered. "Craig's team won a prize for their display and I interviewed him. Them." He looked at her and she looked at him and they both blushed. Well.

I handed Aunt Lulu's blueberry crumble to Molly and drifted in Phil's direction. One of the things about Phil that used to irritate the heck out of me is his unfailingly serious approach to whatever he's doing. He's almost always frowning in concentration and fiddling with his glasses, as though having them polished and poised helps him focus his thoughts. For some reason, I've lately begun to think of this mannerism as endearing instead of irritating. If nothing else, it has an honest unaffectedness that compares favorably to the slick impersonal glad-handing of somebody like Brad Phipps—to pick a name at random.

As I approached, Phil looked up with a smile and nudged the nosepiece of his glasses with the knuckles of a hand holding a long-handled fork.

"So," I said, dodging the fork and coming back close

enough to whisper. "How long's this been goin' on between your daddy and Miz Purvis?"

He grinned and turned a piece of fish. "It's been escalating lately. Started with her bringing food by on behalf of the church sunshine committee whenever he'd have a flareup. It went on like that for a while, then, next thing I knew, I came home one afternoon and caught 'em goin' at it, hot and heavy."

"No!"

"Yep! Just like they are now!"

I considered the older couple, him distorted by arthritis but always up-beat, her overweight and dowdy and unfailingly righteous. "I don't know what kind of woman I thought was his type, but she isn't it." I frowned to convey the notion of serious thought. "Is there anything about her that could remind him of your mother?"

"Not a thing as far as I can see. But you know there's no accounting for chemistry, Trudy." Phil said this seriously, as he lifted a sizzling piece of catfish onto a paper towel. "But in this case, I do have something of an explanation. For a long time before he died, Mr. Purvis was so sick that playing checkers was about all he could do, and she spent a lot of time playing with him. She gives Daddy a pretty good game—a lot of good games—which is more than Molly or I have time for since Daddy's pretty much quit doing anything down at the paper and is leaving it all to us. I appreciate that about her."

Phil was obviously paying too much attention to the fish and not enough to me. He hadn't even realized I was teasing. He should know better. It only makes me worse. "Okay," I said. "If she can cook and play checkers, it might work out for the two of them. Has she started trying to worm her way into your affections yet, yours and

Molly's? Been bringing you milk and warm oatmeal cookies?''

He did look at me then. "You aren't suggesting she thinks she and Daddy…?''

"Don't look so horrified. It happens all the time.''

"That look was merely surprise, Trudy, not horror,'' he said defensively. "It just never occurred to me that Daddy would be interested in a woman. As a woman, I mean, and not just as a checkers player. Or vice versa.''

"I wouldn't worry about it, Phil,'' I said, with what I hoped was obvious insincerity. "I'm sure Molly and I can come up with a really cute shower theme when the time comes. All you'll have to do is let the romance unfold at its own rate. That is, if you're really going to stand by and let her become your mama.''

"You got something against Baptists?''

"Not as a group necessarily, just specific specimens. I think the fish is burning.''

Phil hastily speared the last piece of fish and I found a separate plate to put the extremely well-cooked ones on, for the convenience of anybody who might prefer them that way. With the cooking done, Phil was finally able to give my flippant conversation the attention it deserved. He straightened his glasses with both hands and assumed a thoughtful pose.

"Let me see, now. Ma Purvis? Sounds like a gangster. Anyway, she'd be Pittman, wouldn't she? So Miz Purvis wouldn't work, either, unless she's so liberated, like you, that she wouldn't want to change her name. Mommy? Mom? Mama? Mother? Lou-Ella?''

"That's the spirit! I'm sure you'll work it out.''

"What are you two whispering about?'' Molly had sneaked up on us with the hushpuppy batter. Phil re-adjusted his glasses, took the batter, and turned back to the cooker. I went inside to the kitchen with Molly as Craig ambled over to keep Phil company.

As soon as we'd finished debating whether it was better to put the frozen dessert in a low oven or thaw it in the microwave, deciding in favor of the microwave, we got on to the serious stuff.

"So, Molly, where've you been keeping Craig?" I asked subtly as I piled plates, napkins, and silverware on a tray.

Molly has the same round, innocent face, freckled complexion, and reddish hair that Phil has. She's a couple of years older, she wears her hair longer, and she doesn't wear glasses. Otherwise you could take them for twins. I've noticed she blushes more often, and she was doing it now. "Do you like him?" she asked.

"Kind of soon to pass judgment, but so far I haven't seen anything not to like. Anyway, I'm willing to go out on a limb and guess he's an improvement over You-Know-Who." Molly's last romance, as far as I knew, had been with an older, married sleazeball, and had left her feeling pretty worthless. Her logic, such as it was at the time, seemed to go along the lines of, "If even a sleazeball can't admit he's carrying on with you, how low must you be?"

"What did I ever see in him?"

"Beats me. I'm sorry I brought him up. Forget him. How serious is this with Craig?"

"I don't know yet. It might get to be pretty serious. Neither one of us is in a big hurry."

"Good."

"Y'all comin'?" It was Phil's voice.

"Be right there," Molly called back. "So you do like him?"

"You make a cute couple," I said, hoping she wouldn't

be offended by my blatant reversion to high-school-girlish repartee. I've never been good at that kind of stuff and it was the best I could do. Anyway, it was true. And besides, Craig was employed, acquainted with personal hygiene, and willing to meet the family. That may not seem to be a lot to ask, but you'd be surprised.

"If y'all don't need me in there, I'll help Floyd get settled at the table. Don't forget my slaw, now." Mrs. Purvis was at the screen door.

"No, ma'am," Molly said. "We sure won't. Here," she said to me, pulling a bowl from the refrigerator and putting it on top of my stack of plates.

When we got back outside, me with my tray and Molly with a pitcher of tea and an assortment of seafood sauces, the others had settled around the picnic table. I took the spot on the bench next to Phil, and Molly slid onto the other bench beside Craig. Mr. Pittman and Mrs. Purvis commanded the ends of the table.

"Lou-Ella will say grace," Mr. Pittman told us before anybody could mess up and make a premature grab for the catfish.

"Lord God, our Creator and Savior," Lou-Ella Purvis began in a chatty tone that made clear how comfortable she was talking to the Lord God. "We thank You for America and for the peace that passeth understanding and we thank You for these good friends and family. In the name of the One who fed five thousand with two little fishes and five barley loaves, we thank You for these catfish and hushpuppies and we thank You for the slaw and we thank You for the blueberry crumble I saw in the kitchen. And we ask You to help us please You in our daily walk and all our doings. In Jesus' precious name. Amen."

"Uh-oh! I think she forgot to bless the cocktail sauce," Phil whispered.

I covered my mouth with a paper napkin and muttered back, "But she remembered to watch out for our daily walk and all our doings. You think she meant anything in particular by that?"

"How could you think such a thing?" Phil asked.

"I guess I have a dirty mind. I'm going to have to risk some of that sauce, anyway."

Mr. Pittman was looking at us suspiciously, so I smiled at him as innocently as I could as I reached for the cocktail sauce.

We pitched into the mounds of food. For a few brisk minutes, dinner conversation consisted mostly of "Can I pass anybody the fish?" and "More slaw?" When the feeding frenzy slowed down enough that we were just sipping at our tea and pushing fish bones around on our plates, the conversation branched out.

We heard about the mystery trip First Baptist was getting up and the fact that there were so many old people going that they were hiring a special van for handicap accessibility so Floyd, Mr. Pittman, really should plan to go.

From Craig Bland we heard about how hard it is to teach high school these days, considering the impact of video games and drugs and having to mainstream children with all sorts of problems right into the classroom.

"We have so many kids with medical and behavioral and emotional challenges—we call them challenges these days—that it's a wonder we ever get any teaching done. I heard the other day about a parent bringing a lawsuit against a school because the school—the school, mind you—wasn't providing appropriate medical care!"

"The sins of the fathers will be visited upon the children," Mrs. Purvis contributed to this topic.

I'm in a better position than most to see how creatively some fathers and mothers manage to visit sin upon their children. "We just had a case where a man and woman were abusing her little girl. Mean, awful things. And we were sure it was mostly the man who was doing it, but the woman wouldn't testify against him, not even to reduce her own sentence. She told Hen the world's coming to an end in a couple of years anyway and she wouldn't have to face a judge with what she'd done, she'd face the Lord. Good ol' Hen puffed up and told her, 'You won't be facin' the Lord for long, you pore pitiful excuse for a mother. You're goin' to roast in hell and if God answers prayer, I'll get a chance to help turn the spit.' I was proud of him, but it didn't shake her a bit."

This flight of righteous hyperbole on Hen's part might have been inspired by the fact that the sins of the woman and her boyfriend involved the perversely imaginative use of an electric skillet. I shivered at the recollection of what they'd done to that little girl.

It was only when I noticed everybody staring at me that I realized that as a topic of conversation at a more-or-less family fish fry it was more than a little strong.

"Everybody ready for dessert?" Molly asked, rescuing me.

By the time we had consumed Aunt Lulu's dessert and Phil, ignoring Mrs. Purvis's frown, was picking at the sweet crust around the edges of the pan, I was ready to try to redeem my status as a good guest by making interesting conversation. What was on my mind, of course, was the body under the bridge, but after my earlier *faux pas* I sensed that they might not want to hear about the sand on the dead man's eyeballs. Instead, I offered my new resolution to clean up my property and become a patron of the arts.

Good old Phil did his part. "Y'all should have seen the prices on the stuff we saw up in Atlanta the last time we were there. Hundreds and hundreds of dollars for recycled auto parts."

"I don't see how you can call that art," said Phil's possible future step-mother.

"Nevertheless, the general idea has some Biblical precedent, Lou-Ella," Mr. Pittman offered. "Jesus himself did believe in recycling."

Miz Purvis looked at him suspiciously. "I don't recollect where it says that."

"Right there after the feeding of the five thousand that you referred to when you said grace," Mr. Pittman said. "Didn't Jesus tell his disciples to pick up the scraps and not waste anything?"

While Mrs. Purvis was muttering, "Well, I'll have to look that up. What translation do you use, Floyd?" Phil jumped in.

"What you ought to do, Trudy," Phil said, "You ought to find a place to rent you a welding rig. Then you could clean up your property and make your own sculpture all at the same time."

"I'll think about that," I said. "I had only gotten as far as thinking of renting a truck to haul things off."

"It's a great idea," Molly contributed, no doubt determined to keep me talking about something besides child abuse. "What you could do is have a fish fry at your place and invite everybody you know and let them help. No telling what you'd come up with."

"I have a piece of sculpture that looks like it might have been made like that," Craig said. "Except I'm sorry to say I'm such an ignoramus that it never occurred to me 'til right this minute to call it sculpture. Christmas morning a few years ago I went out on my porch and there was this thing I've always called a hunkajunk, a bunch of parts from tractors and plows and I don't know what all, welded together. Some of my students had made it for me. I didn't want to hurt their feelings, so I put it out in a corner of my backyard and planted a morning glory under it, which pretty much covers it up, at least in the summer.''

"Sounds like you ought to polish it and put it in the front yard," Phil said.

"Maybe you could get them to make some more, if there's a market for that kind of thing," Mr. Pittman suggested.

Craig grinned. "Get 'em off the county welfare and into some gainful employment. I'm for that, whether it's art or not. You know, I could probably get some kind of grant to help out with a project like that."

"There wasn't a girl named Coreen in that bunch, was there?" I asked. "If there was, you might have a high-priced piece out there under your morning glories." That would be the end-all of coincidences, I thought.

"We could put you in touch with a gallery that handles her work," Phil said. "You could make a nice little windfall and get the hunkajunk out of your yard at the same time."

"I could go for that," Craig said, "But this was just a bunch of boys and I don't think they made it themselves, anyway."

"Too bad." Molly looked as dejected as though she'd been thinking this was a serious conversation. That's what love'll do for you.

"I didn't mean to say they didn't do any of it," Craig said, responding to her tone. "But they did have help getting the parts together, somebody with a junkyard over by Mendes.''

I'm not sure where the conversation went after that, because I was distracted again. When Mrs. Purvis said she needed to be going so she could get her beauty sleep for church the next morning, we all pitched in to clean up. Then Phil walked with me out to my car, carrying Aunt Lulu's pan.

"Nice evening. Thanks for asking me over," I said.

"Always a pleasure, Trudy," he said, but I could tell his good manners were on automatic. His thoughts were elsewhere and when he spoke again I realized it was my fault. My needling about Mrs. Purvis had struck a sensitive spot.

"You don't have to talk like that to be a church secretary, do you?"

"Uh-huh. I'm pretty sure there's a test you have to take, part vocabulary, part theology, and part etiquette, including a dress code. Then…" I was really warming up to the idea, but—

"I withdraw the question," Phil said.

"Oh. Okay. But, anyway, I wouldn't worry about it. Really. She's probably on especially good behavior right now, while she feels like she's on probation. I'm sure she'll loosen up, once she's a member of the family."

"You always know just the right thing to say, Trudy," Phil said, shoving the pan at me.

I went home, well fed, content, and with a plan for the morrow, even though Mrs. Purvis might have told me it ought to be against my religion to take thought for that.

SEVEN

On a normal Sunday morning, Hen toddles down to the Ogeechee United Methodist Church with his wife (Teri) and daughter (Delcie) in time for Sunday School, the picture of old-fashioned family values.

Hen will wear a nice sports jacket and slacks instead of his uniform, usually with a blue shirt because Teri's extremely color conscious and she picks out shirts that compliment his eyes. Teri is always—for church or for any other day—dressed in a brightly colored outfit that brings out the sparkle in her eye and the bloom on her cheek and is made of something comfortable and washable that doesn't hamper her movement while she's teaching the preschoolers, which she does as a volunteer at church on Sunday and during the week for a salary.

Delcie, now. Delcie. She's in first grade this year, bright and beautiful, beginning to resist the fussy dresses Teri likes to put her in, but still on Sundays wearing puffy sleeves and full skirts, maybe even a bow in the back. Delcie would rather be making secret lean-tos in the pine-straw or crawling around under my house with the cats than playing with tea sets or even computers, and skirts cramp her style. She adopted one of the cats, black with white mittens, and we saw to it that she got her shots. "Paws" seemed like a natural name for the cat, and Hen, being Hen, raised the question of how to spell it, recommending "Pause," since she's never still. Delcie's new enough to reading that she's fascinated by words, so after Teri took the time to explain about the spelling, Delcie giggled at the joke, but she stuck with "Paws." Paws continues to live with the rest of the throng at my place, not at the Huckabee house. Teri's allergic.

They make a handsome family, especially when they're joined by Aunt Lulu, who has no peers, appearance-wise. Since there's not all that much entertainment in Ogeechee, Aunt Lulu and Pauline Brewton (of Pauline's Cut-n-Curl) entertain a lot of people besides themselves with the semi-annual game they play, inventing a color for Aunt Lulu's hair and a name for the color. Then Aunt Lulu goes shopping for outfits to match the color. Lately it's been "Pineapple Daquiri," I think, so she's been getting a lot of wear out of a two-piece silk suit in a silvery yellow color. As I said, a handsome family.

On Sunday mornings, Hen teaches a class called, for the age-group, "60 More or Less" (mostly more, and mostly females, including his mother). They dote on him. It has to be habit and the social life, even more than Hen or the desire for religious education, that brings these seniors back Sunday after Sunday. Much as I love and admire my cousin (and I really do, but don't tell him I said so), I doubt he can teach them much about walking in the paths of righteousness, even if they aren't all the angelic personages their benign smiles and snowy hair would lead you to believe.

I'm the black sheep of the family since I dawdle around until time for the preaching service. As I've suggested earlier, in Ogeechee there's not much in the way of a social circle for people like me—single and relatively young—and that extends to the churches. Unlike the seniors, I can't even get a satisfying social connection out of

Sunday School. I do occasionally help out—I'll help Teri if she asks me to, and I'm a sucker for anything that involves Delcie—but mostly I stay clear. I'm sure there's a campaign to get me more involved, especially since I'm perceived to be dating a Baptist and there's bound to be apprehension about the possibility of a mixed marriage, as well as lively concern over whether it will be the Methodist church or the Baptist church that loses a member if that happens.

This, however, was emphatically not a normal Sunday morning.

I was ready to have another talk with Oscar Jackson and take another look at his place of business, but I made the mistake of checking in at the station before I lit out. It was a mistake because I had hoped my line of investigation would pan out and I'd be able to quietly solve the case, to the grateful astonishment of the rest of the OPD, especially the chief. No such luck. When I got to the station, Hen was already there at his desk with a wad of papers in his hand and not decked out in his Sunday best.

"You get Dwight to take your Sunday School class?" I asked.

"Naw. Wouldn't work out. Dwight's a Buddhist. Thought you knew. Mama's doin' it."

He waved his handful of papers at me. "The wonders of modern technology have already provided us with a copy of the medical examiner's report. Freely translating from the language of the laboratory, our man died of massive trauma to most of his internal organs. He has bruises on the back of his calves, crushed ribs, a punctured lung. Not to mention the kind of injuries that are generally consistent with those tire tracks running up and down his body.''

I nodded to indicate understanding.

"You surely noticed I said those injuries are generally consistent with the tire tracks.''

"Yes, Your Honor, I did notice that.''

"I put it that way because there are some confusin' discrepancies. Not contradictions exactly, but confusin' discrepancies.''

"I get the part about confusion,'' I said helpfully.

"Well, look here, and learn. There had been a couple of blows to the head—one under the right eye, which you observed, and one on the back of the head—that had time to swell and bleed and discolor, which means it happened some time before the fatal trauma to the rest of him.''

"Do you think he was in a fight?''

Hen spread photos on the table in front of me. "Take a look and tell me what you think.''

I took my time, looking at photos of the body taken from half a dozen different angles, comparing the pictures with what I remembered seeing for myself. "I don't see any other marks on his face. You'd expect more than one blow, wouldn't you? Some other bruises or scrapes. Something. And as far as I can remember, his hands weren't bruised or scraped.''

"That's right,'' Hen confirmed, glancing back at the report he was holding.

"Besides his head injuries, are there any indications that he was in a fight?'' I asked. Hen shook his head. "So, maybe somebody sneaked up and gave him a sucker punch before he could fight back?''

"It's kind of hard to sneak up on somebody from the front,'' Hen pointed out.

"Right." I considered other possibilities. "So maybe somebody knocked him out and then ran over him."

"Remember, some time elapsed between the blow and the running over."

"Right." I hate it when he keeps being right.

"But you're thinking, Trudy. That's good. I like to see that in my people. What else?"

That's Hen's way of saying how much he values my detecting abilities. As a matter of fact, I might as well admit right now that our habit of constantly challenging each other on the job tends to produce pretty solid police work. So I thought before answering. "Well, for one thing, I'd say Mr. Lester DeLoach, a.k.a. Tariq Last Name Unknown, really ticked off people at least twice last night. Maybe one person hit him and made him woozy and careless on the highway and then later somebody else ran over him."

"Maybe."

"Or depending on how ticked this other person was, it could have been the same person, twice. This person could have knocked him out and then put him down there and run over him."

"So we'd be talking about a fairly strong person. Why drag him under the bridge?"

"Was he dragged? I didn't see signs of dragging." Hen isn't the only one who can ask questions designed to make somebody challenge assumptions. He picked up the pictures again and studied them as I talked.

"Maybe if there was a fight, if you could call it that, it took place under the bridge," I continued.

"No signs of that," Hen said, slapping the pictures back on the table. "I'd say the body was not dragged down there. Matter of fact, it looks to me like he was hit up there on the bridge. If the force knocked him over the

guardrail, he could have rolled up against that piling. We
got some clear car tracks and footprints down there near
the body, includin' Tanner's, but not the scuffin' sort of
stuff you'd get with a fight."

"Well, what? What does this tell us?"

"I'm workin' on it," Hen said. "The one thing I'm
sure of is that nobody besides Tanner has come forward
to tell us about runnin' over anybody, accidentally or with
'malice of forethought' as one of my deppities used to
say. I've got the area closed off 'til we can be sure we're
through going over it. Another thing. Those bruises on the
back of his legs look like he was pushed up against something low, maybe the guardrail on the bridge. That fits.
But some of those other injuries were post mortem, including the ones that left those nice tracks."

"So. Let me see if I'm taking all this in. He got beat
up in a fight, but not very much. Then he got knocked off
the bridge and killed."

"Or maybe killed as he was knocked off the bridge.
He was dead before he hit bottom, or his eyes would have
closed reflexively and there wouldn'ta been sand on
'em."

I took a minute to digest that. "Okay. Then he got run
over."

"Generally speakin' that fits with what these pictures
tell us."

"This man must have had a real gift for bringing out
the worst in people."

"Let that be a lesson to you, Trudy. The only other
thing that might mean something is some cotton fibers on
the body that don't match what he was wearin'. Could
just be careless laundry technique, but they made a note
of it here on the autopsy report. And speakin' of fibers,

did I ever tell you about the poor feller I saw who got hit by a tractor trailer and dragged to death? Left a long blue smear on the highway that had us confused at first, 'til we realized it was his blue jeans wearing off.''

I've noticed that Hen begins to sound more callous than usual whenever he suspects I'm about to display normal human feeling. It's probably not a bad way to keep me in balance, since it works on me like a dash of cold water and my reaction is to become more business-like and to change the subject. "Yep, you told me about that, thanks. Did I tell you about my visit with Oscar Jackson?" I asked.

"You know blame well you didn't. Who's Oscar Jackson?"

So I told him about how and why I tracked down Oscar Jackson, and what Oscar told me about Coreen Collins and another man coming down with Tariq. I even threw in something about Craig Bland's hunkajunk for good measure. All of which goes to explain why Hen was with me when I pulled up at J&D Salvage and Towing a little later that morning.

The place was locked up tight, doors, windows, chain-link fence, and everything. It was a business, after all, and it was a Sunday morning. I should have realized the business would be closed. Since Oscar Jackson lived on the premises, it meant we couldn't even get back to his school bus to knock on his door and find out if he was at home.

We examined the "4 SALE" cars, with particular attention to the front ends and tire treads on the truck, without finding anything especially interesting, and then we sat there in front of the building for a little while, hoping Oscar Jackson would show up while we were making a new plan. Just to kill time, I started telling Hen about the bus the old man lived in, but it sparked an idea. "Can you find Frog Pond?"

"I could find you a frog pond any size you want," he bragged. "Any particular frog pond?"

"Not a frog pond. Frog Pond, with a church."

Hen prides himself on knowing every inch of our county and every foot of the surrounding counties, so of course he said he could find it. He did find it, but it gave me some satisfaction that he wasn't able to go directly to it. Down the fourth narrow dirt road we tried, he got help from a small sign saying FROG POND BAPTIST CHURCH 2 MI. By the time we drove up onto the hard-packed dirt under an ancient oak in the yard surrounding the small red-brick building perched on a hill, services were coming to an end.

When the car stopped, we could hear the joyous hand-clapping and soaring voices proclaiming their belief that they were walking in the sunlight of God's love. Hen being Hen, and me being me, we sang and clapped along, enjoying the sunshiny autumn moment there in the churchyard, the thought of malice and murder pushed aside. The small oak-shaded cemetery at one side of the building did suggest death, but it was peaceful death, natural, journey's-end kind of death, without a hint of a world where one person would whale another person over the head, knock him off a bridge, and then run over him. I was mulling over the different ways we could go about trying to find out why and how whatever happened to Tariq happened when the music ended and people began drifting out of the building.

Of course we were conspicuous there in their yard with our police car, and one of the first people out of the church, a wiry, wary man in a neat dark blue suit headed our way. Good social manners as well as good police procedure say you get out of the car to talk to somebody, so we were both on our feet by the time he got to us.

"Somethin' we can do for you?" the man said, with a slight, but perfectly understandable, defensive edge in his voice.

"You could get everybody to go back inside and sing another couple of verses," Hen said appreciatively. "And you could send your piano player over to my church some Sunday to liven things up a little."

"That's what brought you?" Hen's charm hadn't done much to soften the man's suspicions.

"Not what brought us, no. I'm Henry Huckabee, Chief of Police over in Ogeechee. This police officer is Trudy Roundtree. We were hopin' to find Mr.... What was his name again, Trudy?"

"Oscar Jackson," I said.

"Oscar? You after Oscar Jackson?" Our one-man reception committee was aghast. Wariness disappeared behind outrage. "You ain't got nothing on Oscar! Anybody says Oscar ever done anything wrong is lyin'. And you outta your territory anyway." He thumped the Ogeechee insignia on the car door.

"We'll call you as a character reference if we need to," Hen said, undisturbed.

"Calvin Simmons," he said, pulling himself up as tall as he could. He was still glaring at Hen when I caught sight of Oscar Jackson coming through the doorway of the church. I'd thought him an imposing figure the day before, even in his everyday clothes. Imposing isn't a big enough word to cover the impression he made in a black suit and dazzling white shirt. Maybe it's just because he was on the steps of a church, but with his size and that walking stick of his, I couldn't help but think of Moses and his staff, leading his people out of the wilderness.

Presuming on our slight, but, I thought, not actually hostile, acquaintance, I waved to get his attention. He nodded to acknowledge me and in a few moments—slowly enough to make it absolutely clear that I had not summoned him and that he was completely at ease, joining us because he wanted to—he broke away from the knot of women who had him surrounded and began to move in our direction.

"Mornin', Mr. Jackson," I said.

"You back to talk about what happened to Lester?" the old man asked.

"Oh, Lester," Calvin Simmons said. From his tone, he wouldn't have done Lester much good as a character witness.

"Yes, we do need to talk to you some more about Lester. This is Ogeechee's Chief of Police, Henry Huckabee, my boss. We've found out a little more about what happened to your nephew, and we're hoping you can help us."

"No handcuffs?" he asked, leaning on his stick. "Just helping the po-lice?"

"No handcuffs," Hen said.

"You give me a ride home?" he asked.

Hen opened the back door of the car and bowed slightly in a fair, if ironic, imitation of a chauffeur. As Calvin Simmons shrank back, Oscar Jackson took his time arranging himself in the car. By the time he was finished and we were ready to go, the whole congregation had recongregated around us, with expressions on their faces ranging from interest through apprehension to outright hostility.

"Got me another ride home today, Gloria, thank you," Oscar Jackson called into the crowd. "Got business with the po-lice. I'll just have to wait for that fried chicken, if that's all right with you. I'll get word to you if you need to smuggle it to me over at the jail, with a hacksaw in it.'' Oscar Jackson had the perfectly serious, straight-faced manner good comedians cultivate. I remembered it from our conversation about how many Lester DeLoaches I knew.

"With gravy," a woman called out.

"You can see it was his idea to ride with us," Hen said to Calvin Simmons, holding his hands wide and smiling past Calvin Simmons's shoulder at the congregation.

"You call me if you need any help," Simmons said to Jackson, then he turned to face the crowd and raised his voice so that everybody could hear. "It's about that Lester." The crowd parted around us, like the Red Sea before Moses, as Hen eased out of the churchyard. I may have imagined the hisses as mouth after mouth repeated Lesssssster.

EIGHT

IN SPITE OF HIS apparent ease with the situation, some of which he may have assumed for his adoring audience at Frog Pond, Oscar Jackson was quiet until we pulled up in front of J&D Salvage and Towing, responding only monosyllabically to Hen's attempts to make friendly, casual conversation as we rode.

Jackson took his time with the padlock on the door and we entered the building. Then, instead of leading us back to the homey bus I'd been describing in such detail to Hen, and maybe offering us a glass of tea, he stopped when we reached the hook with the engine hanging from it that I'd noticed the day before. Maybe he was pouting because we'd done him out of a chicken dinner.

He leaned against a table. "I don't know nothing about Lester being run over. I already told you that."

"But you do know something you haven't told me," I said. "Yesterday, you said he walked out of here, but you took it for granted he was in the hospital. Why'd you think that?"

He stared and shook his head as though to dislodge a troublesome thought.

"Why?" Hen prompted. "Why would he be walking out of here to go to the hospital?"

"No reason. She just took me by surprise, telling me Lester was dead like that."

"You mentioned the hospital before I told you he was dead."

He arched his back and sighed. "All I did was hit him. I mighta felt like killing him for a minute, what he was doing to Lettie, but I didn't. He walked out of here and if somebody run over him I don't know anything about that."

I had so many questions after that I didn't know where to start. Hen knew what to do. He said almost exactly what he says when Delcie brings home some artwork from school and offers it for him to admire. Instead of risking making a serious mistake and cutting off communication by assuming, for example, that the big square thing is a house and finding out later that it was really a piece of toast, he always says, "Well, why don't you just tell me all about it."

"It was an accident I hurt him as bad as I did," Jackson said, "But, tell the truth, I wanted to hurt him."

"Uh-huh," Hen said.

"It was right here." Jackson waved his stick at the hook. "See, the boy knew he'd been doing wrong, so when I lost my temper and started waving my stick around he dodged back. Now, I admit I did connect with the stick, but he dodged back and hit this here." He whacked at the engine block. "Hit him right there."

"What made you want to hurt him?" I asked, mentally noting that his story accounted for the pre-death head injuries.

"That boy had been stealing from his grandmother and I just then found out about it."

"What's that to you?" Hen asked.

"She's my sister, Lettie. See, Lettie raised me, pert' near, and then all those years later, here come Lester and she helped take care of him, too. Now, she's not doing

very well; it's our turn to take care of her but instead of
doin' right, like he was raised, he's stealing from her.
Made me so mad, I hit him. Now what's Lettie gone do?
Poor Lettie. What we gone do about her?''

We didn't have an answer for that.

"So you hit him," Hen said. "Then what happened?
You still so mad you want to hurt him more? You take
him out and run over him?''

"Did not. I told you he walked outta here. Knew he
wasn't welcome. I made sure he knew that. I felt bad, too.
Losing my temper wasn't gone help Lettie. Anyhow, Lester wasn't hurt that bad. He was mad at me and mad that
the rest of 'em didn't take his side against me—me and
Lettie. Tell the truth, I blamed all of them. Him mostly,
but all the whole bunch. They're a bad bunch, all of 'em.
Started fightin' each other. I don't need that kind of things
messin' up my peace and quiet. I ran 'em all out.''

"Did they all leave together?" Hen asked.

"Nah. That other man—his name'll come to me—he
whipped outta here with that big ol' bike kicking up
gravel. Coreen was right on his heels in the truck, not
even worried they hadn't got the stuff lashed down in it.''

"Wait a minute," I said. "When I was here before,
you said the other man came with them. Where'd a bike
come from?''

He thought about that, then shook his head. "I don't
know. Maybe he rode it down. Or they coulda brought it
down in the truck.''

"Okay. Just trying to get a picture as we go along. You
said this man and Coreen left, separately. But Tariq was
still here? Then what?''

"I left Lester out front and locked the gate behind the
whole pack of 'em. What I care if he had to walk to
Glennville? Not but a few miles. Didn't think it would

hurt him, might give 'im a chance to think about what he'd been doin'. Next thing I know, Officer Roundtree is here telling me a Lester DeLoach been run over. How'd he get run over?''

"We don't know yet," I said. "But we're working on it. Maybe it was an accident. Maybe somebody didn't see him walking along the road at night."

He looked doubtful. "I don't know about that. It wasn't all that dark yet when he left here."

"Tell us more about how Lester was stealing from your sister and how you found out about it," Hen said. "He just volunteer that information to you?"

"It was that other man let it out. See, they brought a truck with 'em to put the stuff in and that other man let out a whistle when he saw it all and said how that would pay the rent for a while. I'da thought he was just jokin', but Lester tried to hush 'im up, so I paid attention. It come out Lester'd been making a lot of money off that stuff and just givin' me a little bit for Lettie. I call that stealin', and from his own grandmother! I don't like that Coreen much, she's got too up-town for her own good, but when we started talking about the money, she turned on him, too, like she didn't know what he'd been up to, either. Maybe he hadn't been passin' along her share. I lost my temper—the Lord's been dealing with me about my temper and maybe this is His last warnin'. When I lost my temper and hit out at Lester, he put up his hand to stop me hittin' him and I saw that gold watch, and I got madder and madder!''

Oscar was brandishing the stick around, angry again as he thought about it. It did look like the Lord still had some dealing to do.

"Let me make sure I've got this right," Hen said, gesturing dismissively at the stick. "When you say stealing, you mean—"

It was about then, when we seemed to be making some progress, that we had an unpleasant surprise. Rufus Badcock strode through the front door, swaggering and glowering. He's a stringy little man and a swagger doesn't set well on him, but he has no idea it makes him look like somebody trying to stretch up to the "You Cannot Ride Unless You're This Tall" mark. Unlike Hen, who, with all his faults, is emotionally stable enough that he doesn't need a gun to make him feel like he can handle things, little old Rufus Badcock seems to derive a real sense of importance from the weight of his weapons and other appurtenances of his office, a sense of importance that is apparent, naturally, only if he is wielding those aforementioned appurtenances.

For once, I didn't see any point in trying to prove female officers are as tough as males. I left it up to Hen to deal with the county sheriff.

"Hey, Rufus," he said. "Looking to junk that car of yours? I don't think Mr. Jackson's open on Sunday."

"Whachall doing out here in the county?" Sheriff Badcock answered. "Donchall know where the limits of Ogeechee run out?"

"We gave Mr. Jackson a ride home from church, Rufus. How about you? You been to church?"

"I come to arrest me a cold-blooded killer," the sheriff said.

"Trudy, what you been up to?" Hen asked, for all the world as if it was a serious question. "Something you forget to tell me about?" I heard Oscar Jackson take a deep breath behind me.

"Probably," I admitted. "But I'd be glad to fill you both in if you want me to. Let me see, now. Last night I trimmed my toenails and scrubbed the bathtub, trying to get that rust stain out of the—''

"You're both about as funny as a rubber crutch," the sheriff said, a simile that struck me oddly, coming from one of the few people I know who might actually think it was funny to hand a rubber crutch to somebody who needs support. "You got yourselves a vehicular homicide over in Ogeechee, but Ogeechee's the only place you're the law. Looks to me like I got myself the man who did it right here."

"Rufus, this is our case," Hen said, without humor this time. "We're investigating and we aren't ready to make an arrest."

"You ain't gone be ready to make an arrest. You got no jurisdiction outside of Ogeechee."

"What makes you think this man's a killer?" Hen asked.

"Why would I want to let him know what I've got on him?" Rufus countered. "Fact is, I got a tip about a fracas out here and this man beating up on the victim."

"A tip from…?"

"Never you mind 'from.'"

"An anonymous tip? You're coming out here to arrest a man and interfere with my orderly investigation based on an anonymous tip?"

"Git on back to your speeding tickets, Huckabee, and I'll get on with my job."

"Your job being to haul in this ruthless mad-dog of a cold-blooded killer?" Hen asked, turning to look at the old man we'd just fetched home from church.

Without missing a beat, Oscar Jackson fell into a slouch and let his walking stick droop, but Hen's sarcasm was lost on the sheriff.

"We'll just let a jury decide about that," Badcock said. "Come on, Jackson."

"On the basis of an anonymous tip about some fracas, you are assuming this man ran over a body that was found miles from here?" Hen was not faking amazement.

"Aren't you going to read him his rights?" I asked, earning a thoughtful glance from Jackson, a nod of approval from Huckabee, and a scowl from Badcock.

"I wouldn't put up a fight," Hen said to the old man, "But I wouldn't talk to him without my lawyer, either. We'll be in touch." For this contribution to civil rights, Hen earned his own scowl from the sheriff, which bothered him as little as it had bothered me.

"That your truck out there?" Rufus asked Oscar.

"No."

"You got the keys to it?"

"How else can I let people try it out?"

"So you could have used it for the crime," Rufus said. "We'll get the lab boys on that. Open and shut. Come on."

We stood by as Oscar locked up. I pointed our car back toward Ogeechee.

"Never mind what Rufus thinks, it looks to me like we've got us some other likely suspects to look at besides Mad Dog Jackson," Hen said.

"Uh-huh. Coreen or that motorcycle man could have been waiting for Tariq on the road. He'd have been an easy mark on foot. But, so far, much as I hate to say it, Badcock could be right. Oscar Jackson could have gone after him. Sounds like he was mad enough."

"Well, I think he's safe for now, whether he did it or not," Hen said. "But we'd better have us a talk with the widow, that Coreen, and get a look at that truck she was drivin'. Wouldn't want to overlook anything obvious."

By now we were back at the station. Hen climbed out of the car but leaned back in to say, "First thing I'm gonna do when the clerk's office opens in the mornin', I'm gonna look up if it's too late to file for sheriff. Somebody's got to do something about that pore excuse for a humanoid."

I've never much liked Rufus Badcock, but I was beginning to wonder if my prejudice, no doubt colored by my relationship with Hen, had been unjust. It looked like there might be something I could learn from him. Try as I may, I've never been able to irritate Hen as much as Badcock can, and he can do it without putting out any apparent effort. And I could see a definite up side to Hen's running for sheriff. If he ran, it would be bound to take some of his attention away from protecting me from the seamier side of life at the OPD, and I'd have a little more breathing space. If he actually won, he wouldn't be my boss anymore. It would be pure serendipity, for me and the county, if he turned out to be good at it. Stranger things have happened.

"You go on home and take it easy for a while. See you for supper over at Mama's?" Hen asked.

"Hmm?" I'd been enjoying my thoughts so much it took me a second to focus. "Oh. Yes." As I drove away I slid happily back into my fantasy. Hen as county sheriff. I'd vote for him against anybody, especially against a pore excuse for a humanoid.

NINE

THE WAY I REMEMBER Sundays when I was a child, Mama and Daddy and I would join the rest of the family at church, then we'd all go to Grandma's house for a big Sunday dinner and we'd idle away the afternoon. That's what I still think of as the standard Sunday, even though I wasn't very old before it broke down. I was still young when Mama and Daddy died in a car wreck and Grandma took over my upbringing. Everything in my life took on a different flavor after that, but one thing that didn't change was that everybody still gathered at Grandma's house whenever they gathered, on Sundays and other times.

When Grandma died, she left a major hole in everybody's life, and one of the ways we re-structured our lives around the gaping hole was that we shifted the family meeting place. Maybe it would have been different if she hadn't left the house to me, a single woman, but she did. Because I had an absolute fit about it, we still have holiday and special celebrations at what I'm still getting used to thinking of as my place. As a routine thing, though, we go to Aunt Lulu's.

Several years back, Billy Watson opened his fish place west of town and people started going by there after church on Sunday instead of going home, to give the women-folk a day off, since so many of the women-folk these days either have jobs outside their homes or have reached the stage of life where they don't need to prove, or don't feel like proving, what hot-shot homemakers they are.

Aunt Lulu's house is a good half-century younger than mine and anybody in her right mind would have to admit it's much more comfortable. As it has evolved, my house (I keep practicing calling it mine) has acquired electricity and a screened-in porch, but Aunt Lulu's not only has closets and central heating, which mine doesn't, it has air conditioning. It's one of those nice brick places out north of town.

Another change to family tradition is that Aunt Lulu has become one of those who goes over to Billy Watson's after church, or to that family-style dinner place over in Bellville, so when I pulled up at her place early that Sunday evening it was for a "simple supper," not Sunday dinner.

Hen, Teri, and Delcie were already there. Hen, as usual, was entertaining. He is a natural born storyteller, with an in-born knack for subjecting the plain truth to strategic nips and tucks like a cosmetic surgeon, in order to put the most attractive face on a yarn. Since his—our—line of work provides an endless supply of fresh material, he is endlessly entertaining, according to the commandments he laid down when he hired me: Thou shalt exaggerate the truth so much that nobody will believe it really happened; thou shalt not indulge thyself in telling stories about police encounters by people your audience knows; thou shalt not cause thy loved ones to worry about what you do for a living.

By the time Aunt Lulu had laid out the "simple supper" of canned asparagus topped with mayonnaise and grated cheddar, canned pears topped with mayonnaise and pecans, cold fried chicken, and her locally famous corn-bread (she says the secret is sour cream, but nobody else can duplicate it), Hen was launched into a tale about a woman—in another town, another time, he claimed—who had to be locked up every once in a while for assaulting her husband.

"Dear Christian woman, though, lovely woman," he insisted. "Always sorry for her sins, sorry for hers and everybody else's. You didn't have to check with the desk to know when Miz Sapp was in because you could hear her prayin' all over the building. Got on everybody's nerves somethin' fierce, the loudness of it, not the fact that she was prayin', Mama. Naturally we all appreciate being prayed over, especially in public and at the top of the pray-er's lungs. It was the fact that it was so loud and it went on so everlastin' long that bothered people. When they'd start bringing in the drunks on Saturday night she'd take on about 'em, one by one, by name, loudly and at length, ending up every time, for some reason, with, 'Thank you and God bless you!' Got so we couldn't arrest a drunk to save our lives whenever she was in; somehow they'd all get the word and manage to stay sober 'til she was out. That woman did more to clean up the town than I've ever done, and I swear, to this day whenever I hear somebody say, 'Thank you and God bless you!' I have a flashback on Miz Sapp."

"I always thought he was making this up," Teri said, "You know how he is. Then one day a woman came by the house selling brushes. I bought a little nail brush from her, just to be nice, and when she left she said, 'Thank you and God bless you!' I heard a crash from the kitchen. Hen had dropped his glass of tea."

"Thought I was hallucinatin'," Hen said, shaking his head.

"Not to change the subject," Aunt Lulu said, changing the subject, "but I want to ask, Trudy, if I can come use your sewing machine tomorrow."

"Of course, Aunt Lulu. Any time. But I didn't know you were a seamstress."

"You're absolutely right, I am not. I never did understand why it would make any sense for me to spend time and money sewing up clothes that might not fit or look right, when I could go down to the store and find something already made and know right off if I'd like it. Now, Mama was a whiz at it. Could just look at a magazine picture of what Alma or I wanted and make it for us, so we never had much reason to learn."

"So if you aren't sewing…?" I queried delicately.

"Well, it isn't sewing, really."

Hen was intrigued by now. "If it isn't really sewing, what do you plan to do with the sewing machine?"

"It's just that the stores aren't carrying what I need right now," she said, as if that explained anything.

"Why is that? Wrong season?" I asked.

Aunt Lulu gave up. "It's the wrong generation. I usually get Wilma Barnard to sew for me when I have to have something made, but this is out of the ordinary. Besides, it's supposed to be a secret."

Now we were all interested.

"Goody!" Delcie said. "It's a secret. Grandma's going to tell us a secret."

"A secret is something you *don't* tell," Teri told her daughter.

"But Grandma's going to tell, aren't you, Grandma?"

Of course she was going to tell.

"I'm goin' to tell you, but you aren't supposed to tell anybody else," Aunt Lulu said, shaking a finger in an admonishing way that made Delcie giggle. "The Geez-erettes are having their swimming party," she whispered.

Some of the older-generation men in town have a semi-secret, completely pointless club known as the OOG. Officially, the letters stand for Ogeechee's Old Gentlemen, but I've never heard anybody actually call it anything more respectful than OOG, or Ogeechee's Old Geezers, or sometimes, simply the Geezers. As far as I know, all they do is go down to Ozzie Rhodes's fish camp once a month and take turns fixing supper for each other. Phil Pittman, who is not an OOG but whose daddy is, says they have dues so they can afford to replace the grease in the deep fryer once a year whether it needs it or not. I imagine whatever the dues are it's worth it to some of the Geezers for the sake of being able to take a nip without having to try to hide the fact from a Geezerette. Uh-huh, Geezerette. According to Aunt Lulu, you don't have to be married to a Geezer to qualify for membership in the Geezerettes, you just have to be willing to make fun of them. A rule I've figured out for myself is that you have to qualify for Social Security.

Again according to Aunt Lulu, it has been a Geezerette tradition, ever since Oleta Griner's son, Russell, put in a swimming pool behind his house, to talk about having a swimming party. The first time the idea came up, Mrs. Griner said, "Y'all go ahead if you want to. I'll be glad to make cookies, but I won't be able to go in because my bathing suit has a hole in the knee." They talk about it every year, and Mrs. Griner makes the same joke about her bathing suit. Now Aunt Lulu was saying they were actually going to do it.

"I didn't make it to church this morning," I admitted. "Do you know something I don't know? Is the world coming to an end?"

"Brother Burns didn't mention it. I don't know why you and Henry can't arrange your work hours a little better. He's the boss, isn't he?"

Henry, for once, sat quietly, letting me answer. After all, she had asked me.

"He is definitely the boss, Aunt Lulu, but we have a man who is dead and the circumstances aren't entirely straightforward, so it's the job of the boss as well as the underlings to look into it without wasting any time."

"Going to church isn't wasting time. Henry's not so perfect that he doesn't need a good sermon once in a while, and neither are you."

I grinned at her. "You know perfectly well what I mean. And I know perfectly well you're saying this to me because you've said it to Hen 'til you're blue in the face and he hasn't changed his ways."

"Maybe he'll listen to you."

"Right. And maybe Martha Stewart will drop by and re-decorate my house. But back to the swimming party. Why now? You've been talking about it since before I came back to Ogeechee. You sure you want to trade talking about it for the real thing? It's liable to be a big letdown. Besides everything else, it's a little late in the season for a swimming party, isn't it?"

"That's why we're doing it now. Oleta says Russell's ready to cover the pool for the winter, and Lalie Coleman's about to have to go live with her daughter in Birmingham, so we just decided to go ahead and do it. We thought it would cheer Lalie up."

"Uh-huh. Lalie and anybody else in the neighborhood," Hen said and Teri gave him a poke in the ribs.

"What does this have to do with the sewing machine?" Teri asked. One of the many things Teri's had trouble getting used to about the house being mine is that the stuff in it is mine, too. In my half-hearted assault on the layers of family history that has accumulated over the years, I uncovered Grandma's treadle sewing machine in a storage-junk-utility room at the back of the house. Of course Teri would put the machine to better use than I do. Of course it wouldn't hurt me to give it to her. Maybe I will one of these days—after I've figured out my motivation and enough time has gone by to make clear to everybody, myself included, that the house and the stuff really are mine, to give or to keep.

This attitude on my part probably has something to do with why Teri and I have never become good friends. There are other reasons, too. For one thing, I've never spent much time with just her, apart from the rest of the family. She and Hen met at some class they were both taking over in Statesboro while I was living away. They got married and produced Delcie during that time, and when I came back and started working for Hen, it seemed to trigger some ill-will on her part. I sometimes wonder if she's jealous of all the time I spend with Hen. Or maybe she doesn't approve of a woman being in my line of work; maybe she thinks watching out for me puts Hen in danger. I know she thinks Grandma should have left the house to Hen instead of me. I'd like for us to be better friends, and I'm working on it.

"When are you going to get to the secret?" Delcie asked. "I thought you said you had a secret."

"This is the main part," Aunt Lulu told her. "You won't tell, will you?"

Delcie solemnly shook her head, her blue eyes big and innocent. Nobody with two brain cells to rub together would have trusted her for a second. The only thing that made it safe was that she had no clue what the secret was about.

"Okay. Here it is. I'm making a bathing suit," Aunt Lulu said, those Roundtree blue eyes sparkling.

Delcie pouted. "People don't make their bathing suits. They buy them."

"Sounds fishy to me, too," I said, pulling her onto my lap.

"Just wait and see," Aunt Lulu said.

"Is everybody making their own suits?" Teri asked.

"Oh, no. Most everybody is being pretty cagey about what they're doing, but I happen to know that Lalie has a real vintage one that belonged to her mother, and Lou-Ella's making one up out of tights and boxer shorts."

"Lou-Ella Purvis?" I couldn't imagine it. My mind simply refused to admit that Lou-Ella Purvis had that much of a sense of fun. It also refused to admit the image of Lou-Ella Purvis in a pair of tights. There was obviously more to that woman than I had realized before. Maybe the Pittmans weren't in as much trouble as I'd thought.

"Oh, yes. It was Lou-Ella's idea to have this as a sort of going-away party for Lalie. She's got Russell Griner to agree to be one of the judges and she thinks she can get Floyd Pittman to be another one and then maybe Phil'll put it in the paper, in the social column."

"Judges? You're going too fast for me."

"The bathing suits, Trudy. Judge the bathing suits."

"You're planning to have a—I'm struggling for the right expression here—a beauty pageant? You might want to give that some more thought, Aunt Lulu. Phil's a demon with that camera of his, you know. What if he wants to run pictures with the story?"

"Hmm. Maybe it's time for the *Beacon* to print something interesting for a change." Aunt Lulu smiled. I think she was trying to see if I, lover-like, would rush to the defense of Phil's paper. I didn't.

"I don't think the world—let alone Ogeechee—is ready for the sight of Lou-Ella Purvis in tights and boxer shorts," Hen said.

I had to agree. And it occurred to me that if Phil wanted to put an end to the looming possibility of Lou-Ella Purvis becoming his step-mother, he could probably do it by giving these bathing beauties a big spread in the *Beacon*. "The whole thing sounds like a lot of fun," I said, truthfully as well as supportively.

"Oh, I expect it will be. Everybody's looking forward to it. Oleta thinks we ought to have seafood for refreshments, so she's making crab dip. I said I'd make that seafood bisque from the Pirates' House cookbook, if I can remember where I put it, and—oh!"

"What's the matter, Grandma? Is there more secret?"

"No, Sweetie, that's all of the secret. I thought of something to tell your daddy. Hen, Oleta says your friend Tanner has a new car. Says he told her his old one got bent up when he ran over somebody, so he had to trade for a new one."

This was nonsense of a different sort at least.

"Good for ol' Tanner," Hen said. "His county check must go further than I would have thought. What's he got now?"

"Oleta says Tanner says it's an Oldsmobile, but she can't tell one hubcap from another, so she had to take his word for it." Aunt Lulu had the faint smile almost everybody gets when they talk about Tanner. The ones who don't have to come into actual contact with him think he's just a colorful character. "He's really been getting on Oleta's nerves, too, calling her on the telephone, like a big-shot business man, to check on the status of his bank account. She says he told her he's calling from his car phone. Sure wish I had his imagination."

"You're doing all right with the imagination you have," I said, "You and the Geezerettes."

"Well, thank you," she said with an unconvincing modest simper. "It must have caused some trouble for whoever he took it from, I bet."

"You've lost me again."

"The car phone."

"Well, Aunt Lulu, it can't be a real car phone, because that would be attached to a real car. I'm assuming Miz Griner didn't say Tanner's driving an honest-to-goodness Oldsmobile."

"No. Just the hubcap. But he really does have a phone."

"Trudy'll check that first thing tomorrow," Hen assured her. "What's for dessert?"

Tanner with a portable telephone? I couldn't remember any reports of missing telephones. Well, maybe whoever it belonged to hadn't missed it yet. And maybe he hadn't missed it because he was dead. Much as I disliked the idea, there was no way to avoid having Tanner at the top of my Monday morning to-do list. Then, as I was dipping into the pear cobbler, I began to see the silver lining to that cloud. If Tanner had taken something from Tariq besides the watch and Hen had failed to discover it, I would get no end of mileage out of it.

TEN

I DIDN'T EVEN BOTHER going by the station before I started work on Monday morning, just formulated a few ideas of where I might hope to find Tanner and set out. Hen likes to have police cars circulating around town all the time, to let the good folks know we're on the job and to keep the bad folks from being too open with their wrongdoing, so it didn't matter whether I found Tanner sooner or later. If I just kept cruising, I knew I'd find him.

The obvious place to start looking was at Tanner's house, but I was too late. He'd already hit the road for the day. Mrs. Griner, who lives just a few houses down and helps him out, told me she saw him going by—only she said "drivin' by" and rolled her eyes when she said it—when she went out to get the *Savannah Morning News* from the box in her driveway and she knew that was just before seven o'clock because she never sleeps past six-thirty no matter how late she's been up, on account of having to feed the darned dog. As far as I knew, it wasn't important to pin down when Tanner left home; all I cared was that he wasn't there, but I thanked her. To give you an idea how focused I was, I didn't even mention the Geezerettes' swimming party.

I drove back through town and turned east on 280, scanning for Tanner. I found him a little north and east of town and was pleased with myself for anticipating that,

the way what passes for his mind works, he'd avoid the
Glennville side of town for a while. He was puttering
along in what I assume was low gear until he caught sight
of me. Then he launched into what he might have thought
was peeling rubber. He dropped his bag of cans and his
hubcap and plunged across the drainage ditch along the
road, disappearing into a field of dry cornstalks. I'm pretty
sure he doesn't like me any better than I like him, but he
doesn't usually run from me. I took his flight to mean he
had something to hide. I hoped it would be something I
was interested in and not just a reflection of his paranoia.

Watching Tanner disappear, I considered my options.
One: I could play hide-and-seek with him among the cornstalks. That would be dirty, undignified, and irritating.
Two: I could stay there by the side of the road with his
hubcap and aluminum cans and wait for him to come to
me. The success of that would depend on (a) how much
he really did not want to talk to me, (b) how much he
cared about that particular hubcap and bag of cans, and
(c) which one of us had more time and patience. Much
as I hate to give Tanner credit for anything, I was afraid
he'd be able to wait me out. Theoretically, there was option three. I could call for back-up. I knew I'd never hear
the end of it if I did that, no matter what Tanner might
turn out to have been up to, so I went back to option one,
with a variation.

I stood up on the back bumper of my cruiser and gazed
out across the field. I saw nothing to tell me where Tanner
was. He was cagey enough to come to a stop, once he
was out of my sight, instead of setting up a commotion
of noise and movement by making his way through the
corn. I was still trying to come up with a pursuit option
that wasn't distasteful when I heard a chirp. I froze and
looked around, trying to match the sound with an insect,

bird, or snake. I didn't see anything. When it chirped again I realized the sound was coming from a telephone, not some unfamiliar kind of wildlife. It appeared to be coming from about three rows in and half a dozen stalks to my left. On the third chirp, Tanner answered and I smiled. Option one, with variation, had paid off.

"No. No. Whadduyuh want? No. Tanner! I don't know. No."

When I parted the cornstalks and saw him crouching there, trying to find the button that would let him hang up on the caller, he looked frantic, almost relieved to see me.

"What's the matter?" I asked.

"He said I missed our meeting," Tanner said, so aggrieved by the accusation that he forgot he was fleeing from my presence. "I never. I never had no meeting."

"Who was it?"

"How'd I know?"

"It wasn't some friend of yours calling you up on your new phone?" I could see him thinking that idea over, so before he decided to adopt it, I suggested, "He probably took you for somebody else, Tanner. I wouldn't worry about it if I were you. Nice phone. Where'd you get it?"

He tucked it under his arm, apparently hoping I wouldn't be able to see it and would forget all about it. "Came with the car," he said.

"Oh, yes. That's right. I heard you'd traded cars."

He gave one sharp, suspicious, decisive nod, sure as he could be that I was going to find some way to take his new car away from him. As it turned out, he was right.

A wicked impulse made me say, "Better let me see the registration, then, make sure everything's in order. Wouldn't want somebody taking advantage of you."

He narrowed his eyes and thought. He was into the car culture enough to know that people with cars have registration papers and license plates, just like they have batteries and flat tires. I waited fairly patiently as he rifled through his pockets, no doubt hoping there'd be something there that could pass for a car registration. There wasn't. Then he had an inspiration. "It's back at the house," he said.

I've heard that before, from smarter people than Tanner. He didn't impress me any more than they do. "You're supposed to keep it with the vehicle, you know. I could give you a ticket for not having it."

"I got it, but it's at the house. Anyway, I ain't drivin' now so you got no reason. I know all about speed traps. Cain't afford a ticket anyhow."

My conversations with Tanner, where I try to create a code that I hope will translate into what I mean to be saying to him, are always a challenge. I had no trouble looking like I was thinking it over. "Tell you what, Tanner. I'll skip the ticket if you help me out a little."

"Maybe. What?"

"I need to take a look at your telephone."

"What telephone?"

"You know what telephone. The one in your armpit."

"I told you it come with the car."

"But you didn't tell me where the car came from. Did you get it from that bridge down toward Glennville?" I could tell by the look on his face that I was right. He had helped himself to a new car (translation: hubcap) and cell phone as well as a watch. "I'm going to have to...to impound your car and confiscate your phone."

Tanner may not have the Intelligence Quotient of a lot of people, but he knows the police vocabulary. He puffed up for all the world like a bullfrog and drew a breath to croak out a protest.

"Unless you want us to lock you up for obstructing justice," I added, pretty sure he wouldn't like the sound of that. He didn't. Just as he was beginning to un-puff and hand me the telephone, it rang again. Tanner flinched and dropped it as if it had suddenly come to life and tried to bite his nose.

By the third ring I had retrieved it. "Hello."

"Well, hello, Sugar." It was a woman's voice, soft and musical, and sounding a little surprised. "What're you doin' with this phone?"

"Who is this?" I asked.

"Who is *this?*" she returned. "And, I asked you, what are you doing with this telephone?"

"I found it," I explained. "Can you tell me who it belongs to?"

"*I* found it," Tanner shouted, practically jumping up and down in irritation at my lie and desperate to explain it to the caller. "And she's trying to take it away from me."

"Shut up, Tanner," I said.

"Who is this?" the woman on the other end of phone asked again.

"This is Trudy Roundtree of the Ogeechee Police Department, and we've just recovered this lost property." I was giving Tanner the benefit of the doubt there, but I didn't expect him to appreciate it. "Who am I talking to?"

"The Ogeechee Police Department, you said?"

"Yes, ma'am. Are you here in Ogeechee?" There was a long silence, but I could tell she hadn't disconnected. "Hello?" There was something familiar about her voice.

I felt like I was on the point of recognizing it, but she wasn't helping.

"Hmm?"

"The man who found the phone just turned it in," I said, giving Tanner a look. "If you'll tell me how to reach the owner, I'll see about returning it."

For some reason, the caller found this suggestion funny. "Usually when I want to reach the owner, I can do it by calling him on this phone," she said, around her chuckles.

"That's my phone!"

"No, Tanner, this is not your phone," I said to him, and by the time I turned my attention back to the caller, she had disconnected, still laughing. Shoot. It would have been a nice short-cut if she'd told me who the phone belonged to. Maybe when I wasn't trying to deal with Tanner and could think about it, I'd place her voice.

"Gimme back my phone."

"Tanner, tell me again where you got this phone."

"I told you. Came with the car."

"That's not good enough. Exactly where did you get it? Did you get it the same place you got that watch?"

"You took my watch, too."

"It wasn't your watch either. Did you get them all at the bridge?"

"I want a lawyer."

"Tanner, listen to me. I will speak slowly. Stop me if I say anything you do not understand. Are you with me so far?"

He seemed to be turning the idea over in his mind, trying to find the trick. Eventually he nodded.

"Okay, then. I do not think you ran over and killed that man. I am not going to arrest you. I am not even going to give you a ticket. You do not need a lawyer. I am taking this phone and this hubcap. They may be evidence in a police investigation. I will give you a piece of paper saying that I am taking them. You are not in any trouble right now. If you do not want to get into trouble, you will tell me where you got them.'' It cramps my style to speak in short sentences, but I was willing to make the effort.

He stomped around a little more, flattening cornstalks in his wrath and emitting the words ''rights,'' ''lawyer,'' and ''police brutality'' from time to time. I listened stoically. He finally calmed down. ''Okay. Gimme the paper.''

''What paper?''

''Saying you're taking my stuff.''

''Oh.'' I wrote out a receipt and dangled it in front of him. He reached for it. I snatched it back. ''Where'd you get the phone and the hubcap?''

He made a half-hearted grab for the receipt, but I kept it out of his reach. ''With the man.''

''What man?'' He lunged for the receipt. I held it away. ''The man under the bridge?''

''Yeah.''

''The dead man?'' I needed to be as clear as possible.

''Yeah. Gimme that.''

I figured that was as good as I'd be able to do. I was just about to trade the receipt for the two items, when I realized there might be any amount of unexamined evidence in his ever-present bag.

''I better take a look at the rest of your stuff, too,'' I told him. He thrust the bag behind him. ''You have a choice here, Tanner. You can give me the bag or you can come along to the station with me and the bag while we look at it there. We are talking about a murder, remember.''

''I never murdered anybody.''

"No."

He was so surprised at my agreeing with him that he emptied the bag. Flattened aluminum cans tumbled out, along with a few empty bottles, a brown paper bag, a bottle partly filled with wine, and another hubcap. I picked up the paper bag.

"Gone take my lunch too?" Tanner asked.

"Not on a dare," I said, but I did verify that it was a sandwich inside before I put it back on the ground. "I'm taking this other hubcap, though. Where'd you get it?"

But Tanner was out of patience with me. He shook his head, which might have meant he didn't remember or might have meant he wasn't going to tell. I went back to my car with my collection. I had a surly Tanner, which was nothing new, but I also had a couple of leads that, with some luck, would help with the murder investigation. At worst, I'd be operating a lost-and-found out of the OPD. At best, I'd trace the phone and at least one of the hubcaps and find the killer. I hoped for the best, as usual.

"You just leavin' me here? How'd you like it if somebody came and took your car?"

Oh, yes. How could I have forgotten? I was leaving him stranded. "I could give you a ride somewhere," I offered.

"Not in no police car," he said.

"It's up to you."

He turned his back, which I took to mean he didn't want to ride with me any more than I wanted to ride with him. As I drove away, my rearview mirror showed him putting the cans back inside his bag, while mouthing something in my direction. Luckily, I don't read lips.

ELEVEN

BEING THE WELL-TRAINED and obedient police officer that
I am, I headed back to the station with Tanner's treasures,
where I would label and stash them in the evidence closet,
ideally to await their moment of glory in the sensational
trial of a vicious murderer who had been hounded to justice by the keen-witted and merciless Trudy Roundtree. I
couldn't be sure that anything I had would actually turn
out to be useful in the case, and considering the source it
was extremely doubtful, but you never know.

I soon recognized how ironic it was that I was involved
in the investigation of a vehicular homicide, since I myself
had become a menace behind the wheel. As I drove, I was
not so much watching traffic as watching hubcaps. Just
suppose one of the hubcaps in my possession had fallen
off the vehicle that ran down Tariq (and you'll kindly note
that I said "vehicle," not "car" or "truck," since a good
investigator does not reach conclusions ahead of the
facts). A low-tech approach to finding the vehicle (and
low tech is my favorite approach) would be to look for a
vehicle in Ogeechee with only three hubcaps that matched
one of the ones I had.

I had never realized before that there are so many differences in hubcaps—big ones, little ones, shiny ones, dull
ones, round ones, flat ones, fancy ones, plain ones. Even
restricting my observations to those roughly similar to the

ones in my possession—and I added to my irresponsible
driving by constantly glancing at them for comparison—
I saw them everywhere. I passed Kathi Harvey, for instance, proprietor of Kathi's Koffee Kup, one of Ogeechee's few reliable breakfast and lunch places, and as I
waved to her I caught myself checking out her hubcaps.
From where I sat, it looked like they matched the newer
one on the seat beside me. Naturally, I could see only one
side of her car. I made a mental note to check the other
side as soon as it was convenient.

By the time I got to the station, I was a mental, but
luckily not a vehicular, wreck. Hen and Dwight were gab-
bing in the file room, so after I got myself a cup of coffee,
I joined them, thumping the things I'd taken away from
Tanner onto the table under their noses. Normally, I don't
go out of my way to spend time with Dwight, but this
time I figured he'd take my spinning mind off spinning
hubcaps. Wrong.

"Whatcha got there?" Dwight asked, looking at the
hubcaps and the telephone.

"I'm surprised a crack detective like you can't figure
it out, Dwight."

"Evidence?" Hen asked, grinning, before Dwight
could respond. He needn't have hurried. Dwight likes to
take plenty of time working out his snappy comebacks.

"Could be evidence," I said. I indicated the newer hubcap. "Tanner says—more or less says—he picked this up
under the bridge where we found the body. He didn't say
where the other one came from. Maybe one of them came
from the vehicle that ran down Mr. Lester-Tariq De-
Loach."

"Nah," Dwight said.

"Nah? What do you mean, nah? Just because I found
it and you didn't? And why didn't you, anyway? If you'd

searched Tanner like you should have, especially after I told you he'd taken the watch, you'd have found this stuff." I was guessing, but it was a good guess. The two men glanced at each other and instantly created a defensive bond.

"Nah, because whatever hit him hit him high," Dwight said.

"Huh?" I responded.

"You can almost always get an idea of what hit somebody by the marks on the body," Hen explained. "Sometimes there's the impression of the grille. Once I saw a body where the impression of a hood ornament was on the chest like it had been engraved there on purpose. Helped us a whole lot when we found a former friend of the deceased who had a nice car—all freshly washed and vacuumed, naturally—with that i-den-ti-cal hood ornament on it. Especially helped when we found out the two men weren't friends anymore on accounta one of 'em's girlfriend had complained to her man that the other one—the dead one—had called her 'the H word.'"

"The H word?" I never will learn not to step into these things.

"'Ho,'" Hen explained. This cracked Dwight up. I could tell by the raspy cackle he uses for a laugh.

Hen waited until Dwight's mirth subsided and then resumed his lecture. "Now this here looks to me like it came from a little ol' sedan of some kind. What Dwight was tryin' to say, Dwight and I think our man got hit by something bigger, judging from where he was hurt. You remember? A sedan mighta got him across the legs or the lower belly. He was damaged higher up."

"Anyway, that's not a hubcap. It's a wheelcover," Dwight said.

"Hubcap, wheelcover—what's the difference?" I shouldn't have asked.

"The difference is in what they cover," Dwight said. "I'm surprised a crack detective like you couldn't figure it out." See what I mean about Dwight? It had taken him all that time to think of this imitation of a smart remark, and then it was pathetic.

"They wouldn't let me take auto mechanics in high school," I said. "I had to take Home Ec. So all I know is that those shiny little round things in the middle of the tires that cover up those ugly ol' things that hold the tires onto the car are called hubcaps."

"He's right, technically," Hen said, pretending not to notice I was *acting* dumb. "You might could learn a lot from Dwight, Trudy. Hubcaps cover just the hubs of the wheels, that part that the tire fits over so it can be bolted to the car. Used to be all they covered was the hub. Left most of the wheel assembly uncovered."

"Nowadays those fancy wheel covers go all the way out to the rim of the tire," Dwight said. "Hardly anything has what you'd call real hubcaps anymore."

"So why does everybody call them hubcaps if they aren't hubcaps?" I asked, reasonably, I thought.

"Just carryover in the use of language," Hen said, in one of those observations that reminds me that he sometimes thinks about something besides police work. "Like people still say carbon copy, when nobody uses carbon paper anymore."

"I don't call 'em hubcaps unless they're hubcaps," Dwight said.

"You're a couple of phoneys," I said. I had heard more than I wanted to about hubcaps, so I nudged the cell phone. "There's the phone, too. Maybe it'll help us."

"You think somebody killed him with a phone?" Dwight asked.

"I saw that on TV once," I said earnestly. "The guy picked up the phone and a little needle came out of it and went right through his ear into his brain. They practically never did figure out what killed him."

Dwight sucked on a tooth and scratched an armpit and studied the phone.

"Go ahead and put that stuff in the evidence room, Trudy, just in case," Hen said. "Then, I want you to cruise up north and have a talk with the widow-woman, get a look at that truck she was drivin', compare the tires with the pictures we got of the tracks. The Atlanta folks broke the news to her, but we don't have what you could call a statement, and seein's how she was in Ogeechee the night her husband died, she might have something useful to say. We'll want to compare it with Oscar Jackson's story."

It made sense, getting the statement and looking at the truck, I mean, not my driving up to Atlanta. It's a truism in police work that, when somebody dies a suspicious death, the first ones to come under suspicion are the family. After all, it is the ones who have to put up with bad habits who are most likely to be driven to murder, whether those bad habits are philandering or stubbing out cigarettes in the sugar bowl. Rufus Badcock no doubt thought he was following that line of thought when he arrested Oscar Jackson on an unsubstantiated tip, possibly hoping evidence would materialize.

"Why not send Dwight?"

"Dwight don't know how to drive in the big city," Hen said. "While you're doin' that, I'll go over and see what's happening at the jail. In our country there are laws about holding people in jail without charging them with a crime.

Our friendly local sheriff isn't dumb enough to think he can get away with charging somebody with murder without some kind of evidence that would hold up in court, so it's about time for Oscar Jackson to walk. Not to mention that there are some other folks over there I oughta check in with."

Hen enjoys his work so much he resists anything that would pull him out of context. I know that sounds like sarcasm, but it isn't. One of the reasons he's so good at what he does is that he knows his territory, and the reason he's so good at knowing his territory is that he's always around with his eyes and ears open. So he exercised his executive privilege to send me on a six or seven hour (round trip) drive, while he meandered over to the jail.

That would leave most of the routine Ogeechee crime prevention to Dwight. He likes mixing with the tough guys, so that meant everybody was happy but me.

"And why don't you take that cell phone with you and drop it off somewhere they have those magic gizmos that can find out what the number is and who gets billed for the service and what calls were made on it on Friday night, just in case it might eventually be helpful to know that." Hen threw this errand in as if it were an afterthought, which I doubted it was.

I had to admit the two chores, getting a statement from Coreen and an identification on the telephone would definitely make the trip to Atlanta worthwhile. It even felt like an honest-to-goodness worthwhile assignment, not just an excuse to get me out of the way so Hen and Dwight and the other fellas could do the real policework.

My disposition improved a notch when Dawn poked her head into the room and announced, "The Hodgeses are at it again."

Ferrell and Nadine Hodges were regular customers,

both somewhere in their late seventies or early eighties. The violence of their domestic squabbles had never been hampered by their age or by the fact that his mobility depended on a wheelchair and she got around with a walker. Their habit had been to get their fresh air and exercise by making their way down to the nearest liquor store to get a bottle of the best their Social Security would buy for them. Then they'd go back home and drink it up, and, when the mood got just right, they'd commence to beating up on each other, with whatever they could reach or throw.

The neighbors had complained about this behavior more than once, since the noise of the fights, let alone the noise of the occasional ambulance and the disturbance in the neighborhood caused by the appearance of the police, tended to drown out prime-time television viewing. Everybody in the OPD had at some time responded to one of the disturbance calls.

"I'd love to help out," I said, "But I'm on my way to Atlanta. Time's awastin'."

Hen looked disgusted, but he said, "Dwight and I'll go see about settlin' down Mr. and Mrs. Congeniality."

I was happier than I had been a few minutes earlier, but I still didn't want to be gracious about it. "I'll go by the house first and get something for lunch," I said.

"The sooner you leave, the sooner you'll get back," Hen said, recognizing my feeble show of rebellion for exactly what it was.

Aunt Lulu's car was in my driveway when I got home. When I went up the back steps I could hear a gentle whir.

When I had uncovered Grandma's sewing machine, under layers of history that would no doubt have been fascinating to an archaeologist, I was inspired to extraordinary feats of orderliness. I created an island of space around the machine, with the admittedly optimistic idea that anybody passing by the door would admire it instead of noticing the mess all around it and would give me credit for having a plan to clean up the whole place. Today what I saw instead of the machine was Aunt Lulu's back, clad in a cotton T-shirt striped in silver, white, and pale yellow. Pineapple Daquiri. She was feeding a bright blue-and-white-striped fabric through the machine, so intent on pedaling and guiding the material that she jumped as though she'd been shot when I simply said, "Hey, Aunt Lulu."

An electric sewing machine might have done real harm to her and required some seam-ripping on the garment she was constructing, but this blessed low-tech model simply stopped in mid-stitch when she froze.

"Oh, Trudy," she said, turning.

"How's it coming?" I asked.

She looked at the fabric in her hands and seemed to make a great effort to understand the question before she answered. "Oh." She clipped the thread binding the garment to the machine and held up what looked like an enormous pair of pants. For a clown maybe. "What do you think?"

I know it isn't ladylike, but I snorted. Aunt Lulu on her fattest day has never topped 110 pounds. I said, "Hen will be so pleased! You're making him a pair of pants to match his eyes."

Giving a snort only a little more ladylike than mine, Aunt Lulu stuck her tongue in her cheek and studied the garment. "Much as I like that idea, this is for me. I'm making a hat, too." She held up a circle of the same striped fabric, with lace all the way around. For somebody who claimed not to be able to sew, she seemed to be doing pretty well.

"Did you say the judging is going to be on the bathing costumes, or on the bathing beauties?"

"This just started out to be a swimming party, you remember. I don't know how it got out of hand," she said.

"I do. Those Geezerettes are an incorrigible bunch of troublemakers."

"We've about decided not to do the contest part. I think we ought to leave the newspaper out of it and just have our fun for our own sake, like we always do." She examined a seam and then added, "We're talking about having a talent show, though, as long as we're all dressed up."

"You could probably sell tickets to that," I said with a laugh.

"Well, I don't know about that," she said, but I could tell my comment had pleased her.

She was obviously eager to get back to her sewing, so I left her and started rummaging in the kitchen for something to eat that I could take in the car. The worst thing about living alone is the meals. Seems like if I ever try to plan meals and shop for food it winds up spoiling because I've been eating at Aunt Lulu's or Phil's or somewhere, so I've given up. I wind up having odd unbalanced meals made up of non-perishables and whatever extra garden produce somebody has handed me.

Lunch today would be a tomato sandwich. I like them with light bread (which means not cornbread or biscuits), mayonnaise (one of the things that works for Phil and me is that he's a mayonnaise person too, not one of those oddballs who likes Miracle Whip), and sliced tomatoes with lots of salt and pepper. Today, to keep the sandwich from getting too soggy and messy to eat in the car, I didn't slice the tomatoes. I'd just bite into them like I would an apple and hope the seeds and juice didn't get all over me before my big interview with the memorably elegant Coreen.

TWELVE

I MADE A CALL to the Atlanta Police Bureau—goodness forbid we'd be as careless of jurisdictional etiquette as Rufus Badcock—and then hit the road. I've made the drive often enough that I pretty much do it on auto-pilot. My mind is free to range hither and thither over various concerns. Sometimes, if my mind is ranging freely enough, I come up with some interesting connections. For instance, with the junk sculptures, my relationship with Teri, my half-formed plan to do some fix-up around my place, and the Geezerette swimming party whirling around together, it began to seem like a good idea to get Teri to help me find somebody to help clean up the place by making sculptures out of my junk and putting in a swimming pool so the Geezerettes could have their party there. It was a lot like the kind of dream you have just before you wake up after a night when you haven't been sleeping well. Luckily, I came to my exit off Highway 75 before the plan jelled.

I stopped to drop off the telephone with the technicians who knew how to penetrate its mysteries, and then picked up the local man who would accompany me on my investigations in his territory.

The homicide investigator who was delegated to go with me to talk to Coreen Collins—Coreen Collins De-Loach?—didn't look very happy about it. Detective

Mack Cordell was about my age and very good-looking in an over-groomed kind of way. He hardly said a word to me as we made our way to Tariq's home address, outside of giving directions that led into a neighborhood with gentle hills where pines had been chopped away to allow for the growth of condominiums.

We got no answer at the elegant brick condominium and decided to try the Upstart Gallery. People handle grief in different ways; maybe Coreen was the kind to work it off. Since I could find my way back downtown without my sidekick's help, he seemed to doze off. I'd have judged him to be the kind of man to make an automatic pass, just to keep in practice, but it didn't happen. Maybe I wasn't his type. The thought didn't upset me any more than his lack of enthusiasm for our chore. Detective Mack Cordell was just along for the ride. If he stayed bored, maybe he wouldn't get in the way of my doing the job I came to do.

Remembering Coreen from that earlier trip to the Upstart Gallery, I had decided there was a bright spot in the assignment. Studying her, maybe I could learn something about how to exude glamor. I expected Mack Cordell would perk up when he got a gander at Coreen. He didn't, but it wasn't entirely his fault.

Glamor must be something you can put on or take off. Instead of the stunning woman in African garb queening it over a showing of her work at an elegant gallery—the woman I remembered—we found a small tired woman in faded denim jeans and workshirt. I quit worrying about stray tomato seeds.

She was supervising workmen who were removing paintings from the walls and crating them. The elaborate head wrap I remembered was gone, revealing hair so close-cropped I suspected she and Tariq might have used the same barber. The change was so dramatic I might not have known it was the same woman except for her distinctive feline-serpentine slither. I was glad to see her in plain-folks clothes.

When we told her what we were after, she told the men to come back in half an hour and with a fluid motion snapped open two folding chairs.

"Have a seat," she said, indicating the chairs. She leaned her head back against a wall, closed her eyes, and slowly slid down into a crouch, both hands folded in her lap. Her movements were smooth and controlled, but now, instead of the lithe grace of a panther, she was sinuous as a snake winding its way down a drainpipe. Yes, she looked tired, but underneath that I saw strength. She'd been through a lot and she was still functioning.

When you're interrogating witnesses, the rule of thumb is that you make them comfortable in direct proportion to how little you think they have to offer and how cooperative you think they want to be. That is, if I'm talking to someone I expect to be hostile, I bring her onto my turf, not hers, and I give her a hard chair under a harsh light and I sit very close to her, invading her space. On the other hand, if I'm talking to somebody just to see what she can tell me, with no idea that I've got to push for anything in particular, I let her set the stage. That's what had happened here, except that I hadn't exactly *let* her. Coreen had us on her turf, sitting on her little hard chairs. As we sat where Coreen indicated, Cordell, to my surprise, gave me a wink. He wasn't really in another world after all.

I smiled, first at this indication of rapport with my fellow officer, then at the widow-woman.

"You won't remember me," I said, "but we met when I was here several weeks ago. A friend and I came to the opening of an exhibit. There was some of your work and some pastel oils.''

She opened her eyes then and looked at me thoughtfully. ''Oh? No, I don't remember you from that.'' She made a brief dismissive gesture with her right hand then folded it into the left hand again. ''Sorry. Those parties are purely cha-ot-ic and I do get pretty much wrapped up in 'em. Part of the payoff for all my hard work.'' Her eyes widened. ''Roundtree. There was a phone message from you. About Tariq, I guess.''

I'd forgotten about that. It seemed like ages ago. ''I'm sorry about your husband, and I'm sorry we have to bother you, but I'm sure you'll want to help us get a picture of what happened the night he was killed.''

''They said somebody ran over him. That's what happened.'' She said it flatly.

Cordell smiled into the distance.

''Yes, somebody ran over him. We know that's basically what happened, but we have to try to find out *how* it happened, what led up to it.''

She frowned. ''You tellin' me you don't think it was an accident?''

''We try not to take too much for granted,'' I said. ''If it turns out to be a stranger who did it, then we might be inclined to believe it was an accident. Even then, failing to call for help would be a crime. But the sheriff has arrested your husband's uncle, Oscar Jackson. If your husband was killed by somebody who knew him, we have to look at the surrounding circumstances a little closer and we're hoping you can help us. Let's start with this: Oscar Jackson says he and Lester got into a fight.''

''Call him Tariq,'' she said. ''He wasn't Lester to me. Beats me what his mama had in her mind, givin' him that name. Tariq now, there's a name with style. Well, if I understand what you're sayin,' you're looking for a reason for Oscar to run down Tariq. I don't mind telling you he was so mad I thought he was goin' to kill Tariq right there on the spot."

"The spot being the workshop at Oscar's place?" I asked.

"Uh-huh."

"Do you know why?"

She stretched out one leg at a time and inched her bottom down the rest of the way to the floor. "It was family stuff. Somethin' about Tariq's grandmother."

"I think you can do better than that. Oscar Jackson has made a statement already," I reminded her.

"Uh-huh. Well, okay. He'd got it in his head Tariq was cheatin' him."

"Was he? Was Tariq cheating him?"

She really looked at me for the first time and seemed to mull over my question. "Might have been, uh-huh."

"Was he in the habit of cheating people?"

She smiled at me. "You're talkin' to me about a man I married and brought into my business. You think I'd do that if I knew he was a cheat?"

I smiled back at her. "I don't know. Maybe not. Or maybe you were crazy in love and didn't learn that about him 'til later."

"And maybe the old man was wrong about the cheatin'. But he sure *thought* he was right, thought it enough to come at Tariq with that stick of his."

"Oscar's admitted that much already," I reminded her. "How about you describe what all happened. From the beginning."

"Sure." She pushed her spine against the wall and relaxed it two or three times before she spoke, getting her thoughts in order. "One place to begin with is I didn't want to go down there with them, so I went with a bad attitude, so I wasn't in any kind of mood to smooth things out when they started gettin' rough. Maybe things would have worked out different if I had.''

She stared into some private distance. After a moment, I intruded. "Why didn't you want to go?"

She blinked herself back into our presence. Then, "I'm a city girl. I got no business, I mean none of *my* business, in a place like that. No offense."

"I'm not offended, but a little confused. I'd have sworn you told us, when we were here at the gallery that time, that you were from Claxton."

"I am, but that's got nothin' to do with it. Bein' born some place is just accidental. It's got nothin' to do with who you are, what you want. I've been a poor country girl. I like bein' a rich city girl a whole lot better."

"Okay, you should've been born a city girl, but why do you say you have no business down there? Those sculptures are your business."

"Well." She shrugged dismissively. "That was Tariq, his idea. He was a *good* promoter."

"Now I'm confused again."

Just as smoothly and comfortably as though she wasn't about to admit to a lie, Coreen laughed. "You're thinkin' I go down there and make those things? Well, that was our *story.*"

Of course. The revelation fit so well with my half-formed observations that I almost wasn't even surprised. "Wait a minute while my gears shift," I said.

"No, you wait a minute, if you're shiftin' into thinking Oscar was mad about that. He knew we were doin' it that way, didn't care. Come on, now, tell me you weren't more interested in that junk when you thought a little ol' *gal* was makin' it."

She was right. From the beginning, I'd been intrigued at the idea. But did Oscar know she was taking the credit and was it really fine with him? I'd have to ask him. "Okay. Then back to your story. If you didn't want to go, why did you?" She had brought that up, after all.

"Tariq was the jealous type. You'd think with all his tomcattin' around he wouldn't be worryin' about me too much, but you'd be wrong. He never heard of 'what's sauce for the gander is sauce for the goose.' He knew how sweet he had it here, with me and the gallery and all, but instead of that makin' him behave himself, it made him jealous about me and my other friends, afraid I might decide I could get along without him. Thing is, he was so gorgeous and so slick and smart and cocky and sure of himself, no matter what he did, he'd've been hard to give up. I'm sure gonna miss that man."

She closed her eyes. This time I waited.

"Maybe he got too slick and smart for his own good, takin' advantage of Oscar like that," she said, after a while. "Anyway, why I went with 'em to get the stuff, longer story shorter, Tariq got it in his head I was gettin' down with somebody besides him and he'd really been watchin' me. Tell the truth, that made it a lot more fun. He thought I wanted to stay here because I wanted to spend time with Brad, and he wouldn't have it."

"Brad?" Was I hearing right?

"Brad Phipps. One of our partners. White boy." Her glance flickered in Cordell's direction. He smiled again, this time at Coreen.

"I know Brad," I said. "We saw him here that night, but he didn't mention he had a business interest in the gallery."

She shrugged, like a cat or a snake might shrug. "Some reason he would? He the kind of man tell everybody his business? No-body wants ever'body knowing *all* their business.''

''Well, was Tariq wrong about you and Brad? Now that you bring it up, when I saw you together that night it did look like y'all were pretty good friends.''

''Well. Friends.'' Her beautiful mouth twisted into an expression of extreme scorn. Who could possibly need friends? ''Okay, friends. Tuesday afternoon friends, maybe. Once in a while, but nothing to get ex-*cited* about.'' She cut her eyes toward Cordell again, but I couldn't tell if that meant she was ex-*cited* or not.

''Okay, so you weren't ex-*cited* about Brad. But was Tariq maybe half right? Was there somebody exciting out there? Could that somebody have been excited enough about you to want to get Tariq out of the way?'' I didn't ask because I expected the answer to be interesting, or even relevant. I was stalling because I didn't want to spend any time at all thinking of the kind of pathetic woman who could get ex-*cited* about Brad.

I was finding quite a bit to admire about Coreen, from the close-cropped, no-nonsense hairstyle that focused attention on her beautiful skull to the lush abundance of her sense of who she was. I liked hearing her talk, getting some insight into a woman who flat-out liked herself. Her next answer surprised me, but didn't let me down.

''Not that I see what it has to do with *your* business, but of course there's always somebody out there who seems excitin' for a while. Brad's old news, but wouldn't you say Andrew has a lot more excitement potential, any-way?''

''Andrew?'' I said. ''That would be Andrew Lamotte, the sentimental oils.'' I said it as much to fill Cordell in, in case he cared, as to make sure I had it right. Andrew Lamotte was about as much unlike Brad Phipps as you could ask for. If you didn't like Brad, you might like Andrew. Come to think of it, Coreen's—is there a word for a male harem?—Coreen's taste represented a real range of manhood—Brad, Andrew, and Tariq. I didn't want to think about what it said about my sexuality that none of them exactly lit my fire. Neither did Mack Cordell, another type altogether. I brought my mind back to the subject at hand.

"Oscar Jackson said you and Tariq had another man with you. That would be Andrew?"

"Uh-huh."

"And you all went down to Ogeechee-Mendes—together?"

"That's right, in that pickup, about as together as you can get. A little crowded, but perfect, when you think about it, me squeezed tight in there between Tariq and Andrew. I tell you, Sugar, it was exciting. Maybe a little dangerous, but exciting. I *loved* it, taking turns making them happy."

She wriggled her shoulders and her fingers and gave me a dreamy, mega-watt smile that made it clear my imagination wasn't up to the situation. I swallowed and took refuge in my cop-ness.

"So you got there and—?"

"And we started loading those sculptures. They may be junk, but 'round here we call 'em sculptures. And then the old man came and there was that *fra*-cas." She laughed. "Andrew said something and Oscar started hollerin' about his sister Lettie, and went after Tariq. Then Tariq got mad, and went after Andrew for settin' the old man off and got mad at me for no reason at all. So I left. Wasn't my kind of a party any of the time."

"Oscar said y'all were fightin' over money, you and Tariq."

"Uh-huh. It was Oscar, his idea that Tariq was cheatin' him."

"No, not Oscar and Tariq, you and Tariq. What was that about?"

"The old man's confused. I was tryin' to calm things down. He just got it wrong."

She was very convincing. I couldn't tell if I was learning anything or not. "Okay. You left. How?"

"Got in the truck and drove off."

"Andrew had already gone?"

"Uh-huh. Left on that motorcycle. He had business in Jacksonville, so we brought his bike down in the truck and he went on from there."

"So you both just drove off and left Tariq?"

She nodded thoughtfully. "Sure did. By then I didn't care how he managed to get home, thought maybe he'd be cooled off by the time he got there. Had no idea what was comin', you know, or I'd've done different and I'd still have my Saturday night man. And to save you askin', I wasn't excited enough about anybody else that I wanted Tariq out of the way either." She shook her head. "Yeah. I left Tariq with a big, mad man who'd just gone after him with a stick. Turned out not to be a good idea, huh? From Tariq's point of view, I mean. That's all I know, though. I left him standin' there with *Mis*-ter Jackson. If somebody did it on purpose, sounds like y'all arrested the right man."

"What kind of truck were you driving?" Cordell asked.

"Me? I thought I said, a pickup." She was studying him through narrowed eyes. "I thought you had your man."

"Just trying to tidy up as we go," I said. "Having a suspect and having hard evidence are two different things. Could we take a look at it?"

"My truck?"

"Your truck."

She seemed to think it over. "Well, I guess so, if it's here. Ramon!" Her change in tone and volume was so abrupt I jumped.

A man appeared in a doorway leading to the back. He was a brawny man, wearing a T-shirt with ragged holes where the sleeves had been ripped out to show off his muscles. Exposure to Coreen's frank sexuality seemed to be influencing me. I don't usually think about sex all that much, but now I noticed that he didn't especially appeal to me, and it surprised me that the thought even crossed my mind. Yet another masculine type that didn't excite me. Reckon freckles and glasses with loose ear pieces fit my ideal of manly charm? Could I be zeroing in on Phil Pittman as Mr. *It?*

"Your truck here?" Coreen asked.

The man, Ramon I assumed, nodded. "Out back," he said.

"That's the truck y'all took to Mendes?" I asked.

Ramon looked toward Coreen. Coreen nodded.

"Let's have a look," I said.

Ramon led the way through a cluttered workroom to an alley behind the building and stopped beside a rusty blue pickup with a white cowcatcher on the front.

"They're police," Coreen told him. "Want to make sure it wasn't your truck that hit Tariq."

Ramon merely nodded.

"You could get on back to work," Coreen told him.

"Sure thing," he said and started back inside. Then he paused. "We're missing one of those quilts," he said. "They leave it in Mendes?"

"I don't know," Coreen said, sounding annoyed. "We'll see about that later."

He stood in the doorway, watching me and Mack Cordell.

"Go on," Coreen said.

"Hey now, it's my truck they're lookin' at. I got an interest here."

"As far as I can see, your truck is innocent of wrongdoing," I told him. Still, Ramon watched while I verified that all four hubcaps were in place and there was no sign of a recent collision. All the creases in the body were edged with rust. The tires on the truck could not have produced the tire tracks in our photos. Still—

"Better get the lab to take a look at it," I said.

Cordell nodded and pulled out a cell phone. Ramon harrumphed and frowned.

A look of anger flitted across Coreen's face, but she recovered quickly. "Okay, then," she said. "Is that all we can do for y'all? I don't know another thing. And with Tariq gone, I've got a whole lot of stuff to take care of here, trying to deal with that."

"Just one other thing or two," I said. "What time would you say you left Mendes?"

She shook her head. "Sure wasn't watchin' the clock. Wasn't dark yet. It was dark by the time I stopped for gas up close to Dublin, though." Her gaze sharpened. "I could look on the receipt and get that time, and you could figure back, probably forty-five minutes or so, but I don't see why you care."

"It might help us establish when he was still alive," I said. "We never know what information will turn out to be useful. So if you could find that for us, we'd appreciate it."

We followed her back inside where she quickly found the receipt, tucked inside a Day-Timer. It showed a time of 7:42 p.m. on the date in question.

"Okay. Thanks," I said, making a note. "Just one more thing. We have a cell phone that was found near Tariq. Did Tariq have a cell phone with him? Could it be his?"

Coreen made a sinuous motion that involved her head and shoulders and was probably just a stretch-and-relax exercise, before she answered. "Most of the time he'd carry a cell phone with him, but he didn't want to look too high falutin' when we went to see the old man, so he left it in the truck. You got a cell phone, maybe it's a clue. It's not Tariq's. I've got that one."

"Okay, then. Thanks for your help. And, again, I'm sorry about your husband."

She gave a brisk nod, and turned away to get on with the re-organizing of her affairs.

I felt like Lt. Columbo when I called her back for another question, following up on something she'd suggested earlier. "So you wouldn't have any trouble believing Oscar Jackson killed Tariq and did it because he thought Tariq had been cheating him?"

She looked at me and shook her head.

"Can you think of anybody else who might have wanted him dead?"

"You mean in case you can't nail the old man for it? Let me think." Then, "I got the feelin' Tariq had something on Andrew that might have put him back inside, where he couldn't ride around on that *Hog* of his. He's got a bad history, Andrew, one of the things I like about him." She darted a quick secretive smile and then added, "Maybe even Brad. I think he was mad with Tariq over some money he thought Tariq owed him, and I know Tariq liked to tease him about his mama. I don't know of anything in particular, mind you, but Tariq had a lot of things goin' on *all* the time and he *might* have sucked ol' squeaky-clean Brad into something he had trouble getting out of.''

Drugs? Smuggling? Art forgery? Her insinuations raised all kinds of questions, but she insisted she didn't have anything in particular in mind, just trying to be helpful.

THIRTEEN

As MACK CORDELL AND I made our exit from the Upstart Gallery, I recognized the burly Andrew Lamotte parking his Hog at the curb. Fate, obviously.

"Andrew Lamotte?"

He dismounted and turned, looking politely inquisitive.

"We're police—Officer Mack Cordell from here in Atlanta and I'm Trudy Roundtree from down in Ogeechee."

He almost covered a wary look by undoing a bandanna from around his neck and wiping his face. He jammed the bandanna into a back pocket, where the trailing end caught my attention. I'd seen that owl design before.

"This'ud be about Tariq, right? Too bad about that."

"Yes. About Tariq. We'd like to talk to you."

"I wasn't even there, man. I was outta there by the time it happened." He looked toward the door of the Upstart Gallery.

"Oh?" I asked.

"Well, from what I heard. I can't help you with that. When I left, everybody was still alive, more than you can say for some brawls I've been in."

"This was a brawl?"

"There a coffee shop around here?" This from Mack Cordell.

Lamotte smiled. "Just around the corner. Got a mongo iced mocha cappuccino."

"Let's do it," Cordell said.

"Mongo iced mocha cappuccino? That's good?" I asked.

"Sounds good to me," Cordell said with the most enthusiasm I'd yet witnessed.

I followed the two men around the corner. If you're trying to figure out whose turf's being invaded and who's being intimidated, a yuppie coffeehouse has got to rate as almost neutral. It wasn't the worst place in the world to take a statement from Andrew.

We sat at a heavy oak table with our three iced mocha cappuccinos and I resumed my questioning.

"I think the last word you used in connection with the night your friend died was 'brawl.'"

"I've seen better, but this was a pretty good imitation."

"Why? What caused it?"

"I guess I did. For once, I wasn't even trying to start trouble. Just wanted to get through the program and move on down to Jacksonville. Had some guys waitin' for me."

"Why don't you just tell us what went on so I don't have to interrupt myself slurping up this pretentious coffee drink to ask questions."

Lamotte grinned and took a big slurp of his drink before continuing. "It was something I said. Lookin' back, I think the idea was for us to get in and out of the place while the old man, Tariq's uncle or grandpa or something, was gone. Tariq had keys to everything—the front gate and the storage shed and all—so it wasn't like we were breaking in or anything, nothing my parole officer'd be interested in, you dig, and I didn't see any problem. We got right on it. Like I say, I was in a hurry to book it. But it takes a while to load that kind of stuff. It's heavy as sin and there's no way to get a good grip on it. If you do find a place to get a good hold, that'll be exactly where you shouldn't grab it.''

"Jacksonville," Mack Cordell said thoughtfully. "Your parole officer know you were leaving the state?"

"Oh, yeah. No point in getting myself in trouble over nothin'. I'm behavin' myself." He watched Cordell for a few long seconds as though waiting for some hassle, but Cordell just nodded and returned his attention to his drink.

"So, anyway," Lamotte resumed, "the old man had been to a church supper or something and got to feeling bad and had somebody bring him home early, so he got there while we were loading. That was cool, as far as I knew. We went on with what we were doing, until I said something—just bein' friendly—like he must be glad to get stuff this valuable off his hands and he said it was just junk and I said his idea of junk must be different from mine, seeing how much money they go for. I don't know exactly what I said, maybe something about who'd think there'd be so much money in recycled junk. We were getting along pretty good, passin' the time while we worked, and I was lettin' my mouth run on. I was talking about how expensive it is to do stuff. I probably spend more on canvas and stretchers and frames and stuff than anybody would think, but that big heavy stuff's more substantial, you know, so people think it ought to cost more. I can't get over what people'll pay for it.''

I was trying not to slurp and distract Lamotte from his chatty description of events.

"How was I supposed to know Tariq had told the old man he was selling the stuff at flea markets or something and wasn't getting much for it? They started yelling at each other about the difference between what Tariq was getting and what he was giving Oscar, and the whole thing hit the fan.

"The old man looked like murder, I can tell you. Looked like he was ready to kill Tariq. He hit him with that stick he carries, and Tariq fell back and hit his head against that big old hook hanging there, and the situation got worse from there. Tariq was trying to protect himself from the old man and kill me at the same time, because I'd let it out. Then, when they started talking money, Coreen got in it. It sounded to me like maybe she thought there was too much difference between what Tariq was giving the old man and what the gallery was getting. Then Oscar said something about some big piece of sculpture Coreen said she hadn't ever seen and she wanted Tariq to leave me alone and explain why it hadn't come to the gallery, so Tariq turned on her. I thought it was kind of funny, everybody gettin' so worked up, but soon as I could, I hauled. I don't need to be around where people are getting violent."

By now both Cordell and I had finished our drinks. Lamotte paused to finish his before he added, "Of course, I didn't really think anybody was going to kill anybody, but even if I had I'd've still cleared out. Wasn't any business of mine."

"Coreen suggested that you and Tariq go back a ways, that maybe he knew something you'd just as soon keep quiet."

His laugh seemed genuine. "The worst there is to know about me is all in the record," he said.

"So y'all weren't mixed up in something you wanted kept quiet?" I asked. "You weren't helping him cheat his uncle and his wife?"

"No. If that's what he was doin' he was doin' it without my help."

"You think he might have been doin' that?"

"He could have. I'll tell you I wouldn't want to be the

one trying to take anything away from Coreen, but he might have been the man to think he could get away with it. Thought pretty well of himself.''

''Are you saying Coreen could have been mad enough at him to run him down?''

''I didn't say that, did I?'' He looked to Cordell for support.

Cordell shrugged.

''You didn't say that exactly,'' I admitted.

''How about you? Is there any way you can prove you really did clear out and kept goin', instead of coming back to get rid of Tariq?'' Cordell asked.

Andrew frowned. ''I don't get you.''

''I think you do.''

''Well, no. Just truckin' on down the road, you know. Not much of an alibi. But I didn't have any reason to kill him, either.'' For the first time, Andrew looked troubled.

''I noticed you wear a bandanna when you ride,'' I said.

''Uh-huh. Keeps the bugs off my teeth.'' He grinned.

''You got one with a little design in the corner?'' I asked.

''Yeah. It's kind of like my trademark.'' He reached around and pulled the bandanna out of his back pocket, smoothing the design against the tabletop. It looked just like the one I remembered from the death scene.

''What would you say if I told you we found a bandanna like this next to Tariq's body?''

''I'd say you're jerkin' me around.''

''Cross my heart.''

He didn't look guilt-ridden, just wary. ''If old Tariq had motorcycle tracks on him I'm probably in some real trouble.''

''If he does, you'll be hearing about it,'' Cordell said. ''You have a lot of those cute little things?''

"Used to," Andrew said. "They were kind of joke presents from one of my crazy old girlfriends. Gave me a gross of 'em, so I started givin' 'em away, like advertising gifts."

"A joke? I don't get it," Cordell said.

"See, my initials are A and L, and that's Al. And this is an owl. Get it?"

I got it then, but unless you can imagine a south Georgia accent, you may not get it. Anyway, the owl was his trademark. I got that.

"Matter of fact, I put a little owl somewhere in all my pictures, kind of an extra signature. It may be a bad joke, but I like it. I ever get big enough for people to forge my stuff, you'll know it's fake if there's not an owl in it."

"I'll remember that," I said. I glanced at Cordell to see if he was satisfied. He shrugged. "Well," I said to Andrew, "You've been very helpful. Just let me clarify one or two more points. When you left Oscar Jackson's place, Coreen, Oscar, and Tariq were still there?"

"Right. And everybody was still breathing."

"Right. Okay. Thanks for your help," I said. Then I had another thought. "Somehow I'm not surprised to find out that Coreen doesn't really do the welding. Do you really do those dainty paintings, or are you fronting for your grandmother?"

Lamotte cracked an ice cube between his back teeth. His good humor seemed restored. "You thinking Tariq was gonna expose me for a fake artist and I killed him to keep him quiet? Nah. I do the painting. I started one of the times I was in rehab. It was supposed to give me something to occupy my brain and my hands instead of picking up a bottle or a smoke or a needle. The funny thing is, it turned out I liked it. Even funnier, it turns out other people liked it and would pay to have it. Seems like I've got an eye for shape and color. Can you beat that?''

"Couldn't beat it with a stick," I said.

"What happens to the gallery with this Tariq out of the picture?" This came from Cordell.

"The gallery will be fine," Lamotte said. "It was Coreen's in the first place, and you ask me, Tariq was all flash, not much help in the business, maybe even a drawback. This business means a lot to her. She grew up out of dirt poor roots and figures she's entitled to some good life. Doesn't mind workin' for it, either. Now Tariq, his idea of work was a little different, more like tryin' not to work. Nah, I'd say the business will do better without him. Something tells me she won't be getting any more of those car sculptures, though. Too bad, too. I kinda liked 'em."

He looked from me to Cordell and back. "If there's nothin' else I can do for y'all, I oughta be movin' on."

I looked from Lamotte to Cordell and back. Cordell had lapsed back into detachment, so I said, "I guess that's it. Thanks again."

Cordell and I compared impressions on the way back to his station house.

"He could have done it to get the woman and the gallery," Cordell said, "and to get out from under whatever Tariq had on him."

To which I said, "Yep, if Tariq had something on him. But he'd have had to get a truck from somewhere. Those were not motorcycle tracks we found."

Cordell thought some more. "Or Coreen could have done it, to get a man she's excited about."

"Yep. I'll keep an open mind, but, anyway, she left before Tariq did. Even if she'd wanted to get rid of him— and he doesn't sound like much of a prize—it doesn't look like that truck hit anything recently. And how could she have known where to find him?''

He couldn't answer that. I dropped him off and headed for I-75.

Neither Hen nor I liked Oscar Jackson in the role of killer, but if Hen's idea had been to see if we could pin this on Coreen, it hadn't panned out. I had heard nothing to make me think she was heartbroken, but nothing to make me think she had run her husband down, either. Little as I liked it, what I had learned, and it fit with what Oscar himself had said, was that Andrew and Coreen had both left Tariq alive with an angry Oscar. He admitted he had a temper problem. He was beginning to look like a good bet, but, as I'd said to Coreen, having a suspect and having hard evidence are two different things.

I pushed it a bit, getting out of town. It had occurred to me that Hen knew very well I wouldn't find anything interesting in Atlanta and had just wanted me out of the way. By now he'd probably wrung a confession out of Oscar Jackson. Of course, if he had, he'd have to eat crow in front of Rufus Badcock, so he probably wasn't too eager to do that.

On the way back south I tried to let my mind range freely but it kept coming back to a couple of specific things: the telephone and the hubcaps. Since you can always find hubcaps—wheelcovers—by the side of the road, I considered them less likely to point to our hit-and-run driver, but you never know. On the other hand, if the telephone wasn't Tariq's, maybe tracing it would lead to something useful after all.

We definitely needed some actual evidence.

FOURTEEN

I DRAGGED MYSELF in to work on Tuesday morning, more worn out from all that driving than if I'd been chopping cotton. It hadn't helped that when I got ready to leave the house I found a flat tire and had to call Dawn and find out who was fixing our tires that week and then put in a call to Felton Massey. I knew better than to wait until Felton showed up to fix it. Nowhere in Ogeechee is too far to walk from anywhere else in Ogeechee if you're in the right mood or mad enough, so I burned off some of my aggravation, and dispersed some of my driving hangover, by walking to the station house. Under other circumstances, I might even have enjoyed the walk. I really don't get enough exercise.

I was writing up my notes on Monday's activity for Hen's benefit when Dawn told me I had a call. She had an obnoxiously coy look on her face, so I knew it was Phil, even without her mouthing his name at me, as if it were somehow against the rules for him to call.

Dawn's quite a few years younger than I am, and she's married—got that way right out of high school just a couple of years ago—and she's absolutely sure I would be happier and better off in every way if I would get married. She has no doubt that any normal woman—and I'm almost sure she puts me in that category—really wants to be married. She makes no secret of her belief that the only reason Phil and I haven't taken The Step is that I don't know how to bring him around, that I have no feminine wiles. She's willing to help. It has occurred to me that she may be working to effect some changes in my behavior, just as I'm working on her. I don't dwell on it.

I gave her a look as far from coy as I could manage and spoke my name into the phone.

"Just wanted to remind you it's not too late to get breaking news in this week's paper," Phil said.

"Wish we had breaking news," I told him. "Maybe the Geezerette swimming party. When is that, anyway?"

"I have better sources than the police on happenings with the Geezerettes. It's pending. I wouldn't be bothering you at work for that, anyway. You did notice I'm bothering you at work?"

He usually calls me at work instead of at home, especially if he's calling earlyish in the morning, since I tend to be cranky before I've had several cups of coffee.

"I noticed. Thanks. You know I really don't mind talking to you on my own time, Phil, but it's sweet of you to call on Hen's time."

"Sweet? Aw, shucks. Anyway—to business—what can you give me on that hit and run?"

"Not a thing, and you know it. We do have the man's name for sure, but that's about all for now."

"I was hoping for a leak from an anonymous source in the department."

"Don't you dare! Are you willing to settle for a statement from the chief?"

"Do I have to?"

"It's that or nothing."

"Is he busy?"

"Who cares?"

"I heard there'd been an arrest."

"That's true, Phil, but—"

"The dead man's uncle?"

"Yes, but I think you ought to wait 'til next week on that."

"Meaning?"

"Meaning I think you ought to wait 'til next week on that."

"Trudy!"

"Phil! Don't be sleazy!"

"Okay. You want to meet me for lunch tomorrow?"

"Good idea. Even police hot on the trail of a murderer get to take a lunch break, and all I have at home is an aging tomato and a stale loaf of bread. Of course, if things start breaking, I might have to stand you up."

"You've stood me up before. I'm learning to deal with it. Kathi's?"

"Sure. Noon?"

"Sure. Now, give me the authorized source, if you please."

"See you tomorrow, then." I turned the call over to Hen, and turned to face a horrible frown from Dawn.

"You just told him you like him better than an old tomato? That's not very enthusiastic, Trudy. Men like it when you butter them up a little more. That's no way to get a man to—"

"But Dawn, I'm not trying to get a man to. To anything. And he knows that isn't what I meant."

"Even if you think he knows, he'd like to hear some sweet talk once in a while."

"Dawn, I—"

For once I was glad when Hen bellowed for me to come to his office. I held up a finger to indicate to Dawn that she shouldn't lose that thought and I'd be back to continue this conversation as soon as possible. Then I grabbed my notes and my coffee cup and scurried.

From the look of Hen's desk, never neat, Phil's call had interrupted him at shuffling papers. Shuffling papers, studying papers, writing papers, that's all part of a policeman's lot, but I've never yet run into anybody who put that into the equation when he or she was trying to decide to go into law enforcement.

"Sit down and tell me about your trip to Atlanta," Hen said, obviously glad to have something more pressing than the paperwork.

"Light traffic all the way up," I said. "Maybe a little heavier on the way back."

He frowned and shook a handful of papers at me in a threatening manner.

"There's a great coffee shop near the Upstart Gallery," I added.

He adjusted his reading glasses and frowned again.

"Those are the high spots."

"Lordy. Well, give me the low spots, then."

"Okay. Coreen and Andrew Lamotte, the other man who was at the salvage yard the night Tariq died, confirm what Oscar said about the fight. Jackson and Tariq tangled, everybody got mad at everybody else, Andrew— he's an artist—left on his motorcycle, Coreen left in the truck they'd brought down for the sculptures. That truck looks clean, by the way, but Atlanta's checking it. And it turns out Oscar's the one who makes those junk car sculptures, not Coreen."

"Yeah. He told me."

I might have known. So much for that little revelation. "And it sounds like Tariq was taking advantage of, or cheating, or stealing from, Oscar, so maybe Oscar did

want to kill him. All I could establish for certain is that
Tariq was—''

Dawn's voice interrupted. "Trudy, you want to take a
call from a Brad Phipps?"

Of course I did. It gave me a way out of Hen's office,
a way out of dwelling on the fact that I had turned up an
embarrassingly small amount of anything useful in Atlanta.

"Take it, then come back and I'll tell you about my
day yesterday," Hen said. "While you're gone I'll work
on these everlasting cotton-picking padiddlin' personnel
forms."

"Brad Phipps? *The* Brad Phipps?" I said into the
phone. "To what do I owe the honor of your call?"

Brad's ingratiating chuckle greeted me. "The honor is
all mine, Trudy. I was wonderin' if you'd do me the honor
of lettin' me buy you a cup of coffee."

"You missed me by a day. It was yesterday I was in
Atlanta. And I did have a great—a mongo—cup of coffee."

"Yeah, Coreen told me. She said you talked to her and
Andrew about what happened the night Tariq was killed.
Does that mean y'all don't think it was just an accident?"

"We're investigating," I said automatically. If I
wouldn't spill anything to Phil, why would I confide in
Brad? "Looking into all the possibilities. Don't want to
reach conclusions ahead of the evidence, you understand.
Sorry about the coffee. It would have been nice."

"Oh, you don't have to be sorry. We can still make it
happen. I'm coming down there tomorrow on business.
Coreen wants me to talk to that uncle of Tariq's, see if I
can work out something with him, some arrangement so
they can keep on doin' business."

"Are you serious? Why would he want to come to an

arrangement to do business with somebody who's been cheating him out of money and taking credit for his work?''

''Well, now, Coreen says Oscar was goin' along with her sayin' she makes those things, so that part shouldn't be a problem. And she says Tariq was stealin' from both of 'em, her and Oscar, so that makes 'em fellow victims, gives 'em a common bond. I'm supposed to take the approach that if he's worried about his sister's financial situation he'll let bygones be. It's my job to make him see that was all Tariq's doing. Coreen didn't know what he was up to, so he shouldn't blame her.''

''I wish you luck. Mr. Jackson might not be in a very good mood, though. You did know he's in jail?''

''Yeah, I heard. Should be easy to find him, then. So, can we have that coffee?''

Why not? ''Why not? Even police hot on the trail of a murderer get a coffee break.'' I could see where a promoter type like Brad might automatically keep in touch with people, even ex-girlfriends. But what about me? Why was I agreeing to this?

''Good,'' he said. You know the territory. Where's a good place?''

''I don't think there's anybody in town with an espresso machine,'' I said.

''I can drink the plain stuff,'' he said, ''especially if I can get a piece of pie or something to go with it.''

''You're in luck, then. Ogeechee does run to that kind of place. Kathi's Koffee Kup.''

''Okay, I can find that.''

''Yeah, it's easy to find. If you come in through Vidalia, turn right at the light, onto Main Street. If you come through Aline, the highway becomes Main. Just go straight. It's in that first block. What time?''

"About two all right with you? I've got a couple of things to take care of before I leave here. Two o'clock? Kathi's Koffee Kup." I could picture him penciling me in. "See you then. And I'll meet with Tariq's uncle after."

And he was off, no doubt hot on the trail of some client, leaving me to wonder what was going on. Was I losing my mind? Did I just make two dates for the next day at Kathi's? I hadn't done that since I was in college, and then I must have been trying to prove something.

"You're sure popular today," Dawn said.

"Yeah. Quite a surprise, huh?" I said.

"Do you still like that Brad?"

"The embers of that feeble passion died out a long time ago, Dawn," I said.

"I don't know what that means, but from your conversation, it sounds like you like him better than you do Phil."

I opened my mouth to explain, but I couldn't. Dawn rushed on. "At least you didn't compare this one to an old tomato."

"I didn't compare Phil to—"

"Are you just leading Phil on to make Brad jealous so he'll be interested in you again and you can go back to Atlanta?"

I was about to say something snappish about how much attention she was paying to my telephone calls—the downside of having people call at work—when Dwight came in and poked his head into Hen's office. A second later Hen bellowed for me again. He must have been as eager to get away from the paperwork as I was to get away from Dawn.

Hen's office is large enough for two people, but not three, so the three of us went into the file room for our briefing. Hen took a chair and leaned back so he could put his feet on the table. Dwight took a chair and leaned forward with his elbows on his knees in a position that looked very uncomfortable to me. I leaned against the edge of the table.

"Let me tell you what Dwight and I have been doin'," Hen said in my direction. "After you left for Atlanta, I went over to the jail and while I was there I had a chat with Mr. Oscar Jackson. Wanted to see how he and Rufus were gettin' along."

"So. How *are* they getting along, anyway?"

"They've come to a parting of the ways," Hen said, "Rufus havin' not a pea-pickin' particle of evidence on which to hold on to the man."

"What about that anonymous phone tip?" I asked.

"Well, I'm glad you asked. Since I was still down at the jail when Rufus finally realized, just like we knew he would, that you can't hold somebody indefinitely on something like that, and he let Mr. Jackson go, I gave Mr. Jackson a ride home. We talked about that very thing, the anonymous tip. I had been giving considerable thought to it. Not to the tip, exactly, but to who the tipster might be. I'd been tryin' to figure who would have known enough about what was goin' on that night to make the call. The only people we know who were there—Tariq's wife and that biker-artist—didn't add up to a good fit, to my way of thinkin'. As far as we know, they didn't even know Tariq was dead when Badcock got that call. Anyway, if one of them did it, why attract our attention by makin' a call like that?"

"You're not asking me, are you?" I asked. A glance at Dwight, who was now embracing himself, scratching both armpits, and looking pleased with himself, alarmed

me. I had a vague feeling that the two men were setting
me up for something.

"No," Hen continued. "That was what I had been asking myself. At the moment, it's a rhetorical question. But
I did pose it to Oscar. He couldn't do any better than I
could when it came to figuring out who could have made
the call, but the call itself, the sneaky mean-spiritedness
of it, made him think of a cousin of Tariq's, somebody
from the other side of the family—the DeLoach side, not
the Jackson side. He said Tariq—or, rather, Lester—sort
of used to hang out with this cousin, and it was the kind
of stunt he'd pull, not bein' concerned about whether it
would hold up, just happy knowin' he was makin' trouble
for somebody."

"This cousin, this mischief-making cousin, is the idea
that Tariq might have gotten in touch with him?"

Hen gave me a triumphant look.

"Go on, Hen. Tell me." I could tell he was dying to.

"Figuring the man who would make an anonymous
phone call, especially—if—since—he didn't really know
what he was talking about, might not be the kind to stand
right up and admit it if we asked him, Dwight and I tried
a little strategem."

Dwight scratched even harder and began to grin. I could
hardly wait to hear about the strategem, and Hen was
ready to tell me.

"Ol' Dwight here—"

But Dwight couldn't stand it. He interrupted with a guf-
faw. "I went by to see him. Told him we had another
question or two about his tip on Mr. Oscar Jackson and
Mr. Lester DeLoach. And he said yeah, what else did we
need? And I said we needed to have a good long talk with
him, now we knew for sure he was the one who called. I
let on as how makin' an anonymous telephone call to

waste the police's time mighta got him in some trouble he would rather do without, but we could give 'im a break if we wanted to. So he was willin' to talk.''

I didn't want to think about how much Dwight would have enjoyed intimidating the man.

Hen was containing it better than Dwight was, but he, too, was oozing self-satisfaction. And he was ready to pick up the story. I was so relieved that their satisfaction had nothing to do with me that I listened attentively.

''This particular cousin, a Mr. B.C. Bacon, known to his friends as Fatback, is not a fan of Mr. Jackson's. He says he never had any idea of putting Oscar in trouble, but there is nothing to compel us to believe that. I got the idea Oscar's just a little too straight-and-narrow for B.C. Bacon, and Mr. Bacon took this opportunity to cause him a little trouble. He did act all surprised at how much trouble it had caused, but that's beside the point. The gist of what he had to say is that he got a call from Tariq on Friday night and Tariq told him he'd been in a fight with the old man and was stranded out on the highway and needed a ride.''

This sounded promising. ''So Bacon knew Tariq had already left Jackson's. But if he knew that, he knew Jackson hadn't beat Tariq to death.''

''Uh-huh. I'm thinkin' of tryin' to get Rufus to haul him in for givin' misinformation to the po-lice. Oughta be just about his level of police work.''

''From what I heard, Bacon didn't exactly give misinformation, just irrelevant information,'' I said, to be contrary. ''Tariq was killed by a vehicle, not by a beating. Is the idea that Oscar let him leave but then came after him and ran him down? Everybody agrees that Tariq and Oscar were left alone at the junkyard. And when we went out to Frog Pond to see him, he didn't have a car. He told

LINDA BERRY

151

somebody or other he didn't need a ride home because we'd give him one.''

"That's right.''

"And yesterday Andrew Lamotte told me Oscar surprised them on Friday night because he wasn't feeling well and got somebody to bring him home early.''

Hen nodded approval. "That sounds a whole lot like either he doesn't have a car or he doesn't drive. Oscar himself says he couldn't pass the eye test last time and doesn't have a license or a car.''

"But just because he don't drive these days don't mean he never did,'' Dwight said. "And if he ever did, he still knows how. So he could. We cain't rule him out.''

"Good point,'' Hen said, "and even if he doesn't own a truck of his own, there's that one for sale sitting on his lot. He could have given Tariq a head start, enough time to get away from the yard, and then gone to run him down.''

"Well, it's a theory. Or how about that cousin?'' I suggested. It seemed as likely as anything else.

"We thought of that,'' Hen said, "But if he did, it would have been colossally stupid of him to call attention to himself with this telephone call to Rufus.''

"Not necessarily. Not if he thought he'd remain anonymous.''

"You do have a point there, Trudy. Maybe Dwight better go talk to him again.''

Dwight grunted and looked pleased at the prospect.

"And Bacon said Tariq called him from the highway?'' I asked.

"That's what he said.''

"Did he say which highway?''

Hen grinned at me. "Trudy, I do declare, sometimes I'm proud to know we swam out of the same gene pool.

You are askin' all the right questions. That would be highway twenty-three and fifty-seven.''

"So, why did Tariq wait 'til he got to the highway to call for a ride? Why didn't he call from Oscar's?"

"Oscar wouldn't let him," Dwight said. "And where's he gonna find a pay phone in Mendes?" He scratched mightily again. "And why y'all call him Ta-*reek*, anyway? Man's name was plain ol' Lester. They're always makin' up these fancy-soundin' names that don't mean a thing."

"You're right, Dwight," I said, so dumbfounded that Dwight had actually raised a reasonable question about the phone that I reacted to that instead of his puerile comment about the names. I resisted the temptation to repeat my little spontaneous rhyme or to tell him how little I had always admired the name Dwight. "As far as that goes, I don't picture any place along the Glennville Highway with a pay phone, either. Not one that a stranger would be able to find."

"Maybe I've been wrong—maybe you *could* detect your way out of City Hall," Hen said.

"And when I asked Coreen if Tariq had a cell phone that was missing, she said he had one but it was in the truck. He didn't have it with him. Since the phone I took away from Tanner isn't Tariq's, maybe it will help us to find out whose it is."

"Yes, indeedy," Hen agreed. "We can hope so."

We had a moment to speculate on how helpful that phone might turn out to be, and then my next phone call came. This turned out to be the most significant call I got that morning, no offense to Phil or Brad.

The call was from Atlanta, where the techno-geniuses had come up with the information I had asked for about the telephone. They had a number. The area code that came with the number for the phone placed it in the Atlanta area. They had a name and a billing address that made me draw in my breath so sharply that Dawn asked, "Trudy? Something wrong?"

"No," I said, but I felt lightheaded as my brain expanded to make room for another suspect. A clanky whine brought me back to earth. "Is that something coming in on the fax?"

It was. As promised, the Atlanta people had sent a list of outgoing calls made on that mysterious phone on Friday. Crossing my fingers for luck, I grabbed the phone book for Ogeechee and surrounding areas and looked up B.C. Bacon. Give the lady detective a sugar-cured ham!

"Hey, Hen!" I called, on my way to the file room where he and Dwight were dawdling while I was having brilliant insights. "Want to know how Tariq called his cousin?"

One mystery solved. But that wasn't the best part. It looked like my Wednesday was going to be enlivened by more than back-to-back assignations at Kathi's Koffee Kup. I could hardly wait to see Brad's face when I asked him to explain how his phone came to be next to a dead man. And then I started wondering why my buddy Coreen hadn't been helpful enough to tell me it was Brad's phone I had. I knew she knew because now I realized that hers was the familiar voice I'd talked to in the cornfield. Had she and Brad cooked something up?

FIFTEEN

KATHI'S KOFFEE KUP is in a significantly central spot, just two doors down from the post office and maybe a block and a half from the courthouse. With that location, anybody who has any business at all in downtown Ogeechee will find it handy. Kathi has made a good little business out of the place by not trying to do anything fancier than she can do well. Homemade biscuits and cinnamon rolls along with grits and eggs, bacon, sausage, and ham, draw in a breakfast crowd; homemade soups, sandwiches, and pies take care of the lunch bunch; a two-choice menu that changes with the day of the week makes it possible for her to stay open for supper without losing money. I know a lot of small places, and maybe some larger ones, depend on bulk-purchased pre-prepared foods from Sam's Club or Wal-Mart, but Kathi doesn't, and it's working for her.

The morning had started off badly again. To my intense irritation, I'd found another flat on my car, a different tire. When I called Felton again I asked him if he'd rotated the tires and put the bad one in a new spot. He said, a little huffily, that not only had he not done any unauthorized work, he hadn't been able to find anything wrong with yesterday's tire except that it didn't have any air in it. He suggested that since I was also missing the wheel cover on that tire, maybe I'd taken a big bump I didn't remember and run across something that created some slow leaks that would be hard to find. He said he'd see about today's emergency as soon as he could.

I walked to work again, puzzlement and irritation keeping me company as I tried to figure out what could have caused the flats. Telling myself that the exercise was good for me didn't help any more than it had the day before. At the station, I tried to distract myself with an assault on accumulated paperwork, but that was a bad choice of things to do when I was already in a bad mood. Dawn, of course, was sure my problem was girlish flutters because of my back-to-back dates later in the day.

My mood was not improved when Felton brought the car by and made a point of telling me he couldn't find anything wrong with that tire, either, but it was also missing its wheelcover, so maybe I ought to take it a little easier when I drive. I thanked him for his advice.

"I sure hope you get in a better mood before all your dates," Dawn said. "You catch more flies with honey."

I thanked her for her advice, too. Actually, thinking about a piece of pie at Kathi's did improve my mood a little even as I puzzled over the two mysterious flat tires and missing wheelcovers. How could I have taken a bump that big and not remember it?

In Ogeechee, a noon date doesn't mean you're actually there at noon; it means you leave for wherever you're going when the courthouse clock starts striking. When the clock began to strike noon, I was cruising a spot on the west side of town where a low-rent motel with a big back lot between it and a dense growth of trees seems to attract people who prefer to carry on their business in the shade instead of the bright light of day. I knew Phil would start walking toward Kathi's when he heard the clock. I did not swing past the *Beacon* offices so I could give him a lift. Dawn's wrong about me on more than one count. For one thing, I do like Phil, a lot. For another, I have my own notions of how to play hard-to-get.

I got to the cafe first and took one of the tables near the big front window, not the one under the hanging basket with the spider plant. I know it isn't real spiders, but still.

Phil came in and dropped a copy of the Beacon on the table in front of me. Below the fold, under the headline, ATLANTA MAN FOUND DEAD IN OGEECHEE, I read the brief article.

The body of Mr. Lester DeLoach of Atlanta was discovered early Saturday morning by Tanner Whitcomb of Ogeechee, near the Ogeechee city limits, apparently the victim of a hit-and-run driver. Ogeechee Chief of Police Henry Huckabee says police have several leads and are investigating the death as vehicular homicide.

"Very restrained. I'm glad to see you thought better of your aggressive bulldog journalistic exposé" I said.

"Can't afford to alienate the local police," he said. "No telling when I might need a favor."

"We don't do favors," I said righteously. "We serve and protect the entire citizenry of Ogeechee equally, without fear or favor."

"Uh-huh," Phil said. "Hen told me he thought Rufus would have to let Oscar Jackson go, so he thought I ought to give it a few days and see what developed. What's the soup today?"

"Vegetable," I said. It's often vegetable, since it's a way for Kathi to keep from wasting whatever vegetables are left at the end of the day before.

"Believe I'll have some soup and cornbread," he said. "Too bad she can't get your Aunt Lulu's recipe."

"She has it; it just doesn't come out the same," I said. "Anything here about the swim party?" I asked, unfolding the paper.

"Next week, I think. I have it on good authority."

"Lou-Ella Purvis?"

"You think I'd divulge my sources?"

"Yep. And how about the wedding plans?"

"They may hinge on how the beauty contest comes out."

"Next week could be a big week for the *Beacon*," I said. "Maybe we'll have the murder solved by then, too."

"You know something you and Hen aren't telling me?"

"You think I'd divulge it?"

He shook his head in exasperation. That's pretty much the level of excitement of our conversation. Wednesday's a relaxing day for Phil, the day the paper's done for the week, so he was in a laid-back mood. And I was trying not to anticipate what would come of my meeting with Brad. One of the nice things about the way Phil and I get along is that not every encounter has to be highly charged. He ate his soup and watched me read his paper while I ate a chicken salad sandwich. I commented on whatever took my eye. The lunch hour passed.

"I'll wait on dessert," I told Phil. "I've got another date in a little while." Dawn would have been proud of me. I think. I don't know what she'd think of the fact that Phil didn't even try to pry, or act jealous. Personally, I don't think it's lack of masculine passion; he just doesn't think I'd divulge it.

By the time Phil left, the lunch crowd had thinned out and I was the only one still in the place. Brad was due before very long, so I kept my table and worked on writing up notes on my morning's activity. Boring. It isn't that I wish there were more violent crime in Ogeechee, but it is true that the hit-and-run mystery was more interesting than most of what we have to deal with. The kind of murder we usually get is very straightforward—somebody gets drunk and goes after somebody else in a bar, or goes after his wife (or her husband) at home. Violence, yes. Mystery, no. I was still trying to untangle my thoughts on the subject when Brad arrived, jangling the bells on the front door when he came in.

"It's for me," I called to Kathi when she poked her head through the service window from the kitchen, where she was working, getting over the lunch rush and getting ready for the supper rush.

"You're lookin' good, Trudy," were Brad's first words to me. "I really go for a woman in uniform."

I had to smile. Even knowing he's full of bull doesn't make it less pleasant to hear. "I'll take your order," I said. "Kathi's famous for her cinnamon rolls and pie. What'll you have?"

"Police work pays so little you're moonlightin' as a waitress?"

"This is a small town, remember? We all know everybody's business, but we help each other out too. The owner's busy in back. I'll go tell her what we want." This place was less neutral than the coffee shop near the Upstart Gallery, but I wanted to make sure Brad knew we were more in my space than his.

"Okay, then. I'll have coffee and…what kind of pie does she have today? Peach if she's got it."

"I'll have to ask." I went back to the service window to speak to Kathi. "I've got a tourist with me. What kind of pie today?"

"Pecan and peach. And there are a couple of cinnamon rolls left."

"One cinnamon roll, one peach, and one pecan pie, Kathi, and warm them up for us, please. I'll get the coffee." I found two more mugs behind the counter and poured. To my annoyance, I even remembered that Brad drank his coffee with plenty of cream and sugar, or used to, so I picked up a bowl of those little half-ounce cream packages.

Brad was doing his best to act nonchalant, but it wasn't quite working out for him. What gave him away was that he didn't even ask why I'd brought three mugs of coffee to the table. He spilled a little of the sugar from the packet and carefully mounded it up with his forefinger, before he mustered a smile and aimed it in my direction. "I just can't get over you being a policeman. Woman. Person," he said.

"You don't have to get over it, Brad," I assured him, amused to realize I was much more composed than he was. Maybe just being in my town instead of his qualified as hostile territory for him. Maybe he knew I knew about his phone. Coreen might have told him even if she hadn't seen fit to help me out.

"As a matter of fact, it turns out that I'm not bad at being a police officer, and I like it, which surprises me some. I took the job in the first place to annoy Hen. My cousin. The chief of police." I kept adding descriptors, waiting for a sign that Brad was taking it in. "The chauvinist pig. Who's about to join us for dessert."

On cue, Hen jingled the door bells, just as Kathi came from the back with the warm goodies. Brad jerked nervously and messed up his neat little pile of sugar. Kathi placed the cinnamon roll in front of me and raised an eyebrow questioningly as she held the peach pie toward

Brad. When he nodded, she put the pecan pie at the third place, waved toward Hen, and disappeared back into the kitchen.

I performed introductions as Hen settled himself at our table. "Hen, this is my friend Brad, about whom you have heard so much. Brad, this is my cousin, Henry Huckabee. He wants to talk to you at least as much as I do.

"So," I said, seeing no point in wasting time now that Hen had joined us. "You're down here on business for Coreen. Are the two of you going to run the business now that Tariq's out of the picture?"

"She doesn't need any help running the place," he said, "but I'll probably keep on doing her P.R."

"Are you part owner?"

"What makes you ask that?"

"Coreen told me you had a financial interest in the place," I said.

"Well, yeah. When they wanted to get into that bigger space, I co-signed the lease and helped them out with a loan. I guess that's an interest."

"Enough of an interest that getting a partner out of the way would qualify as a motive for murder?"

"What? Murder? Motive?" He attempted a smile. "Are you trying to pull my leg?"

"It never entered my mind," I said. "Brad, you know we found a cell phone near the body."

"Uh. Yes. Coreen said you found a phone. She said you thought it might be Tariq's."

"Y'all must have had a nice little laugh about that, since you know—knew—who it did belong to," I said.

He kept his eyes on his coffee cup. "She didn't tell me you found it with the body."

"Don't hold it against her. Maybe I forgot to tell her that."

Brad took a long sip of his coffee and when he put the cup down, he did it so forcefully some of the light brown liquid slopped over onto the table. "You don't think I... Well, I did know you had my phone. Coreen told me. She said she'd tried to call me on it and you answered. I just thought it must have fallen out of the car sometime or other when I opened the door."

"Maybe that is what happened," I said. "Sometime or other when you opened the door out there on the highway."

"I suppose you could try, 'It disappeared sometime Thursday,'" Hen suggested, "Or maybe 'I don't know who took it, but I wasn't within two hundred miles of Ogeechee, never been here before in my life.' Of course, we're a little bit on the alert now and it might not work."

I added, "Here's the situation, Brad: We have your cell phone, and we have a man who says he picked it up near Tariq's body." Well, more or less, that's what Tanner had said. Close enough for our current purposes. "What we would like to have is an explanation of how it got there."

"Maybe I can explain that," he said.

I went to refill our coffee cups, so he had plenty of time to decide how he wanted to explain the phone. To Brad's credit, he didn't require prompting. When I returned to the table, he launched right into it.

"When I tell you, it'll make me look like a real weirdo or something," he said, "But that's better than having you think I'm a hit-and-run driver. Well, here goes. I followed them down here Friday night—Tariq and Coreen and Andrew. It wasn't easy keeping track through all that traffic in Atlanta either, I want you to know."

"You followed them? Why on earth?" I asked.

"Well, maybe I put more money into the gallery than

I made it sound like a minute ago, and I borrowed some of it from Mama. Coreen had been making a go of it for a while, so it looked like a safe investment. But then she hooked up with Tariq and… I was beginning to get strange vibes. I started wondering if everything was on the up and up. Andrew told me Tariq had a history with the law, and I got to thinking what a good business an art gallery is for fiddling figures. I mean, it's not like you've got a mass-produced inventory with a fixed-price structure. It's whatever deal you can make with the artist, what the market will bear.''

"That's an interesting train of thought, Brad," I said. "Do go on."

He took a deep breath. "The business looks like it's doing as well as ever, but Tariq said you have to keep up appearances, and he kept putting me off on repaying my loan, which meant I had to put Mama off, so I was getting a little antsy about it. You know Mama, Trudy. You know how she can be."

"Oh, yeah," I said.

"Then when this mysterious trip came up I decided to follow them. To answer your question, I guess when I followed them I thought I was looking out for my investment."

"Did it have to be secretive? Why didn't you just come with them?" Hen asked.

"I offered," Brad said. "But they said they were coming in a pickup, so there wasn't room for me because they had Andrew. He had some sort of a biker rally in Jacksonville he was going to, but the idea was they'd haul his bike down in the truck and he'd help them load and then he'd go on. I guess it made sense, but in my frame of mind, that just made me more suspicious, like they didn't want me to know what they were doing. They probably didn't, actually. Even if all they were doing was picking up those sculptures Coreen was supposed to be making, that's not something they'd want everybody to know."

I nodded encouragingly.

Brad took a sip of coffee and continued. He seemed calmer now that we'd gotten the unpleasantness about the phone out of the way. I'm sure he had no doubt he could explain everything to our satisfaction, if we'd just *let* him.

"It's a long, boring drive down here, as I'm sure you know, and I was sorry I'd started following them, but it was hard to know when to quit. It was a little more interesting than it might have been because I wanted to stay close enough not to lose them, but far enough away that they wouldn't notice me. When they pulled in at that junkyard I went on past a little way and pulled off the road where I could watch the place without being easy to spot, myself. By then I didn't even know why I was there, and I really didn't know what to do next, now that I'd followed them to where they were going. I hadn't thought any further than that."

"Is this story going to get to what happened to your phone?" I asked the question before Hen could.

"Sure. I think so. That's why I'm telling it anyway." Brad took his time letting a bite of Kathi's peach pie melt in his mouth. Hen and I waited patiently, working on our own desserts.

Brad wiped his mouth with his napkin. "From what I could tell, they had the run of the place. Opened it up and went to work."

"In detail, what does that mean—went to work?" Hen beat me to the punch this time.

"In detail? Okay. Tariq started unlocking the place. Andrew rolled his bike down off the truck, so they could put the stuff in. Coreen sort of stood there tapping her foot, looking bored. Then they went in, and in a little while Andrew and Tariq came back with a hand truck and one of those sculptures. From that distance, it kind of looked like an enormous crab or maybe a lobster. That stuff isn't too representational, you know, but maybe the distance helps—you just get the shape and don't get distracted by noticing the details, like what kinds of pieces of junk went into making it. Maybe I've been looking at that stuff from too close up all this time. I like it better from a distance. I watched them wrestle it into the back of the truck. Then they went back inside and in a little while they came back with another piece, bigger, that could have been a dead tree with a bird, an eagle or something, up in the top. And about then a car drove up and this old man got out and they all went inside.

"I was bored and hungry and feeling pretty stupid. I mean, even if I had seen them loading drugs or assault rifles or illegal aliens, I don't know what I'd have done about it. I sure wouldn't have charged in to stop them, I'll tell you that.

"I had just about decided to leave, before they caught me and I had the embarrassing job of trying to explain what I was doing there, when all of a sudden here came Andrew barrelling out into the yard. He piled on that bike of his and took off back toward the highway, the way they'd come.

"Well, it wasn't particularly boring anymore. It was like when you've had a bad day and can't unwind enough to sleep but don't know what to do with yourself and you turn the TV on without any sound. You know?"

"No." Hen and I said it in unison and we were all so surprised we laughed. When he went on with his story, Brad seemed a little more relaxed, even though it was the part of the story that was most important.

"Well, anyway, it was obvious something was going on. It couldn't have been five minutes before here came Coreen with Tariq and the old man right behind her, out of that Quonset thing. It was like one of those jerky old silent movies, and I didn't even need sub-titles to tell me they were all mad at each other. Coreen headed for the truck and climbed in, and Tariq followed her and tried to stop her and then tried to get in, but she must have locked the door. The old man wasn't paying her any attention, he was so busy going after Tariq with a big stick. Tariq was dodging away from the old man and trying to get in the truck. It was pretty wild. I know I'm not beginning to give you an idea how it looked."

"I'm getting a picture," I said.

"Well, then Coreen peeled out, not worried about whether Tariq was holding on or not, or whether that high-priced sculpture was bouncing around. I guess with that stuff, though, nobody would ever notice another dent, huh?"

"Probably not," I said.

"Are we going to get to your phone?" Hen had finished his pecan pie, so he was now less inclined to be patient.

"Comin' right up. I think. I just thought you'd need to know all this to understand."

"Okay. We left off with Coreen bouncing out of there in a truck and Tariq on foot with Oscar after him," Hen prompted.

"Right. So, Coreen went back the way Andrew went and when her dust cleared, I could see Tariq was trying to go back inside but the old man kept poking and prodding at him with that stick to get him away from the door, like he was a lion tamer or something and Tariq was the lion. Finally, the old man clobbered Tariq hard enough that Tariq fell down, so the old man went inside.

"Didn't look like Tariq had any friends at all. Anyway, my silent movie shows this man outside a run-down old junkyard. Charlie Chaplin would have had some really sad piano music going there. For a little while Tariq kept trying the door, rattling and banging and yelling, but it didn't do any good. He stood there for a few minutes and then he started walking, back the way everybody else had gone, the way we came.

"I figured the show was over, end credits were running. I went after Tariq. I don't know what he had in mind, but from what I'd seen, he had a long walk ahead of him even if he wasn't planning to walk all the way back to Atlanta. I pulled up beside him and offered him a ride. He got in the car quick enough, but instead of being glad to see me, grateful, he started picking a fight with me as soon as he had the door closed. I could understand why he wouldn't be in a good mood, just from what I had seen, and besides that it looked like somebody had poked him in the eye, but he was beyond reason. The way he had it doped out, I had followed them down there because of my fatal attraction for Coreen."

I had been wondering about that, myself. This seemed like a good time to ask, "Do you have a fatal attraction for Coreen?"

He blinked and pushed his coffee mug away before he answered. "There's no denying Coreen's a beautiful woman. Don't you think so?" He looked at Hen.

"Hen hasn't met her," I said, "But I certainly agree. What did your mama think about it?" The question was prompted by some genius of a mischievous imp. Brad was startled, if not appalled. Did I imagine he shuddered?

"No tellin' what Mama would do if I had anything to do with a black woman and she ever found out."

"Well, now." I know I grinned. "That's two different things, Brad. Your doin' and her findin' out. I understood Coreen to say y'all are, or were, pretty good friends. I think she called you her Tuesday-afternoon man. Is that some kind of a code?" He blushed. I swear he did. "And Tariq knew about it. He didn't threaten to tell your mama on you, did he? What *would* she do? Did you kill him to keep him from tellin' on you?"

He gripped his coffee mug like a lifeline. "No, I didn't." He didn't. Of course not. "You know me, Trudy. You know I couldn't do a thing like that."

I smiled at him.

"Hmm," Hen said. "Let's clear up a few details, Mr. Phipps. You say you picked up your friend Tariq, a.k.a. Lester DeLoach. He picked a fight with you. And?"

"We hadn't gone far at all. I had started back toward home, but the way he was acting, I wasn't sure it was safe to try to drive with him in the car. I let him out pretty quick after we got back on the main road."

"The main road being the Ogeechee-Glennville road?" Hen asked and I decided to let him handle the questioning for a while, since I was behind on my cinnamon roll.

"Uh-huh."

"You let him out? He just got out when you politely asked him to?"

"I didn't exactly ask him politely and he didn't exactly just get out."

"So how exactly would you describe what happened?"

"I stopped and told him to get out, but he wanted to keep arguing, so I reached across and opened his door and gave him a push."

"Gave him a push. Did he topple out? Land on his

head?'' I stopped licking my fingers long enough to pose the question.

"No, Trudy. He got out, on his feet, and I drove off. I did not run over him." He looked from my face to Hen's, no doubt searching for some expression that would suggest we were believing him.

"That was all very interesting, Brad," I said, "But you know what? You still haven't mentioned your phone."

He looked surprised, as though he'd forgotten all about the phone. "Oh. Well, I don't really know, but if he had my phone, and I guess he did if you say so, he must have taken it with him when he got out. Maybe he thought he'd call a cab or something. I don't know. Anyway, I didn't miss it right away. I don't use it a lot and didn't have anybody I wanted to call from Ogeechee on Friday night. Actually, yesterday when Coreen told me you had it, I didn't believe her. I thought it was still in the car, but it wasn't. But you knew that. That has to be the explanation, though. That's the only way he could have gotten it. Do you have a tape recorder or something? Or are you taking notes? For whatever record you're keeping, I did not drop my cell phone at the scene of the crime in the process of running over Tariq."

"I'll make a note of that, for the record," I said. What Brad was telling us might have been true. On the other hand, once he learned his phone was in Ogeechee he'd had plenty of time to try to work out a story that would account for it, either telling the truth or putting the best possible spin on the facts. Except for the physical presence of the phone, he probably would have denied being here and nobody would have known any different.

I didn't want to let him think he was off the hook, just because he can tell a plausible story. "Any idea what time all this was happening? Any way of proving any of it?"

He gave me a wide-eyed look that said better than words how hurt he was that I didn't believe him implicitly. Hen and I stared him down. Hardly anybody's a match for the double iceberg glare. Brad summoned a ghastly grin, still doing his best to present himself as a candid, cooperative witness. "I wasn't paying attention to the time. It was after ten o'clock when I got back home, though. So, it might have been, what, six-thirty? Seven? It was beginning to get dark when all that happened at the junkyard."

"That sounds about right. Sunset's about seven-thirty these days, give or take," Hen observed. He drained his coffee mug and set it down with an authoritative clunk. "Well, Mr. Phipps, it looks like you got elected Chief Suspect in this here game of Clue," he said.

"You're kidding," Brad stammered.

"I'm not kidding. The phone ties you to the scene of the crime, a scene where you very reluctantly admitted to being. I might as well tell you that didn't make a very good impression."

"I explained that," Brad said.

"You came up with a story when you knew you were on the spot," I amended.

"Is the car you're drivin' today the one you were drivin' Friday night?" Hen asked.

"Uh. Yes. It's the only car I drive."

"Let's go take a look at it."

The three of us had just reached the door when a screech from outside drew our attention. Becki Harvey, Kathi's daughter, had pulled to a stop in Kathi's white Oldsmobile in front of the cafe, close enough to the curb that the rubber on her tires protested. That's not all the tires had to complain about, either, I noted with interest.

The one on the right front was not as well dressed as its peers. It was missing its wheelcover.

Becki flounced past us into the cafe, without so much as a nod or a smile, just as though somebody always appeared to open the door for her every time she wanted in. We went on outside to examine Brad's car for some sign he might have collided with Tariq. Hen crouched in front of the grille of Brad's sporty little red Miata and studied it. He stood and stretched, brushing his hands together to clean them. "Nothing wrong here that I can see. No indication it's ever touched anything rougher than a chamois. What's eatin' you, Trudy?"

"Hen, I think I have that missing hubcap-wheelcover from Kathi's car in the evidence room," I said. "I'll be right back."

It's only a few blocks to the OPD from Kathi's, so I was in, out, and back on the sidewalk in front of the cafe, holding a wheelcover that would have looked right at home on that right front tire, in hardly more time than it would take you to say "biscuits and gravy."

Hen and Brad were peering into the Miata's trunk when I returned. It was obsessively neat, just what I'd have expected, and lined with a heavy blanket that would protect the precious car as well as be ready to offer warmth in an emergency. So very Brad!

Hen slammed the trunk shut as he turned to take the wheelcover from me.

"For now, Mr. Phipps, I am tentatively downgrading your status from Prime Suspect to Prime Suspect With a Lot of Question Marks, meaning we have some other lines of investigation we are goin' to pursue, such as the drivin' habits of Miss Becki Harvey. Trudy will explain your status to you while I go talk to Becki." It was one of those displays of confidence and rapport that comes once in a while and reminds me that Hen really does value, trust, and appreciate my contributions to the police force.

Hen headed back inside, dangling the wheelcover, but turned to say, "We'll be talking to you again, I'm sure, Mr. Phipps."

"What did he mean when he said you'll explain it to me?" Brad asked, already recovering some of his self-confidence now that Hen was gone and he only had me to deal with.

"It means we aren't crazy about your story explaining the cell phone but we're still investigating and are not ready to make an arrest. We have only your word for it that this is your only car and that it's what you were driving Friday night." I continued in a motherly way, "You see, the trouble with sneaking around is that it makes it hard to come up with an alibi. For now, you're free to go about your business, but don't leave the country, okay?"

As I watched Brad drive away—south, toward Mendes, instead of back across Court Street toward the jail—I wondered if he'd actually made an appointment with Oscar Jackson, if he knew where to find him. Even if he wasn't still in jail, Oscar Jackson managed to do a lot of gallivanting for a man without wheels of his own. Wheels of his own. Interesting thought. Were those sporty wheels really Brad's? He had said it was the only car he drives, not the only one he owns. I made a note of the license plate.

I was still standing there, thinking this had turned out to be some of the most fun I'd ever had on a date with Brad, when Hen stomped out of the cafe, slamming the door behind him.

"That's one young'un needs to have her tail feathers plucked," he said by way of greeting.

"Becki Harvey, I presume?"

"How'd that girl get to be such an all-fired blight on society in only sixteen years?"

I chose to answer the question. "It may be inevitable."

"Lord help us! Think it'll happen to Delcie?"

"Delcie's lucky enough to have more good people on her side than a lot of kids do," I assured him. Becki, on the other hand, is the daughter of a single, hard-working parent, widowed several years back. Becki, in my opinion, suffers from the all-too-common fate in such situations. She knows she's the most important thing in the world to her mother and she takes advantage of it. Spoiled rotten.

"But I don't know if that matters much," I continued. "If I remember right, one of our nation's preeminent family gurus—a Christian man, at that—says the best thing to do with teenagers is to put 'em in a barrel and feed 'em through a knothole 'til they grow out of it."

"I'll consider that when the time comes," he said. "For right now, I've invited Miss High and Mighty and a few of her friends to drop by and visit us in a little while so we can see what they can tell us about how that hubcap got from Kathi's car to the scene of the crime."

SIXTEEN

WHEN I LEFT the cafe, instead of going straight back to the station house, I went south. I hoped a return visit to the bridge, with the information we now had about Brad's telephone, Kathi's wheelcover, and Andrew's bandanna, might bring me to some new revelation. I parked well short of the bridge itself and walked the rest of the way, across the bridge for a distance, and then back. I stopped at several different places and tried to visualize, based on the injuries in the medical examiner's report, where Tariq would have been standing, from which direction he would have been hit, what kind of vehicle would have damaged him in just that way, and how he wound up under the bridge. I could not imagine a scenario that would account for the presence of all those clues to what had happened.

All I really gained from the exercise, as far as I could tell, was a little fresh air in a peaceful setting. When I got back to the station, I found a mob scene. Okay, not a mob, just a larger than usual crowd. This would be Becki's bunch, the friends Hen had invited over for a chat, and their parents. I was mentally sorting them into family groups, with one teenaged boy left over, when Dawn, with uncharacteristic assertiveness, said, "Chief'll want you in the interview room, Trudy."

I nodded at Dawn and went on down the short hallway into the city offices part of the building.

The police department uses the back half of the building that also houses the city offices. We are in a constant wrangle with the city over space, since what we have is basically four rooms—Hen's office, which barely has room for him, a desk, a bookcase, and a spare chair; a file room, which has file cabinets, a table with a typewriter and the computer set-up, three or four chairs, and wall-mounted large-scale maps of the town and surrounding areas, as well as a bulletin board; an evidence room, which is a pretentious way of describing the shelf-lined closet with the locked door where we keep anything we might need to support a case; and the dispatcher's office and public area, into which seven people besides Dawn and Dwight were crowded at the moment, sitting on an assortment of chairs that had been pulled from all over the building. We seldom have that many visitors all at one time.

As I've just explained, the police department doesn't have anything that could be dignified by the term "interview room." When we need to, we use the city council's meeting room. A big conference table stretches across the end of the room at the far end from the door. This is where the council and the mayor sit. Three rows of pews occupy most of the rest of the space, giving the place the air of a small chapel. This is where citizens sit during council meetings. I can't be the only one who's had the thought that it was more than the good price on the pews—the city bought them from a church in Lyons when they remodeled—that made the mayor so avid to have them. Some people claim the mayor thinks he rules by divine right.

I was not surprised to see Hen in the high-backed leatherette swivel chair the mayor occupies during city council meetings. He was leaning back in the chair, his hands supporting his head.

"Come right on in, Officer Roundtree. You're just in time to help us out here. Unless I've gotten confused on account of having to listen to lebbenty-leben people talking at me all at the same time, I have just been hearing a confession to the killin' of our Mr. Lester DeLoach."

"Oh?" I said. I gestured to the room behind me. "A conspiracy, was it? Are all of them in on it, too?"

"That's what we're about to find out," Hen said. "We've gotten far enough to know that Miss Rebecca Harvey here, sixteen years of age and in possession of a relatively new driver's license, has something she wants to tell the police."

The only other people in the room, Becki and Kathi Harvey, were seated on the pews. From Becki's expression, Hen had overstated her enthusiasm for talking to the police.

"Now, Becki, catch Officer Roundtree up on what you've been telling me," Hen said.

Becki immediately set about confirming Hen's low opinion of her. "I don't see why," she answered. "I told you already."

"Humor me," Hen said, looking like he needed some humoring.

Becki rolled her eyes and adopted a pose that neither Hen nor I needed the police academy's course in kinesiology to help us read as extreme boredom brought on by having to endure the company of adults. Becki spoke only after she was sure her body language had spoken loudly and clearly and when it became apparent that we were going to wait her out. Only her mother fidgeted during the delay.

In a rushed monotone, Becki said, "We went down

under the bridge after the game and that man must have been there but we didn't know it but then when we heard there really was a dead man there we thought we ought to tell somebody and so we came to tell you. So we're telling you, but it was an accident. He must have been asleep or something not to get out of our way. Can we all go now, please?'' She paused and looked expectant, as if to say that was all and nobody could possibly have any questions after such a lucid account and her good manners in saying please at the end surely deserved a reward.

"I don't remember the part about your public-spirited decision to come forward and help us out with what you know. That report must have gotten lost in all the other paperwork we have around here, but there's no excuse for it. Officer Roundtree?"

"Yes, sir?"

"Remind me to fire Dawn, first thing in the morning."

"Yes, sir."

Becki did not appear to be amused or impressed by our little routine, but Hen didn't seem to be amused or impressed by her, so there was no love lost. "No, Becki," he continued, "My understanding of the way this interview came about is more along the lines of how Officer Roundtree recovered a hubcap—excuse me, a wheelcover—that somehow or other came off your mama's car down under a bridge with a dead man. That the way you remember it?"

Becki stroked her fingernails.

Instead of yelling at Becki, which wouldn't have surprised me, Hen turned to Kathi. "Now one explanation could be that Kathi herself took her car down there. You got a boyfriend you smooch with under the bridge, Kathi?"

"No."

"You go fishin' down there?"

"No. Hen…" I could tell Kathi was trying to rise to Hen's light tone, but her worry about Becki was weighing her down. Becki, on the other hand, was clearly disgusted, whether at Hen's unconvincing amiability or at the notion of her mama making out with some guy, I couldn't say.

Hen gave Becki a brief smile. "Just a few questions to help me figure out just how much trouble y'all are in, and then you can go." He turned to me. "You pay attention now, Officer Roundtree, because we're going to be talking to the others, too, and it'll be interesting to see if the rest of them can tell the story with such clarity and detail."

"Yes, sir," I said.

"I told you," Becki said defensively. "Don't you believe me?"

"And we do appreciate it," Hen assured her, sidestepping the part about how much of it he believed. "Especially your bein' nice enough to go over it again, for the benefit of Officer Roundtree here. But there are a few things we haven't discussed yet."

Kathi could control herself no longer. "She said she was going to drive straight to the game and straight home afterward," she wailed.

"Kathi, to be fair, now, you gotta admit the highway is the most direct route between your house and the football field," Hen said. Kathi made a face at him, but nodded grudgingly. Hen and Kathi had been in high school together and seem to understand each other pretty well. Hen leaned back in the thronelike chair until it protested with a squeak, and went on to prove he was impartial and wasn't taking up for Becki. "Of course, it would be stretching some to say the part of the road under the bridge is the most direct route between any two points."

The inarticulate sound that came from Becki's throat seemed to have equal parts "adults are so stupid," "how can they be so mean to me," and "was ever anybody so mistreated!"

"Okay, Becki, just for the record." Hen glanced down at a notepad and wrote something down before he looked back up at her. I noticed one of the photos of the tire tracks at the death scene lying beside his notepad. "You were drivin'?"

"I told you."

"Right. Just answer and this'll go faster. What time would you say it was when y'all were down there?"

"I don't know. After the game."

"Right after the game?"

"Pretty much."

"So we're talkin' about...what?...ten-thirty, eleven o'clock?"

Becki shrugged.

Hen made another note. "And the other passengers were?"

"You know."

"Tell Officer Roundtree."

"Rusty, Clint, Merry." That accounted for the teenaged part of the crowd out there with Dawn and Dwight.

"Rusty your boyfriend?"

"Sometimes."

"Merry your girlfriend?"

"No." Not even close, from the expression on Becki's face.

"Glenda Albritton told me Merry needed a ride to the game," Kathi said, "So I told Becki she could have the car if she'd take Merry." She was hoping the younger girl would dampen things down, I would have bet.

Hen nodded acknowledgment of this information and aimed another question at Becki. "Clint part of your regular crowd?" Becki rolled her eyes. "So what was he doin' with you that night?"

"He hangs around Rusty. Rusty said we might as well let him come since we had Merry, anyway."

"Okay. Once more over the part where you think maybe you ran over a man but didn't know it."

Another heavy sigh. "If we ran over him, he must have been up against the concrete that holds the bridge up. It's rough and rocky under there, not like it's a real road, you know. All I know is we felt a bump. Rusty and Clint said we'd run over somebody, but we thought they were kidding. If we ran over him that must have been when."

Hen made another scribble.

"Got any idea how long you were down there by the bridge?"

"A while."

"Good. That helps." His sarcasm was lost on her. "Any other traffic while y'all were down there?" I could see the wheels turning as some possibilities occurred to Becki. She perked up a little.

"No, but maybe they came later? Maybe—"

"Maybe," Hen cut her off. "All right, then. Why don't y'all go back out there and wait 'til I say you can go home. While you're waiting, see if there's anything else you can think of that you ought to tell me. This is serious stuff, Becki. I can't ignore it, and it won't do you any good to act like it isn't serious. It is against the law, just as it should be, to run over somebody and then drive off and take your time thinkin' about what you want to do about it. I'll let you know what we'll have to do about it after I've talked to the others. Y'all just go back out there and wait. I'll get back to you."

They left, Becki sauntering casually, to show how little her situation bothered her, and Kathi looking over her shoulder beseechingly at Hen. Kathi looked a lot more worried than Becki did. What do kids know?

When the door had closed behind them, Hen looked at me and raised his eyebrows.

"I hate it when I come in during the second act," I said. "What's the story so far?"

"That's about it, so far. You're in time for the interestin' experience of comparin' stories."

"You mean to tell me you don't think they're all going to tell the same story?" I got wide-eyed and batted my lashes.

Hen gave me a half-smile to acknowledge my attempt at humor. "Substantially, yes. They'll have worked out the main lines. It's the parts they wouldn't have thought about coordinating that will be interestin'. Dwight's out there to keep 'em from doin' any more collaboratin'. Why don't you go fetch the Albrittons and let's see."

Merry Albritton's a high school freshman who babysits Delcie on the rare occasions when Hen and Teri want to break away and go somewhere for an evening without her and Aunt Lulu is unavailable. Usually Merry's bubbly enough to live up to her name, with that bouncy step and bouncy hairdo that seem to ensure you'll be chosen cheerleader, but as the family led the way back to the conference room, she looked miserable. Gordie, who sells real estate for a living, usually manages to look if not cheerful, at least pleasant. He wasn't doing very well at the moment. Glenda, like Merry, had clearly been crying.

"Y'all come on in, have a seat," Hen said, much more affable and backwoods than he'd been with the Harveys. "'Preciate your comin' in. We've got us a bad situation here and we need for Merry to tell us what happened.

We've pretty much got the gist of things, but it's always helpful to get it from more than one point of view.''

Glenda couldn't stand it. ''Merry didn't have anything to do with it, wouldn't even have been with that bunch if I hadn't…'' She stopped to blow her nose. ''If somebody did run over somebody, it wasn't Merry!''

''I know that,'' Hen said. ''Merry's not even old enough to be drivin'. You weren't drivin', were you, Merry?'' Merry shook her head. ''Who was drivin'?''

''Uh. Becki.''

Lie. Even without the telltale pause, what were the odds those boys, macho high-school football players, would have let a girl, any girl, drive them around?

''And you didn't see a body?''

''No, sir.''

''Well, that's a relief. We won't have to send you over to the prison. Might need you to babysit.'' Merry darted him a wary glance, not really sure how much she could relax.

''Okay, now, Merry. It is really important for us to learn everything we can about what actually happened to that poor man. You try not to worry about what somebody else remembers or what they might tell me. You just try to do your best to help me see the situation. Don't tell me anything you don't honestly remember just because you think it's something I want to hear, and don't use your imagination to fill in any gaps in what you actually do remember. Understand?''

''I think so.''

''Good. Then, let's start with when the game was over.''

''Okay.'' The contrast with Becki was profound. Merry actually sounded like she wanted to be helpful. Of course, nobody was saying she ran over somebody either. But she did wait for more prompting.

"What time would you say that was?"

"I guess maybe ten-thirty or so. I wasn't noticing."

"It was after midnight when Merry got home," Glenda said. "I was just about to send Gordie out looking for her."

Hen glanced at her, then back at Merry. "So you all got in Becki's car. Where was everybody sitting?" She looked puzzled.

"I'm just trying to picture everything. Tell me how y'all were sittin'."

"Hmm. Oh, Becki and Rusty were in front. I was behind Becki. Clint had to sit in back with me."

I was saddened by all the social turmoil that answer suggested. Hen went on. "Okay. Good. Now, Merry, just tell me what happened." Hen leaned back and smiled at her.

Merry darted a nervous glance at her mother. "Nothing happened, exactly," she said.

"Well, now, I've heard that Rusty and Clint told you and Becki that there was a dead man down there." She nodded, looking miserable. "Now, I would call that a happening. Merry, pay attention now. Here are the possibilities I see: either the boys lied to you about seeing a body, or they didn't. What do you think?"

She actually appeared to think about the question before she answered. "I don't know. It's a funny thing for them to make up. Well, not *funny* funny. You know."

"Okay. Good. That's what I think. Based on the fact that there actually was a body there, I'm inclined to think the boys did see it, which means the man was there when y'all got there. Am I right so far?"

"She's told you that!" Gordon Albritton said.

"Just trying to take things in order, Gordie. Calm down. Now, Merry, when do you think you—the car you were in—might have run over the man?"

She shuddered and thought about it. "It could have been when we drove down or when we left, either way, or both, I guess, if he was against the concrete like somebody said. It's real narrow there for a car. The bushes came right in the window and scratched me." She patted her neck.

"But you yourself didn't see him—you're just going by what the boys said?"

"No. I mean. Yes. That's right. The car was stopped— Becki stopped the car—right up against the bushes and we couldn't get out, just the boys." She was doing a good job, making sense. Her tension showed only in the way she constantly caressed the scratches that began near her right ear and disappeared into the collar of her blouse.

Hen looked thoughtful. "So, let's say the man really was there. Stick with me now. I need you to help me understand the next set of possibilities. One is that the man was alive when y'all drove down there and the other is that he was dead. You with me?" She nodded and momentarily stopped touching her scratch. "The boys told you he was dead?"

"Yes," she whispered.

"Okay. Now." Hen rocked back in the chair, then came back with a thunk and settled his forearms on the table. He rubbed his neck in what I took for unconscious imitation of Merry's fidgeting. "You got any idea how they would know that?"

Merry grimaced. "No. The whole thing was awful, terrible. Even without that part. When we first drove down under the bridge, I guess maybe we went over a sort of a bump, but nobody paid much attention. The road's pretty bumpy. Maybe it isn't even a road. Anyway, we went on past there and turned around and, you know. And then when we started back, going back up to the real road, and went under the bridge again, there was that bump again and Rusty and Clint got out and looked, to see if we had a flat or something, and when they got back in the car they said we had run over somebody and he was dead but we—Becki and I—thought they were just trying to scare us or something, and we left and that's all. We didn't talk much on the way back. They took me home first."

"Okay," Hen said. "Thank you, Merry. You've done a good job of helping us get a sense of things. That'll do it for now, but I want y'all to go back out there and wait 'til I'm through talking to everybody else. We may need to talk to you again."

Next we got Mayor Ozzie Rhodes, his wife Eula, and their grandson, Rusty. Mrs. Rhodes is in the Garden Club with Aunt Lulu, where she is known to have no opinions of her own, operating almost entirely out of concern for her husband's political goals and agenda. She's the kind of middle-to-elderly aged woman you'd never notice in a crowd, not stylish or witty or attractive or noticeable in any way—probably the ideal serviceable political spouse. She's also a member of the Geezerettes, and I had a giddy moment of imagining her in a vintage bathing suit.

If I'd had to guess ahead of time which one of that group would be most likely to come in talking, I would have picked Ozzie Rhodes. He didn't let me down. Being in politics, the mayor's used to speaking up, and he expects to be listened to when he does. Besides, he would have been irritated at the sight of Hen sitting in his chair.

"Okay, Huckabee, let's get this straightened out. I don't appreciate your keeping us cooling our heels out there."

"I'm mighty sorry, Mr. Mayor," Hen said, shifting a little in the mayor's chair as though to get more comfortable, and not looking at all sorry, "But that's some of the basic investigative know-how the city pays me so handsomely to use. On the one hand, we don't want witnesses to cook up a story that ain't absolutely gospel truth, and on the other hand, sometimes when a miscreant has to cool his—or her—heels, he—or she—will get nervous enough to confess."

"You're not dealing with a bunch of miscreants here and you know it. You've got a bunch of scared kids. We're all doin' the right thing, trying to teach these young'uns respect for the law, and you have no call—"

Hen stood up and slapped his hands on the top of the council meeting table. It's an intimidating pose and the mayor was so startled he quit talking. Hen started.

"With all due deference, Mr. Mayor, I do have call. I am called on to uphold the laws that make our community the safe and attractive place it is. Now, not to be too narrow-minded about it, we all know the right thing would have been for one of these young'uns to hightail it over here, or make a phone call, as soon as they got the idea they were in the company of a corpse, whether or not they thought they had anything to do with it becoming a corpse, and not for them to wait 'til they got caught before they decided to come in."

"That isn't—" the mayor began.

"Oh, yes it is." Once again, Hen tactlessly interrupted the mayor. Worse, he dismissed him, turning instead to Rusty. "I hear you told the girls you'd run over somebody. Didn't it occur to you that you might oughta tell the police, too?"

"Not at the time, no sir," Rusty said.

"Why not?" Hen asked.

"Just not thinking straight, I guess."

"On accounta?"

"What are you gettin' at, Huckabee?" The mayor simply could not be quiet. "What are you suggestin'?"

"I'm not suggesting a thing," Hen said. "I'm just trying to see if I can find out what happened down under that bridge and why this carload of young'uns didn't think they needed to tell anybody about it. Rusty?"

"Well, we'd been horsin' around, feelin' good, you know, because we beat Metter."

"Horsin' around," Hen said.

"You know."

"I'm just a dumb policeman in a little ol' two-stoplight town, so maybe I don't know. You better tell me in just a little more detail what you mean by horsin' around."

Rusty wasn't sure what to make of that, but the mayor snorted. "We were just fooling around—talking about the game and stuff," Rusty said.

"Drinkin'?"

"Uh." Rusty was a lot more interested in his cross trainers than in meeting Hen's eye, or his grandparents'. Finally he said, "Well, Clint had brought some beer, yeah."

"Clint did." Hen nodded in understanding. "You keep that in the car or we gonna get you for litterin' on top of everything else?"

"Uh."

"Oh, for Pete's sake, Huckabee," Ozzie said. "Let up a little."

"Well, your honor, sir," Hen said, "we are investigating a murder here, and it might be helpful to be able to see which stories fit the evidence on the scene—like tire marks on the man's body. All right, son, let's get on to the part about the dead man.''

"Well, like, see, we, Clint, we.'' Rusty looked helplessly at his grandmother. She did not come to the rescue. He drew a deep breath and tried again. He smiled an aw-shucks-I-guess-I'll-come-clean kind of smile. "Well, okay. See, we didn't figure Becki's mother would care if she didn't exactly head right home, since we'd beat Metter and all, so we took our time. And, uh, when we turned off the highway to go down under the bridge, well, there's not a lot of room for a car down there, and we cut sort of close to the concrete there, and I guess that could be when we ran over him. But we didn't see him. I'm just guessing.''

"So. When did you decide you had run over somebody?''

"When we—Clint and me—Clint and I—got out and walked around.''

"Yeah. Beer'll do that to you,'' Hen said. "And?''

Rusty looked around at all four of us, inviting us to be bewildered with him. "I didn't really think it was somebody. I thought we were just kidding, you know. Clint and me—Clint and I—when we started back and felt that bump the second time, we got out and looked and thought it looked sorta like a person and we decided to tell the girls we'd run over somebody. You know, try to scare 'em a little, make 'em scream.''

"How'd you know he was dead and not somebody who needed help?''

"I said. We really didn't think it was anybody. I mean, not a body. So there wasn't any reason to tell anybody. Besides the girls, trying to scare them.''

I could tell Rusty liked this version of the story a lot.

"Now, son," Hen went on. "When you say '*we* had run over somebody,' don't you mean *you* had?"

"I don't understand."

"I think you do."

"Are you sayin' you think Rusty was drivin'? He doesn't even have a driver's license yet," the mayor said.

"Which might have clouded his thinking," Hen agreed. "And I'm suggesting he might have thought it would be more convenient to see if Becki would take the blame for whatever happened. Maybe he thought it would go easier on her than it would on him. Somebody oughta warn that girl about men like him."

Rusty fought a visible battle between being worried about his situation and being pleased that Hen had called him a man. "Didn't she say she was driving?" he asked.

"Yes, son, she did, but that just means I got me more than one liar."

"You calling my grandson a liar?" Ozzie asked.

"Not only that," Hen said, "I'm also suggesting alcohol might have been involved—and don't bother telling me none of these kids is old enough to drink. We all know that."

"Yes, sir." For a drunken hit-and-run teenaged driver without a license, the boy did make a good impression. Definitely the kind of man girls ought to be warned against.

Hen took a deep breath and let it out slowly. "Okay, then, folks. I guess that's all we need from you right now. Looks like I have one more young gentleman to interview before I let y'all go, but I can tell you right now what I'm telling the rest of this bunch. You're in trouble. I just don't know how much yet."

"Yes, sir," said Rusty.

"We'll see," said the mayor.

Eula wiped her nose.

I followed Rusty and his grandmother out to the dispatch room, leaving Hen and the mayor to say their goodbyes privately. The Harveys and the Albrittons were still there, as ordered. The other teenaged boy looked up at me.

"This is Clint Wacker," Dawn informed me.

"Clint, where's your daddy?" I asked, "He on his way? We need to wait for him before we talk to you."

"I'll be all right," he said.

An uproar drew our attention to the half-door that keeps the public out of the dispatch room. A big, rough-looking man in sweat-stained jeans and work shirt was yelling at Dawn, intimidating her with his size and his bluster. The room had seemed crowded before he arrived. Now it was overcrowded and overcharged.

"What's the trouble, Dawn?" I asked, to announce myself, hoping my uniform might have a calming effect.

She looked at me with relief. "This is Mr. Wacker," she said. "Clint's—"

"You arrested my boy. What's he done?" I'm harder to intimidate than Dawn is, but this might have been the man to do it—big, loud, rough.

"He hasn't done anything, as far as I know, Mr. Wacker. We—"

"Then what you doin' hauling him down here? I get a call he's in jail and I have to leave work to come see about him."

"He's not in jail, as you can plainly see," I said, trying sweet reason. "This is not the jailhouse. We wanted to talk to him, and there's a law which you should appreciate that says we can't talk to minors without a parent or custodian present."

"You mean I'm losing time at work for nothing?"

The man couldn't seem to make up his mind exactly what he was mad about. A man like that, it probably didn't matter.

By now Hen was finished with Ozzie Rhodes and the ruckus had attracted his attention. He moseyed over. "Afternoon, Mr. Wacker. Thanks for comin' by. We'd like to talk to your boy about—"

"He ain't under arrest, he ain't talkin'."

Even Hen's size, uniform, and maleness didn't have an immediate calming effect, so I felt a little better about my failure. Hen must have used up his bad temper on the mayor. He said in a reasonable way, "Why don't you and your boy just step in here a minute, and we'll get this over with and not have to bother you again."

Clint looked from Hen to his father. His father harrumphed, but followed Hen. Clint followed him and I followed Clint. This interview didn't take long, partly because the parent did not try to help or apologize. He just sat and glowered. Clint's version matched the others, except that he said Rusty brought the beer.

"Okay," Hen said. "That's it for now. I think we have a pretty good picture of things. But, Mr. Wacker, I want you to take care of this boy, you hear? I might be needing to talk to him later and I wouldn't want to have him impaired in any way."

"You mind your own business."

"That's what I'm doin', and don't you forget it. Now come on out there with the others so I can make this next little speech just one time before I send you all home."

Back in the dispatch room, Hen waited until all eyes— the frightened ones, the defiant ones, the bored ones, the belligerent ones—turned to him before he spoke. "You young'uns have perched me right up on the horns of a wigglin' dilemma and it is not a comfortable place for me to be. On the one horn, there's the fact that you have broken a number of laws and are up to your collarbones in something serious. The car you—Rusty—were drivin' made nice clear photogenic tracks all over a man. I can't just shake my finger at you and say, 'Naughty naughty, don't do it again.' On the other horn, there is the fact that I know you are not hardened criminals and I don't want to give you the electric chair, even if I could. What you need to do here is behave yourselves just as much as you can while I mull over the situation.''

He looked slowly from one face to the next, not skipping the adults, ending with Clint's father. ''Any questions?''

There may have been any number of questions, including what kind of an animal a dilemma might be, but nobody raised them.

''Okay, then. We'll be in touch.'' Hen turned and went back into the conference room, as far as I could tell not because he had left anything there but because it made a better exit.

Watching the crowd disperse, I noticed that Kathi Harvey went to her car but Becki didn't. Becki followed Rusty Rhodes to a spot near the far edge of the parking lot, by the fence that separates us from the firehouse. I couldn't hear what they were saying, but it sure looked like Rusty was getting an earful. I hoped it was about what a lousy trick it was to try to keep himself out of a little trouble by letting her take the heat for running over a man. Maybe, if she was lucky, she'd learn enough from the experience to turn herself around.

But I didn't think she would.

The best I could say about the whole thing was at least I didn't have to go home with any of them. I wonder where you'd go to find a barrel big enough to hold a teenager.

SEVENTEEN

THE PLACE SEEMED very quiet when the last of the teen-agers and their families were finally out of there. It was still only Wednesday, but things had been happening so fast ever since that strange phone call from Mrs. Over-street about Tanner on Saturday that we were grateful for a lull. We needed a chance to have a session of sift and sort, looking at what we had and trying to figure out where that put us, so we'd know where to go next.

Hen, Dwight, and I took advantage of the OPD's pres-ent possession of the conference room and met there, where all three of us could have a nice chair instead of having to take turns sitting on the table in the file room.

"These kids kill him?" Dwight asked as soon as we were settled. Since he'd been keeping the peace in the outer room he hadn't heard all the details.

"Check me if I'm wrong, Hen," I invited, knowing he'd do it even without an invitation. "But these kids didn't kill him. If I can remember all the way back to Sunday, the autopsy report showed that he was dead be-fore those tracks were made up and down his body. Tracks that match the crime scene photos, by the way, so I guess we can quit studying tires. On the other hand, they did confess. Whatever else, we can't complain that we don't have plenty of confessions."

"Uh-huh," Hen said. "Looks to me like the best thing

to do about those kids, in the interest of the future of the community, is try to scare the stuffin' out of 'em. I'm thinkin' about a deal where they do some community service and I don't look through the statutes and ordinances for things to charge 'em with. What do you think?''

"Lock 'em up for a while," Dwight said.

"What do I think?" I asked. "I think community service could be a good idea. It would be the best possible thing for Merry's social development. At least it might open her eyes about the bunch she's trying to hang around with. I think Clint's daddy will take it as an excuse to beat up on him. I think Becki and Rusty are beyond redemption and any way you decide to handle this will serve as an excuse to drive them even further in the direction of career criminality—her into prostitution or drug dealing, him into politics or public relations.''

Hen smiled at me. "Cain't argue with any of that, but I cain't tell if you think the community service is a good idea or not.''

"Oh, yes, definitely. I don't think you have to put them in jail, but they shouldn't just skate away, either.''

"Put 'em on a chain gang." Dwight again.

"Actually, in the interest of inter-agency cooperation and keeping the peace, we wouldn't want to horn in on the folks that really do run the chain gangs and upset the delicate balance of their social hierarchy," Hen said, just as though he took Dwight's suggestion seriously. "But I do like the way you think, Dwight, and I'll see what we can do about it. Now, let's take us a look at where we are on this murder investigation. As Trudy so intelligently observed, we've got plenty of confessions. But just for now, let's make it hard on ourselves. Let's play like the confessions aren't worth a sack full of road apples.''

That made sense to me, considering the confessions.

We had a confession from Tanner. Unquestionably, Tanner was guilty of slovenly personal habits, a bad attitude toward women and particularly women police officers, and a perpetual state of diminished capacity. But he had to be innocent of vehicular homicide.

We had a confession from Oscar Jackson that he had attacked his grandnephew, but not that he had murdered him. He was angry with the victim and did have something of a motive. He might have been guilty of a bad temper, but he and the Lord were working on that, and there was nothing outside a mean-spirited anonymous telephone call to suggest he did it.

We had a confession, more or less, from the teenagers, that they ran over Tariq. This bunch was guilty of a whole range of things that go along with being adolescents—arrogance, insecurity, bad judgment, and poor social skills, for examples—as well as behavior that could be punishable by law, i.e., leaving the scene of a crime, and failure to report a crime (whether they'd actually committed the crime or not). On the other hand, from the forensic evidence (specifically the post-mortem tire tracks and injuries), we could be sure that while they may have run over Tariq, they did not kill him.

We did not have a confession from Brad Phipps, who, as Hen had put it, occupied the status of Prime Suspect, a status based on the fact that Brad does drive, does have a motor vehicle, may have had personal and/or business reasons for wanting Tariq dead, and was on the scene of the crime with the victim at about the time the victim was killed but had tried to conceal that fact. The spotless Miata didn't prove anything. He could have used the same old truck that Oscar could have used. He'd have seen it during his covert operation, and even Brad might have known how to break into and hotwire an old truck like that.

We had a lot of conflicting information that we were sorting out—like Kathi's hubcap and the tire tracks—but we had nothing that amounted to solid evidence against anybody, certainly nothing that we could take into court, unless we wanted to add to the general fund of hilarity in the county and put ourselves on Rufus Badcock's level of police work.

"Let's take this one step at a time," Hen said. "And you interrupt me if you think I'm stepping off the right track. Now, the simplest explanation, and one that would be real restful for us, is that this is an anonymous hit-and-run, with the killer unknown to the victim, without a motive, and, as far as we know, committed by some careless and irresponsible vacationer who is now miles away on a beach somewhere drowning his guilt in piña coladas."

I opened my mouth to protest this scenario, but Hen held up a hand to silence me.

"But I don't really think so," he continued. "I think we're looking for somebody who knew this Lester-Tariq and meant to kill him, or at least didn't mind killing him. Now, Trudy."

"I agree," I said. "Pure accident is just too far-fetched."

Dwight nodded and leaned back in his chair so he could take a nap without falling on the floor. Logical analysis doesn't pique his interest. He's more into physical intimidation.

"And I think we can narrow the field a little," I said. "I think we can focus on the Atlanta people. Tariq hadn't been around here enough to make enemies locally."

Hen frowned. "Maybe, maybe not. He did grow up here, didn't he? We've agreed to eliminate Oscar Jackson for now, in the absence of any real evidence, but what about other relatives? We've turned up a cousin. Maybe there's somebody else.''

''And maybe there's more to that cousin than we know,'' I suggested. ''Maybe he got that call from Tariq and drove over there and ran over him for reasons that go back to their childhood,'' I said.

''Dwight? You want to get in on this?'' Hen invited. Dwight grunted. Not quite a snore. ''Okay,'' Hen continued. ''Dwight's gonna put that on his list of things to talk about when he goes back to see Mr. Bacon. Right, Dwight?'' Grunt. Hen continued. ''As far as I'm concerned, our best bet is that Brad Phipps of yours.''

''He's not mine, but I agree. It isn't much, but he's the only one we know of who was still anywhere around when Tariq—excuse me—bit the dust.''

''You're gettin' hard, Trudy, jokin' about a thing like this. That was plumb unfeelin'. I been trying to tell you this job was no place for a lady.''

''And I've been trying to tell you I'm no lady, Hen. I thought you knew that. But that topic will keep. Let's not get sidetracked. What we need here is good old MOM— motive, opportunity, and means. We have clues putting almost everybody in the neighborhood, if not on the scene, so we could call that opportunity. As far as motive goes, we do have at least half-baked motives for everybody involved except the teenagers—Brad, Andrew, Oscar, and Coreen. We might even dig up something for that cousin.''

''It's the means that stump me,'' Hen said. ''The vehicles we've looked at are clean.''

''The only thing I can think of that would make it more confusing would be motorcycle tracks under the bridge,'' I said. ''There weren't any, were there?''

''Not after all that traffic and stompin' around down

there." Dwight wasn't asleep after all. Another example of a time I've been wrong about people.

"I'd like to pin it on Coreen," I said. "She's gorgeous and successful. But I think we'd need a little more to go on than that before we arrest her."

"A little more than that? You mean something like evidence?" Hen asked.

"Uh-huh, something like that. She might have wanted to be rid of Tariq. Say she was tired of him fooling around with other women. A woman scorned. Besides that, both Andrew and Brad suggested Tariq wasn't exactly good for the business she loved and had worked so hard to build up. I'm guessing that if he damaged her female pride and her business he'd be damaging the two most important things she had. Maybe she decided to—"

"It's a great piece of creative story-telling, Trudy, but we're back to evidence. We've got to have something to prove it—positive proof, mind you, not merely absence of evidence to the contrary."

"Yes. Well. Like what?"

"Like something that would show that somebody who had something to gain from his death was actually there when he died, in a vehicle that could have done it."

"We have Brad's phone and Andrew's bandanna," I suggested.

"They can both be explained away. Matter of fact, you could almost say the presence of those items is so conspicuous it's evidence that neither of them did it."

"Using that logic, the absence of something to tie Coreen to the scene means she did it."

He grinned at me. "I wouldn't go that far."

Temporarily out of ideas, Hen and I studied the peaceful form of Dwight.

"Speakin' of motive," Hen said. "Cain't say I took to

that Brad of yours. Do you think he could have killed Tariq to keep him from talkin' to his mama?''

''Maybe. You'd have to know Brad's mama. But there might have been something else going on between them, something about money. Anyway, you've been in this business long enough to know you can't tell what would be enough to make any particular person kill any other particular person.''

He grunted. ''Yeah. Speaking of Brad, how are you and Phil getting along?''

''What?''

''I'm not asking because I want to pry. Mama wants to know.''

''You're interrupting our discussion of a murder investigation to ask about my private life? I think you ought to get out more!''

Our raised voices roused Dwight, and after very little more discussion, we all agreed that analyzing the present status of the investigation wasn't getting us anywhere. We'd have to go out and beat the bushes for something else. But, as Hen said, knowing where to find the bushes to beat was the hard part.

EIGHTEEN

DURING THE NEXT few weeks we followed up on every idea we had, but the murder investigation stalled out.

For one thing, our Prime Suspect with a Lot of Question Marks developed an alibi. When Brad realized the time might be important, he mentioned he'd eaten supper at Kathi's on Friday night before he started back north. Kathi confirmed he came in soon after she'd turned on the outside neon lights, which made it close to seven-thirty. He was there at least half an hour, having supper and finishing up with a piece of peach pie. Since Tariq had made several brief calls on Brad's phone during that time, possibly trying to find someone with whom he was on good enough terms to come to his assistance, it was pretty clear Brad had left him alive. Of course, he would have had an idea where to find Tariq, and he could have gone back, so we didn't completely cross him off our list. When I ran the plates on the red Miata I learned it was registered to Brad's mother, which didn't prove much of anything except that I had some of the right instincts about Brad. A small triumph, but the only one I'd had in a while, so I enjoyed it.

With Brad's suspect status downgraded, we looked a little more closely at Bacon. If Tariq wanted a ride, he'd have told Bacon how to find him. When we talked to him again, though, he told us he hadn't responded to Tariq's call for help. Why not? Well, he had a poker game going on. Could Mr. Bacon prove he was telling the truth? No, not exactly, but the friends he was playing poker with would—and did, when we talked to them—swear that he took a telephone call about that time but that he didn't leave his house. Bacon obviously subscribed to the thinking of Mark Twain, who said something like, "Since the truth is our most valuable commodity we need to be very careful how we use it." He certainly wasn't wasting it. He did volunteer one new bit of information, assuming it was information and not the figment of a guilty conscience. He said Tariq told him he had somebody else he could call. He said he told Tariq to call him back if he couldn't get anybody else and he'd see about helping him out, but Tariq didn't call again.

Checking up on the other phone calls from Brad's phone in that time period yielded only one other call of interest. He'd called his own cell phone, the one Coreen had said was in the truck. When we asked her about that, she admitted he had called her, thinking he could talk her into coming back for him, but she said she declined. Still, she, too, could have known where to find him.

However, the lab experts had found nothing to suggest that either the truck Coreen was driving that night or the one for sale at Oscar's had anything to do with the crime. With no further leads for us to follow, the police investigation of the hit-and-run was in a lull.

On the other hand, my private life during that period was as complicated as ever.

I had realized that one reason I've never developed much of a friendship with Teri is that we haven't had a chance to find out who we are outside the family circle. I began to think it was important to have some one-on-one time, so I had decided to see if I could talk her into helping me get some of the more pressing things done around my place, thinking that might help build a bridge.

I felt like I was making a little progress, having talked her into coming over and helping me begin compiling a list of things that needed to be done, playing to her great strengths—organization and administration. We had gotten as far as making lists of lists, subdivided by what kind of help I'd need to hire (plumbers, painters, carpenters, fumigators...) when my progress on this front was dealt a couple of serious blows. Yes, it was my fault. At least one of them was.

The aggravation with my tires had made me edgy. I had finally realized it wasn't accidental, wasn't a hard-to-find slow leak, wasn't something I had driven over, wasn't some kind of gross ineptitude on Felton's part, but was some kind of deliberate harassment. I couldn't help wondering who I'd annoyed or threatened enough to bring this on, and it was affecting my sleep and my usual sunny disposition. I had begun thinking of my street as a cul-de-sac, mentally shying away from "dead end."

As far as I knew, nobody had intruded into the house, but I became much more careful about locking the house when I wasn't around—a good habit I've been slow in developing. So far, so good. What I did wrong was not let Teri know I was doing a better job of locking up. When she came over with a handyman one day to get an estimate on the work, they couldn't get in. She took it personally, as a slap in the face and a slur on her integrity. I explained and gave her a key and it helped some, but not enough.

It was almost a relief to be able to turn to police work, especially to police work that had nothing to do with the murder case. Such as—

Hen fielded one of those recurring Ferrell and Nadine

Hodges domestic violence calls, and his frustration over
our stalled murder investigation coupled with the fact that
he got hit in the belly with a flying Southern Comfort
bottle, caused him to lose patience and take action that
was probably long overdue. He got after the Department
of Family and Children's Services (abbreviated DFACS
and pronounced DEE-fax, in case you ever want to drop
it into a conversation), and the next thing Mr. and Mrs.
Ferrell Hodges knew, their little nightly routine had come
to an end.

My lasting memory of this case is of Nadine Hodges
screaming, as she was being wrestled into a van by two
brawny nurses, "Damn that Henry Huckabee. He put my
husband in the veterans' home and he's putting me in the
nursing home. If I could reach my gun I'd put him in the
funeral home!"

Sometime in there, too, Rufus Badcock released the
wrong prisoner in an arrangement under which a minor
felon was to be given a bus ticket out of state with the
understanding that he would be making a big mistake if
he ever showed his face in our parts again. There seems
to be no doubt that the prisoner tried to point out that he
was not the Bobby Roberts they thought he was, but the
people charged with administrating this plan weren't
about to let an uppity black man tell them anything about
how to do their job and he prudently abandoned his efforts
to be helpful. Also, very prudently, especially considering
how short a time he had to think about it, he decided not
to take full advantage of his free ride to Charleston, but
got off the bus when it stopped in Pembroke and quietly
melted into the piney woods. Nobody in our parts has seen
his face since, so that part of the plan is actually working
out.

Dwight's big thrill was being attacked by a naked

woman wielding a bedpan when he responded to a call at the hospital. Apparently she had a bad reaction to some medication and was convinced that her clothes were choking her and there was no air inside the building. Given that conviction, it was natural she'd go outside and resist efforts to make her go back inside. She was a good-sized woman and had intimidated the daylights out of the hospital staff. Her reaction to Dwight's presence was not to calm down but to hide, she thought, behind a tree that was half as wide as she was. She hit Dwight on the head with the bedpan when he thought he was sneaking up on her. The impact made such a clang that Hen swears everybody in that part of town cut short their lunch hour, thinking the courthouse clock had struck. In spite of his stitches, Dwight claims to believe her behavior wasn't all that out of line. He says the only thing wrong with the woman was PMS and he expects all women to act like that every once in a while. Have I mentioned he's a bachelor?

That particular day was a busy one for us. I wish I'd been there for Dwight's coronation, but at the time I was officiating at a traffic accident involving a logging truck and a van that had, mercifully, just dropped off a load of people at the Methodist church for the monthly senior citizens lunch. The van driver, as far as I could tell, had been so relieved to be rid of his cargo that he was moving a little quicker than he should have been and failed to take into account how s-l-o-w-l-y a logging truck makes a ninety-degree turn. Damage was minor, but it did shut down traffic at Ogeechee's main intersection for a while. The nearest thing we have to a by-pass is accessible only to locals who know which side streets will take them around the main intersection. We had a mess at Court and Main for a while and my job was to re-direct what traffic

I could and try to keep other people from running into each other.

The attraction at the senior citizens lunch that day was the Geezerettes. My tongue-in-cheek suggestion about selling tickets to what had become a beauty pageant and talent show had taken root and borne strange fruit. The actual swimming and bathing suit aspects of the party were put aside in favor of having the talent show part at the senior citizens luncheon. They even deigned to go outside their own group for the talent and they wound up with quite a program, ranging from a barbershop quartet of OOG's to a rinkytink piano solo from a woman in Glennville who used to play at a juke joint. They asked for donations to benefit a senior book-delivery program at the county library and raised nearly $200.

I stopped by after my stint of directing traffic, to let the people who had come on the ill-fated van know they'd have to wait while somebody found them some alternate transportation, and I got there in time for the end of the show. When I came in, Aunt Lulu and Oleta Griner were standing together watching a man do a magic trick. They were wearing their regular knit pantsuits, not swimming costumes.

Aunt Lulu bustled off to get me a plate of spaghetti and Mrs. Griner said, "I've been meaning to call you."

"Oh?"

"It's about that Tanner. We may have to do something about him. He gets worse all the time."

"Oh?"

"He's started going out ramblin' at night, up to goodness knows what while the town's asleep. I hear him crunchin' on my gravel. Wakes me up, when I have such a hard time gettin' to sleep in the first place, and... Are you all right?"

My face must have been a study. Tanner. Hubcaps. Of course. I had taken his hubcaps away from him; it would make sense to him to get even by taking mine. "I'm slow-witted, but okay except for that," I assured Mrs. Griner. "We'll talk to Tanner and see what we can do."

Soon after that, Dwight talked to Tanner and found in his possession the missing wheelcovers from my car. Dwight threatened Tanner with dire consequences if he relapsed into bothering my car, and the OPD considered the case closed.

On the non-criminal side of things during those weeks, Oscar Jackson suffered a mild heart attack and spent a few days at Cowart Memorial. When I stopped by to see how he was doing, I found another visitor, Calvin Simmons, who seemed to blame me for the whole thing.

"Y'all hounded him to it, you sure did, arresting him like that," Simmons said.

"The Ogeechee Police Department had nothing to do with arresting Mr. Jackson," I assured him.

"That's right, Cal," Oscar Jackson said. "Only thing they done wrong is not find who did kill Lester."

"We're working on that," I said. "This isn't *Murder, She Wrote*. It just about always takes more than an hour in real life to solve a murder mystery and accumulate enough evidence to take a case to court."

Simmons snorted at me.

The most interesting news I took away from this visit was that with the assistance of Calvin Simmons (who turned out to be Oscar's lawyer as well as the president of his fan club), and perhaps motivated by his own reminder of mortality, Jackson had actually come to a business agreement with Coreen and Brad. I considered this a tribute to Oscar's pragmatism, Calvin's business acumen, and Coreen's charm, but there was even more to it than that. Oscar explained he was just looking out for Lettie's interests.

"She must be quite a woman," I said.

"You got no idea!" he said.

"How do you know I don't?" I asked, annoyed, for some reason. "From what you've told me about her, she must have been a lot like my grandmother. Strong. Good. Your Lettie took in Lester. My grandmother took me in and raised me. She—"

"Hey, calm down some! I didn't mean to set you off!" Oscar was laughing at me. "Ever see somebody with such a short temper?" he asked Calvin Simmons.

"Just you," Simmons answered.

We got along on a more relaxed level after that and they went on to tell me about how Coreen was already planning a big exhibit of his work.

"I'd like to go see that," I said. "Let me know when it happens. I expect she'll have a great party when the exhibit is ready. You'll be a celebrity."

"Don't know about that," Oscar said. "Don't know that I'd go. Ain't been to Atlanta for a long time."

"You'll probably see a lot of changes, then," I said. "Think about it."

"I'll do that."

Then, one night, or more accurately, in the early hours of one morning, I was jerked awake by the sound of a screaming cat. Outdoor cats do disappear from time to time, of course, prey to ranging dogs, or merely an interest in greener pastures. I have such a large number of cats around that I'd probably not miss one, and I've adopted the easygoing attitude that they serve as a low-key security system. Don't laugh. I'm not dimwitted enough to think that they'd care if somebody robbed me or murdered me in my bed, but there's a good chance an intruder would stumble over one or step on one. That's what I figured had happened that night.

When I heard the cat, I bolted for the back door, bare-footed, wearing only the oversized shirt I sleep in. I saw a shadowy figure near my car. The figure ran and I ran after it, following the driveway around to the front of the house. From the front of the house, there are two obvious ways to go on foot. The street—the cul-de-sac—leads back to Main Street. I saw no movement under the street lights in that direction. There is also an unlighted footpath, usually overgrown by weeds and overshadowed by syc-amores. It covers the approximately three hundred yards between my house and the courthouse and it runs behind the county jail. Naturally, it was this dark path my intruder chose, with me on his—I say "his" for convenience—heels. I was well into the shadowed path before the adren-aline began to ebb and I began to notice how painful the sticks and stones were on my bare feet. About that time I also began to realize how stupid it was for me to be chasing him in the dark, barefoot and unarmed, especially since I could no longer see him.

I slowed and stopped. I heard nothing except my own breathing, nobody thrashing through the underbrush, but when I turned to go back home, I saw the glowing tip of a cigarette near the back of the jail.

The dim moonlight helped me make out the bulky fig-ure of a man. He stepped out into the path.

I took a few steps to keep myself between him and my path home, putting my hands on my hips and standing with my elbows akimbo, much as a cat arches its back and fluffs its fur in order to enlarge itself and present as intimidating a presence as possible.

"Did you just see somebody go by here?" I asked. I noted with some relief that he wasn't panting and that he'd hardly have had time to light up if he'd been the one I was chasing.

He took a leisurely drag before he answered. "Just a crazy barefooted jogger."

Maybe my relief had been premature. I decided a good offense is the best defense. "What are you doin' back here?" I asked next.

"Havin' a smoke. How 'bout you?" He seemed to begin moving in my direction.

"Jogging," I answered. "See ya!" I said jauntily. I turned briskly and tried not to limp as I sped back down the path, trying to convey devotion to my workout regime, not fear. Before I washed my feet and tumbled back into bed, I called the jail and let them know somebody was loitering in back. Who could guess what mischief he might have been up to, even if he couldn't have been the man I'd been chasing?

The next afternoon Delcie called, distraught. She couldn't find Paws anywhere, not under the house, not on the back porch, not in the garage. I had no better luck. When Paws didn't appear the next day either, we had to admit she was gone. Hen, to me, suggested she'd been catnapped, or maybe catnipped, but he had the good sense not to try that particular exercise in punning on Delcie. And here's where the other blow to my relationship with Teri comes in: Delcie, knowing I'm the one who loves cats, came to me for comfort instead of Teri.

We cried together over the loss and I tried to explain how losing things we love is part of life. I tried to explain how missing Paws was a tribute to how much we loved her, so it wasn't entirely a bad thing. I tried to suggest that Paws might have just decided to go explore the big, wide world, but that pained us in another way. How could she not love us as much as we loved her? How could she choose to leave? I tried to explain, and as I dug into myself for words of comfort for the child, I realized I was helping myself reach a new place in my grief over Grandma, even over my husband's death. They hadn't chosen to leave me, after all, and it was all right for me to miss them. Delcie and I tried to be sensible about our loss, but we still cried and none of the other cats would fill the gap. It never occurred to either one of us, I'm sorry to say, that Teri would have cried with us, not over the loss of Paws but because we were crying.

And that's how we rocked, more or less gently, into autumn.

NINETEEN

IT WAS ABOUT the middle of November when we got the announcement about the reception at the Upstart Gallery, the gala occasion of the first exhibit of Oscar's work where he would get the credit. Oscar was going to be a celebrity and Phil and I immediately took on the project of making sure he would be there. Phil had convinced Oscar a photo-feature in the *Beacon* would be a good idea.

It would be Oscar's first visit to the gallery, probably his first exposure to the art world (if you don't count his bad experience with Tariq), and his first trip to Atlanta since he went up for a family wedding in nineteen and fifty-six, he thought it was, or maybe 'fifty-seven. He wasn't much for the big city.

In his own quiet way, Oscar was in a tither, as Aunt Lulu would have said, and right up until the time we actually hit the road, I wouldn't have bet a dead nightcrawler either way on whether he'd actually go, but he was ready when we pulled up at J&D Salvage and Towing. He came right out as soon as we stopped, wearing his church suit and carrying a little overnight bag.

We'd arranged to take Delcie with us, too, because I'd been wanting to take her to the zoo. She was also my insurance against a dreary ride. Delcie's fun to have around, and besides my idea that the trip would give her a treat, I was sure her presence would lighten things up and give Oscar something to think about besides worrying about his opening.

This odd double date turned out to be a brilliant idea. Oscar Jackson and Delcie got along like nobody's business. When she couldn't get him interested in playing road sign alphabet or cow poker, she started asking questions, things an adult couldn't, or wouldn't, ask.

"Why do you carry that big ol' stick?" she asked.

"It's my booger stick," he told her, with that straight-faced delivery of his.

"What's a booger stick?"

"It's a stick for keepin' off the boogers, child. What you think?"

"I thought boogers came out of your nose," she said.

"That's one kind of booger, all right," he said without cracking a smile. "Another kind is spooky, mean things."

"Like the boogeyman?"

"Could be. You say boogey, I say booger."

"Booger man sounds really gross," Delcie said. We had a few minutes of quiet while Delcie thought about that grossness and I tried not to. Then, "You don't really chase off boogers with that stick," she said.

"If I have to, I do. But mostly what I do, I use this stick to help me walk."

"Why?"

"Because I got this one knee that sometimes gives out on me and I don't want to fetch up with my nose in the dust. You sure are a question box."

"Yes, sir. My mama says that's how you learn."

"Your mama must have a lot of patience. You don't watch out, all those questions, you gone grow up to be a po-lice woman."

"My daddy's a po-lice man," Delcie told him, imitating his pronunciation and completely missing the dig at me.

"Uh-huh."

The two of them bonded so thoroughly that, without planning it (and I know they didn't plan it because I'd been eavesdropping), they began ganging up on Phil and me.

As everybody knows, one of the realities of traveling with children, even really lovable children, is that no matter where you're going, the ride is too long. We weren't even halfway to Macon—which is just a little more than halfway to Atlanta—when Delcie said she was thirsty.

I was in the middle of saying, "You should have thought of that before we left home," when Oscar interrupted me to say, "Wouldn't hurt my leg a bit if I could have a stretch." So Phil pulled off at the next exit and Oscar made a big show of limping back and forth, leaning heavily on his stick, to show how much he needed to exercise his leg, while Delcie swigged down a can of Coca-Cola.

We started off again and had gotten about as far as Stockbridge, and I was beginning to think we'd make it without another stop, when Delcie had to use a restroom. I was in the middle of saying, "Are you sure you can't wait? We're almost there," when Oscar said, "I wouldn't mind havin' a drink." This time I caught him winking at her.

"Don't push your luck," I told him, turning around to frown at him over my seat back. "You're taking advantage of your celebrity status and acting like a spoiled child because you know we'll humor you."

"He's not spoiled. He's just thirsty," Delcie said, obviously delighted with her new playmate.

"You calling this sweet baby a spoiled child?" he asked.

I gave up. As often happens, Phil was way ahead of me. He'd already slowed the car, ready to take the next exit. Not that it's all that big a deal, but we normally make the trip without a stop.

"Lordamercy." If Oscar said it once, he said it a dozen times as we negotiated the maze of highway ramps and over-and-underpasses on our way to the gallery, swiveling his head from left to right like the cliché tourist in the big city.

He amplified his comment all the way up to "Good Lord, have mercy!" when we pulled up at the Upstart Gallery. Smack dab in the big front window was the largest piece of his work that I'd ever seen. Details were hard to make out through the glare of the glass, but as we were watching, a couple inside the gallery came into the picture and paused to study the sculpture. They moved back and forth around it, to see it from different angles, and when they moved out of sight, they went with smiles on their faces.

I turned to see how Oscar was taking this tribute to his work. He looked thoughtful. "Who'da ever thought my old cars would wind up in a fancy place like this? Made more sense to me when I thought Lester was takin' 'em to flea markets and sellin' 'em to poor folks to give 'em a laugh. The world's a funny place."

"The art world is a funny place of its own," I agreed.

We had no sooner stepped inside than Coreen swooped down on Oscar and began gathering patrons around to introduce him. She was glamorous again, this time in a caftan of brilliantly colored tie-dyed silk that shifted with every movement and suggested some nervous Polynesian bird. Leaving Oscar to deal with that however he could, we lesser mortals, led by Delcie, made our way to the refreshments.

I had expected, as one wordsmith (Yogi Berra?) put it, "*déjà vu* all over again," since this was another reception featuring the junk car sculptures at the Upstart Gallery. There were undeniable similarities between the two receptions, including the junk car art and most of the important people. A big difference was that the main man was missing, and I realized with a shock that I was almost certainly socializing with his killer. Which one of them was it?

I didn't want it to be Brad because I'd dated him and didn't like to think I could be attracted to a man who could do such a thing. I didn't want it to be Oscar because I liked the way he got along with Delcie. I didn't want it to be Coreen because I really liked her style. I didn't want it to be Andrew because I wanted to believe in his rehabilitation, but in a pinch, he's the one I would pick because he was the one I was least attached to. He could paint in prison. He'd told me so himself. All I needed was evidence.

The food was another big difference. Instead of the sushi and imported beer I remembered from the earlier opening, this buffet table featured spicy chicken wings, pickled okra, French-fried sweet potatoes, and pitchers of iced tea. Once again, I found myself admiring Coreen. This menu might have seemed exotic to Atlanta art patrons, but it underscored the down-home, country roots of the featured artist and his work and, perhaps not incidentally, might have made him feel more at home. Even better from my narrow and selfish point of view, there were several things on the menu that Delcie would eat.

Clearly, Coreen had done a good job of pulling herself and her business together around whatever hole Tariq left, if he left a hole. This time, instead of contrasting the rough scrap sculptures with Andrew's dainty work, she'd come up with another kind of contrast—also metal, but jewelry, jewelry that had a southwestern, desert look—earrings, bracelets, rings, necklaces of intricate silver work, set with polished stones. Some of the larger pieces were mounted on the wall, some were shown off in Lucite cases on the floor.

I was pleased to see that Delcie was getting a kick out of the sculptures. I explained to her what Brad had said about not getting a clear look at the sculptures helping him appreciate them, and thereafter Phil and I had to hold on to her to keep her from bumping into things as she walked around with her eyes squinched up.

As we made our squinched-up circuit of the room, we found ourselves standing beside Brad Phipps and Andrew Lamotte in front of a small piece, almost entirely of chrome, that might have been a very large mosquito.

"Welcome, Trudy, and…Phil, is it? You didn't tell me you had a little girl," Brad said.

I was about to explain that I didn't have her all the time, just borrowed her for special occasions, but Phil cut in, "She's our first," he said, earning a perplexed look from Delcie and, no doubt, an exasperated one from me.

Phil pulled Delcie away, saying, "Let's go see what the jewelry looks like if we squint at it," leaving me to smile innocently at Brad.

"Looks like things are on track for the Upstart Gallery," I said. "I'll admit I'm a little surprised that you were able to talk Oscar around, all things considered."

"You can't afford to let emotion cloud your judgment in the business world, Trudy. Everybody has to do business with people they don't like personally," Brad told me.

"And bide your time and hope you can get 'em back another time," Andrew added. He was probably serious.

I turned to Andrew. "This jewelry isn't yours, is it?"

He laughed. "No, ma'am. Nostalgic oils are my specialty, remember? This is somebody from Arizona who got in touch with us—with Coreen—and Coreen thought the stuff would work with Oscar's."

"I think she was right," I said. "Two takes on metal work. I can dig it."

The knot of admirers around Coreen and Oscar was breaking up. Coreen glanced around the room. Catching Andrew's eye, she made a sharp movement with her head.

"The queen is calling," Andrew said. He and Brad moved in her direction and I went to join Phil and Delcie. I found them twisting their heads back and forth and squinting up at the unfinished elephant head I'd seen on my first visit to Oscar's place. It had been finished and was mounted on the back wall, where it looked like a monstrous trophy.

"We aren't at the zoo yet," I whispered. "Stop acting like monkeys."

We moved on to the large piece we'd seen through the window. Now I could see that it was a bare tree rising out of a pond. We'd passed dozens of natural examples of the scene on our way up that very day. This tree had a large bird on an extended branch. Even with my eyelids drooping I couldn't identify the bird, but it was definitely some kind of big bird. Around the base, rising out of the pond, were a few scraggy stumps.

The name of the piece on the card was "Three Jeeps," which we all thought was far too unimaginative. Phil suggested calling it "Frog Pond Pond" in honor of Oscar's church and converted bus, Delcie was holding out for "Big Old Tree," and I was trying to think of something clever of my own so that I could avoid taking sides, when Oscar joined us.

"What's that supposed to look like?" Delcie asked.

"What do you think it looks like?" he returned.

"A big old tree."

"Good. That's what I wanted it to look like," he said.

"I told you so," Delcie said to me and Phil, then back to Oscar. "Where'd you get the idea?"

"Just came to me," he said.

"Do you plan it out ahead," she asked, "or just start and see what it looks like?"

I thought Delcie was coming up with some really great questions, and Oscar was answering them seriously. I liked it that he was taking her seriously. And I liked it that I was learning without having to risk insulting him by asking a dumb question.

"I always have an idea in my head," he said. "Don't put nothing on paper, if that's what you mean."

"Is that supposed to be a specific kind of a bird, or just a bird?" I risked.

Oscar studied the sculpture as though he'd never seen it before, as though he, too, was trying to figure out what kind of bird it was. His silence dragged on. Could my question have been *that* stupid?

"What's the matter?" I asked.

When his answer finally came, I didn't understand it.

"She take the credit for so long, she can't get rid of the notion she really is the one makes these things? She think it makes it all okay? Makes her the real one if she changes it around some?"

"Oscar, I have no idea what you're talking about."

Delcie was standing openmouthed. Phil tried, "Don't you like the way they're showing off your pieces?"

Oscar might not have heard the question. He was in full

fume. "Calvin warned me. Shoulda listened to him. I'm not a big-time artist and I'm not a lawyer, but I get an idea in my head, I got it in my head, and sometimes I make somethin' out of it." He made a sweeping gesture toward the other pieces in the gallery. "And the idea I got in my head now is that all along they been takin' and keepin' what shoulda been mine—mine and Lettie's. That woman said Lester was cheatin' both of us; I say maybe not. Maybe it was her, all along! They been makin' money off what I been doin'. You call it sculpture or old car parts, it was mine. I made it and it was what I made that made 'em the money. Now what I made ain't good enough, she thinks she got to change it."

Good grief! For a man who was usually calm and controlled, even gentle, Oscar Jackson was working up to a real tantrum. I don't necessarily mind being part of a scene, but I do like to know what the ruckus is about. He was waving his booger stick, so we were all giving him plenty of room when I tried again.

"There's something wrong with the sculpture?" I guessed.

"What she do with the nest?"

Had the trip unhinged him? "What nest?"

"Up there on the limb, by the bird. Supposed to be a nest there."

There was nothing that could have passed for a nest up there. At least I thought I understood the problem now.

"Maybe there's a good explanation," Phil suggested. "Maybe it fell off."

"Don't worry," Delcie said, taking his hand. "If it fell off, you can put it back."

"Yes. Great idea," I said. "I'll bet it just fell off and they weren't sure how—or where—to put it back. Let's ask Coreen where it is."

We didn't have far to look for Coreen. Along with everybody else in the place, she'd been looking and listening to our little scene. She glided to Oscar's side, calm and self-possessed, as usual, her plumage settling gracefully around her.

"What's the trouble? Somethin' the matter, Oscar?"

He turned to her, waving the booger stick in the general direction of the metal tree limb.

"What you do with the nest?"

"Nest?" Her puzzlement looked genuine.

"For the bird." He planted the booger stick on the floor with a thump. I liked it planted. I took it for a deescalation in hostilities.

"There wasn't any nest," she said. Then she made the mistake of trying to joke about it. "What does that ol' scrap metal buzzard need a nest for, anyway?"

"He needs a nest because I gave him a nest!" Oscar thundered. I thought he was showing a surprising measure of artistic temperament for somebody who was merely an untrained backwoods native primitive artist. I could see a little of that temper he and the Lord were working on. Maybe he *could* have run down Tariq.

Coreen realized her mistake and became serious. "Oscar, I swear there was never a nest on there. You can ask the boys who helped me unload."

"I don't care who you get to swear and I don't care what they swear. I know what I know. I know it had a nest on it when you left my place with it."

They glared at each other. Judging that it was only a matter of seconds before the booger stick came into play again, I recklessly intervened, trying to make peace.

"Any chance you're mistaken, that you put the nest on a different piece?" I asked.

Oscar scowled.

I cast about for help and found Andrew. "Andrew was there when they picked it up, wasn't he? Maybe he'll remember."

"Oh, yeah, there was a hubcap there, something you might call a nest, on that branch, all right. Couldn't help but notice it when we were loading that thing. The one good place I mighta been able to get a grip and there was that stupid hubcap. No offense, Oscar."

Coreen shrugged her shoulders, setting her silk a-shimmer, and turned on her coquettish manner. "All I can *say* is I don't remember any nest, what-*ev*-er it was made out of. Maybe it fell off. It's a marvelous piece even without that, though."

"That's not the way I made it, not the way I wanted it," Oscar said stubbornly.

"We'll fix it, then. I *promise,* we'll look around for it in back just as soon as we get a chance," Coreen said.

"Maybe the bird with the nest flew to another tree and this is that tree," Delcie said.

Her fanciful engagement with the sculpture brought smiles and chuckles from behind us. More important, the situation was defused. The booger stick stayed on the ground.

The party was on the wane by now. Possibly everybody thought it would be downhill from Oscar's tantrum and if they wanted excitement they'd better go elsewhere. Noticing a yawn from my favorite six-year-old, I led our contingent to the buffet table for one more round of hot wings and we left for the bed and breakfast place that Phil and I use as our headquarters when we come to town.

The hostess beamed at us. "I have your rooms and the Special Occasion Suite all ready," she said. The special suite was for Oscar and his special occasion.

"Country ham, biscuits, spiced grapes, grits, and eggs any way you like them for breakfast," she said. This announcement was for the benefit of Oscar and Delcie, since it was the standard fare. The only variety Phil and I had ever noticed was in the kind of jelly or preserves she offered.

"Dream about the zoo tomorrow," I told Delcie when we were tucked in. Maybe she did. As for me, I dreamed that I was a bowling pin with dozens of hubcaps rolling at me, trying to knock me down.

I guess we enjoyed our visit to the zoo the next morning, but my mind was still on hubcaps. I was glad when we started home, and I was glad to see we were all—even Delcie—so tired or preoccupied that the ride home in the darkening afternoon was almost silent. We didn't even have to stop. We dropped Delcie off at home, Phil carrying her inside without even waking her.

By the time Oscar got out of the car in front of the junkyard, my thoughts had begun to fall into some order.

"Oscar, let's say that hubcap was on the tree and got lost." I was right in thinking I wouldn't have to clarify what hubcap I was talking about. "Could you replace it? Do you have another one?"

"You're asking me do I have another hubcap?"

Phil said, "She means do you have another hubcap just like the one that was on the sculpture?"

"Got three more."

"I tell you what, then," I said. "Let me have one of them. It's a long shot, but it might pay off." Long shots do pay off once in a while. That's why there's a need for an organization like Gamblers Anonymous.

"You want it now?" He didn't look eager to go get it.

"Can you find it in the dark?"

"I'll be right back." He sighed and made a show of

hobbling off. Too bad for him I'd learned what a faker he could be.

He was gone only a few minutes. He must have known exactly where to find it. I spent the time studying the lineup of vehicles for sale.

"What you want it for?" he asked.

"It might prove something," I answered. "Oscar?"

"What?"

"Is that truck in a different place than it was when we left yesterday?"

He didn't even look. "Might be. Sometimes people take it for a test drive."

"No kidding. Did somebody take it for a test drive the night Tariq was killed?"

"Coulda been. I don't watch it."

"Could it have been moved without your knowing it?"

"Maybe. Sometimes Cal brings people by who want to drive it."

"It's Calvin Simmons's truck?"

"That's right."

"He have any reason to want to be rid of Tariq, besides being a good friend of yours?"

"No." Oscar leaned on his booger stick and stared at me.

"It's been a long day," Phil said, starting the car and slowly pulling away from the angry old man.

On the way back to my place, as I cuddled the hubcap that might prove something, I remembered Calvin Simmons at the Frog Pond Baptist Church hissing out the name of Lessssster.

TWENTY

FIRST THING NEXT MORNING, Hen, Dwight, and I were looking at my collection of hubcaps, which I had spread out on the table in the file room.

I muttered one word that would have given Lou-Ella Purvis palpitations, but on the whole I felt I was behaving in a very mature way in view of the fact that the hubcap Oscar Jackson had brought to me the night before didn't match any of the others. Specifically, it didn't match the ones picked up near the death scene. It would have been so *tidy* from my point of view if the hubcap missing from the dead tree sculpture had fallen off when Coreen's truck collided with Tariq. It would have tied *somebody* to the scene! It would have been evidence!

"You got the hots for Tanner, trying to attract his attention?" Dwight asked, smirking insufferably and jerking his jaw toward the hubcaps. "This what you'd call your dowry?"

Dawn saved Dwight's life at that point by calling me to the phone.

"That Coreen called me on the telephone just now," Oscar Jackson informed me. "Says they found that bird's nest back in the back somewhere. Says she's having her boys load the thing up to bring down here so I can fix it."

I mentally said that offensive word again, revealing to

myself how much I had hoped that missing hubcap would mean something useful to our investigation.

"I think you must have gotten her attention with your tantrum at the gallery," I said.

"Uh-huh," he agreed. "She's bringing it down herself on Saturday. I think she's trying to make up with me."

"She knows a valuable commodity when she sees one," I said. "Don't let her dazzle you, now."

"I reckon I'm pretty much dazzle-proof," he said. I could imagine him hefting his booger stick.

"Good luck," I said. "And thanks for letting me know about this."

When I got back to Hen, Dwight, and the hubcaps, Dwight was grinning. He has a sixth sense when it comes to things I'm not going to enjoy.

"You remember those kids and us talking about having 'em do community service?" Hen said.

"Yes."

"We've got that set up. Seems like poetic justice to have 'em clean up a stretch of highway."

"Chain gang. That's what I said all along," Dwight said.

"Maybe it isn't a bad idea even if Dwight did think of it," I admitted. "Have you talked to the mayor about it?"

"Don't plan to, unless he brings it up," Hen said. "This is a police matter."

"He won't like it," Dwight said.

"Nope, I don't think he will, but if he kicks up I'll explain to him how much worse it could be," Hen said.

That's how it came about that the next Saturday morning found me supervising a group of four not-very-happy teenagers out on the highway north of town. I was in a foul mood and was determined to make the kids suffer to the full extent of the law. The deal was that the four kids were to clean up a mile-long stretch of highway, bringing in anything at all that wasn't supposed to be there. Considering that civic-minded people do this kind of thing on their own, I didn't consider it serious punishment, but it was something. At least it would show them they were accountable for their behavior. I tried not to think I was being punished (for what sins?) along with them.

Predictably, Merry was early, dropped off by her father just as I was finishing marking off the area they'd be cleaning up. Clint and Rusty came together and were just about on time. Becki was late.

It was a chilly morning and we'd actually have been more comfortable walking and doing a little physical work to warm up, but I wouldn't let anybody start until Becki got there. I told Rusty, the only one who complained, to take it up with Becki. I had decided it was my job to see that they fulfilled their punishment to the letter, and I was determined to see that all of them put in equal time. We waited in uncomfortable silence until Kathi drove up and let Becki out. I wondered if Becki was doing without driving privileges these days.

"Okay," I told them when we were ready to get started. "I'll put two of you at each end of our stretch. You're through when you meet here in the middle, unless I get the idea you weren't doing a thorough job. In that case, we start over. Everybody got that?"

Becki rolled her eyes, the boys shrugged, Merry nodded.

None of us was having a good time, but I tried to make sure they were having less fun than I was, making them sort whatever they picked up—metal, paper, glass, plastic, dead things. I cruised back and forth, keeping tabs and examining what they accumulated before they put anything into the trash bags I brought along.

My bad temper had made me separate the natural pairs, putting Rusty and Merry at one end, Clint and Becki at the other, to work toward the center. The four distinct personalities were highlighted once again in this activity.

I don't think Rusty, himself, for example, was especially attracted by (or to) dead things. I think he was bringing them up just for me—the flattened bird, three rotting fish, a well-gnawed T-bone. I'm sure Rusty was proud of the ant-ridden armadillo, and I'm afraid I hurt his feelings when I didn't examine it closely but instructed him to go ahead and put it in the trash bag himself.

Rusty, in his pursuit of something putrid, might ignore a plastic bag or a beer bottle. Merry, predictably, was conscientious. She picked everything up. I noticed that she turned her back to the highway whenever a car came along, obviously ashamed to be there.

On the other end of the designated area, Becki was ambling petulantly along just as though she expected her maid to come behind her and pick up. As a matter of fact, that's pretty much what Clint was doing. He might have been a robot. Equally impervious to her scorn and the shame of the situation, he was just doing what had to be done. A very mature attitude for one so young, I thought.

Returning from a run between one end of the cleanup area and the other, I found Clint, as usual, methodically walking the area between the road and the trees, bending every few steps to pick up something. Becki was nowhere in sight.

"Where's your buddy?" I called from my comfortable seat inside the car.

He looked at me and then cast a quick glance all around. "Looks like she disappeared," he said. He sounded surprised.

"Did you notice anything, like strange lights from the sky?" I asked.

He rewarded me with a smile.

"More likely she slid into the woods," he said.

It hadn't occurred to me that any of them would try to make a break for it. Maybe Dwight had been right about the chains. My thoughts must have been reflected on my face.

"She likes to sneak around for a smoke," he said. By now he was close enough to the car that we were talking at a normal volume. He dropped his voice to a whisper. "It's supposed to be a secret from the general public."

"Well, you've blown that," I said. "Telling the police."

He smiled again. "Especially a po-lice who's dating a newspaper."

It astonished me to learn that he knew that. Could it be that this young'un saw me as a person, not just an anonymous authority figure? Well, why not?

"I saw Mr. Bland's hunkajunk," he said, taking me by surprise again.

"Oh?"

"I liked it."

"I haven't seen it," I told him. "But I've seen some other things by the man who made it."

"Mr. Bland said the sheriff arrested him. Do you think he ran over that man?"

"Maybe, but I don't think so. We're still investigating," I said.

"Do you think he ever needs any help?"

This boy was full of surprises. "You mean with his sculptures? I don't know, but I could ask him next time I see him."

"Thanks," he said.

"Meanwhile, how about you go see if you can haul Becki out of the woods."

"Sure." He left with a smile on his face.

He was about halfway to the trees when Becki strolled out of the shade and into view, absolutely nonchalant.

"Pickin' up much trash?" I called.

With a transparently phony smile, she said, "I thought I saw some trash back in there."

If she had seen any trash, she hadn't brought it out with her. True to form, Clint bent over and came up with something.

I couldn't blame Becki for not wanting to touch it. It might once have been an attractive quilt, representing hours of some needlewoman's skill and artistry, but all that was left was a rotting mess. It had obviously been there through many seasons, its exposed cottony innards contributing to countless bird and squirrel nests. As we added it to the other trash, a faint bell rang in my memory. The muscle man at the Upstart Gallery—Ramon—had asked Coreen about a missing quilt. Something like that on the front of a truck, between the truck and the victim, could explain the lack of evidence of contact.

I was so pleased with where this thought was taking me that I, at least, enjoyed the rest of the hard time the high schoolers were putting in. I called Oscar to verify that Coreen had come down—with Ramon's truck—as planned, then I called Hen.

TWENTY-ONE

HEN CALLED THE CRIME SCENE technicians in Statesboro, gave them directions to J&D Salvage and Towing, and told them what we were looking for. They'd already gone over the truck without finding anything, but usually you have more luck on a treasure hunt if you know what the treasure looks like. Now we knew that if there was treasure here it would look like the unidentified fibers the lab had found on Tariq's body.

While Hen was setting things up with Statesboro, I wound up the roadside maintenance project and pronounced the teenagers finished with their penal servitude. I hit the highway for Oscar's place as quickly as I could, but was the last to arrive. Hen was talking with the Statesboro boys when I drove up. Ramon and the other muscle man I remembered from the Upstart Gallery were part of the same huddle.

"You already been over my truck," Ramon was complaining when I joined them. "This double jeopardy or something?"

"We ain't gone put your truck in jail, no matter what," Hen told him. The way he emphasized "truck" I think Ramon got the idea that he'd be smart to back off.

When Hen noticed me, he gestured toward the Quonset and we went inside, leaving Ramon and his sidekick to supervise the technicians. We found Coreen and Oscar in the workshop, gazing at the dead tree with the bird and the newly affixed nest. I wouldn't have thrown a tantrum about it, but I did think the thing looked better with a nest.

"Well, if it ain't the po-lice," Oscar said.

"Coreen, meet Henry Huckabee, Ogeechee's Chief of Police," I said.

"Don't arrest this old man," Coreen said, smiling generously at Hen, making a good impression as usual. "I'm figuring on him makin' both of us so rich we won't know what to do."

"Matter of fact," Hen said, smiling back at her, "we're more interested in talkin' to you."

"I already told you everything I know about this," Coreen said, gesturing at me but smiling at Hen.

"But what you don't know is we've got a bunch of technicians out there seein' if the truck can tell us something else."

"Didn't you already do that?" She was still smiling. Either she had a clear conscience or she had nerves of steel.

Oscar stood attentively, one hand on the booger stick, one resting on his sculpture.

"They're looking for fibers to match the fibers on Tariq's body," I said. Hen and I had discussed whether or not to tell her what we were after, and we had decided it couldn't hurt and might even help. If she'd done it, it might unnerve her enough to make her confess. We'd misjudged either Coreen or the situation. She squinted at me thoughtfully, then took on a distant, focused look that suggested, to me at least, furious thought.

"You know I was drivin' the truck, so if you find matching fibers—"

"Like from that missing quilt Ramon mentioned," I inserted helpfully.

"Then you'll quit lookin' for any other explanation, won't you?" Coreen finished.

"Uh-huh," Hen said.

I made it even more definite. "If we can prove that was the truck that killed Tariq you're in deep trouble."

"I don't care what you find, I know I didn't run him down. I drove away from here in that truck, that's right, I did, but there has to be some other way to account for it," she said, frowning. The silence stretched out, with Hen, Oscar, and me all watching Coreen. Then she suddenly brightened. "I know! Why didn't I think of it before! Andrew! It could have been Andrew! Must have been!"

"Andrew?" Hen asked. "We could talk about *why* Andrew, but the really big question is *how* it could have been Andrew."

I could practically see the starch coming back into Coreen's spine as she talked. "Andrew! Of course! Maybe if you looked you could find something to prove it was him. There are always clues, aren't there, at the scene of a crime, if you know what to look for?"

There was Andrew's distinctive bandanna, of course.

"He didn't mean 'How could we find evidence against Andrew?'" I said, not letting on how interested I was in her certainty that there'd be some. "He meant how could he have done it when you had the truck."

What seemed like a major objection to her theory didn't faze her. "Well, he knew where I'd be, where the truck would be. All he had to do was—"

"Whoa, hoss," Hen said. "What do you mean, he knew where you'd be? The way we got it, your story has been that when you left here you went right back to Atlanta. Seems like you'd have noticed if Andrew took the truck away from you while you were driving it. Unless you're saying the two of you were in it—the truck and the murder—together?''

"Murder? Of course not!" She gave a sensuous wiggle and sent me a sidelong glance. "But, you remember, I told you how ex-*cit*-ing I found Andrew? Well, after he left here that night, and then I left without Tariq, I called him up and suggested we get together before he went on down to Jacksonville.''

"You called him? How'd you do that?" Hen asked.

"On his cell phone. He always carries it with him when he travels, in case he runs into trouble with the bike or something. For a guy who looks so rough and tumble, he can be really con-*ven*-tional. I told him where to meet me, and I went there and waited, but he never did show up. Never did. When I asked him about it later, he said I told him somewhere else. Now I know why! While I was in there waiting for him, he came, all right, he just didn't come *in!* He came and got the truck and went off and ran Tariq down with it.'' Her eyes narrowed as though struck with a sudden thought. "Now that I think about it, I remember when I came out I *did* think the truck was in a different place from where I parked it. I didn't think much about it then, thought I was just imaginin' it. But maybe I wasn't! Maybe it had been moved!'' She flashed a sudden smile. "That's got to be what happened!''

I smiled back. "So we'll find that call when we check your phone records?''

Her eyes widened and she shook her head. "You don't believe me, do you? Oh, I wish I hadn't made that call from a pay phone! Then I could prove it!''

"Why'd you call from a pay phone when you had a phone with you?''

"Well, I'd stopped to get a sandwich and I'd left my phone in the truck. It seemed more convenient." She had it all figured out.

"Would that be before or after you picked up your gas receipt in Dublin?" I thought it was a terrific question. If she said she'd called Andrew *before* she got gas in Dublin, the next question was why hadn't she waited for Andrew closer to Ogeechee instead of leaving him farther behind. If she said she called him *after,* then that made a mess out of her story about calling him right after she left Oscar's.

"Hmm. I'll have to think about that," she said.

"Take your time," I said, sure she'd be able to explain it if she had enough time.

"Hey, in there!" It was one of the technicians.

"Hey," Hen answered. "You got something?"

"Oh yeah," the technician answered. "We went over both those trucks, like you said, and I think we found just what you were looking for."

I could have hugged him. Evidence at last! But which truck did it come from? If it was the 4 SALE truck, did Brad do it, using that blanket from the trunk of his mother's Miata to drape the truck? If it was Ramon's truck, did Coreen use (and then "lose") one of the quilts from the truck? Could her far-fetched story about Andrew be true?

TWENTY-TWO

MONTHS LATER, in what should have been springtime but felt wintery, a crowd gathered on the courthouse grounds for the unveiling of a monumental sculpture by that newly celebrated local artist, Oscar Jackson.

Our little corner of the art world had begun to settle down after the combined forces of the Atlanta and Ogeechee police departments and the Georgia Bureau of Investigation had built a good case against Coreen in the murder of Tariq.

I had asked Andrew about her story that she'd called him to set up a meeting.

"She's hot all right, and I might have gone for it, but if she called me I didn't get it."

"She says you carry a cell phone when you ride."

"I do, but I keep it off unless I want to make a call. Once when somebody called me it took me by surprise and I nearly went in the ditch, so I don't do that anymore."

It was such a flimsy story in the first place that it said a lot about Coreen's impact on me that I even asked Andrew about it.

When Coreen saw the way things were going, she put her undeniably fertile mind to work and came up with a story about how she'd regretted leaving Tariq behind at Oscar's and went back to get him but she was unfamiliar with the truck and ran over him instead and then was frightened and panicked. But it was an accident, truly, truly.

The only part of that I believed was the part about her going back. Coreen frightened? Coreen panicked? She'd have had better luck with that story if she hadn't draped the cowcatcher with a quilt and dropped Andrew's bandanna at the scene. I could easily imagine her saying to Tariq on the phone, "Now, Sugar, you be sure you're standing up by the road when I come by. I don't want to miss you." Or something like that.

I'd learned a lot about myself during this investigation. I already knew I'm often wrong about people. I hadn't known how vulnerable I was to razzle-dazzle, or how obvious it must have been to Coreen that I admired her and would have liked to be able to prove her innocence. And I learned that all that wasn't enough to keep me from doing the best job of police work that I could. By the time Coreen was through shinin' me on, or, as Hen might say, by the time she'd learned that this ol' dog don't do the buck, I wasn't even sorry to realize she'd have a rough time with her plea that Tariq's death was an accident.

We were all still waiting to see what the courts would make of it. In the meantime Brad and Andrew were making a good show of carrying on the Upstart Gallery. Working the publicity angle, Brad had convinced Oscar that offering one of his pieces to the town of Ogeechee would be a great public relations (and therefore a great business) move.

After much debate (I even went to some city council meetings myself, so I know how much debate), it was decided to accept the sculpture and to position it at the intersection of Main and Court streets, the most visible spot in the town, on the courthouse grounds. Naturally, there were differences of opinion—about the piece itself; about the prominence of the location; about the precedent; about the size, shape, and color of the thing; about whether it would constitute a traffic hazard, visual obstruction, or controversy; about anything you can think of, including whether the city wanted to have something that really didn't look like much of anything, donated by an artist they had heard of only in connection with a murder. Was it really art? Would it be an embarrassment? A white elephant? Would it rust?

Here's where Brad stepped in again, convincing enough of the city council that, whether they personally liked it or not, it would be a feather in the city's cap to have a piece by the renowned artist Oscar Jackson on display— a piece representing new thinking about art and the world, compared with the stodgy bronze statues of men on horseback that litter less imaginative cities all over the country. It isn't often a town like Ogeechee gets handed a chance to be *avant-garde,* so we went for it.

The arrangement—which made sense to me whether you looked at it from the Ogeechee point of view or the Oscar Jackson point of view—was that the piece would be on loan to the city indefinitely. That would let Oscar sell it if he wanted to and if the city didn't seem to appreciate it as much as they should, which was entirely possible.

The day for the unveiling had been set—and advertised in *The Atlanta Constitution* and *The Ogeechee Beacon*— well in advance, so we were committed to go ahead even when the sun reluctantly came up on one of those damply misty days that seems twice as chilly as it really is because you aren't prepared for it.

One of the nice things about a small town, unlike a big city where there's always something going on, is that everybody appreciates a break in routine and turns out for a special event. This particular event had the extra cachet of not even being one of the routine celebrations like the Easter Egg Hunt or the Cow Patty Bingo and Barbecue fund-raiser for the fire department on the Fourth of July. It was undoubtedly something special.

In consideration of the fact that the chief of police had exercised his discretion in the matter of how far he wanted to pursue some irresponsible teenagers driving off and failing to report their discovery of a dead body, and had been very understanding (not to say lenient) when the aforesaid teenagers had actually turned out to be helpful, for those and no doubt for less obvious reasons that he had decided would be politically expedient, Mayor Rhodes had declared the day Oscar Jackson Day.

It wasn't a huge crowd that gathered that chilly afternoon, but the City Council and the Frog Pond Baptist Church were well represented, as well as the county high school, the Geezerettes, the Ogeechee Police Department, the media in the person of representatives from the *Beacon* and reporters from art publications, and members of the general public who were attracted by the novelty and the promise of a free party afterward. The atmosphere, something between a carnival, a football game, and a revival service, bore little resemblance to any artist's reception I'd ever seen, which was not a bad thing.

Those of us who were gathered were warm with good feeling and, for many, a sense of accomplishment.

Of course those words—good feeling and a sense of accomplishment—speak volumes. On the good feeling side of the accounts we had the resolution of the murder case, which had proved to both Hen and me that I am a good police officer. So there.

Also on the good feeling side, I guess, Brad almost

made me raise my opinion of him. His publicity campaign called a lot of positive attention to Ogeechee and Oscar Jackson, and, oh yes, of course, but only in a minor way, to the Upstart Gallery. Even I had to admit that was fair. We all know it's an ill wind that blows nobody good, and the publicity about Tariq's murder and Coreen's guilt had inevitably included a full exposé of the way they had exploited Oscar's work.

Oscar had been balky about having a big to-do at first, but he became agreeable once Calvin Simmons helped him get it in his head that if he would be more or less cooperative with reporters and feature writers he could go about the sculpture business exactly the way he had been doing (because Calvin Simmons would look out for his financial interests) and he'd make so much money he'd be able to quit worrying about Lettie.

Once Oscar got used to the idea of a big fuss, he began to enjoy it. With a wonderful instinct for making the most of the moment, he had insisted that the only way he'd go along with the plans that seemed to him to be getting entirely out of hand was if his sister, Lettie, could be there. Lettie was there, a tiny, frail woman, who was solicitously looked after by the Frog Pond congregation whenever Oscar left her side. There was always somebody near Lettie's wheelchair, making sure she was well wrapped up against the weather and constantly assuring her that, yes, it was a wonder. "Well, my goodness!" she said over and over again.

My conversation with Clint Wacker by the side of the road during the community service stint had planted a couple of ideas. As a result of one of them, Molly Pittman's Craig Bland, working with the industrial arts teacher at the high school and Oscar, had enlisted a group of students to work with Oscar and help with the installation and the veiling of the enormous piece.

Community interest had grown with every day the wooden frame surrounding the piece was in place, patrolled by students who were taking seriously their charge to keep the sculpture under wraps. The secrecy involved would naturally appeal to teenagers and even the breaches of security, which were surely numerous, tended to heighten rather than diminish interest. From the school's standpoint, the kids would be learning something useful as they worked with the artist. As a bonus for the community, getting them involved with the project might just tend to reduce vandalism. I gave Craig high marks for civic spirit, imagination, and initiative. From what I gathered watching Molly Pittman flitting around the high-school group, the Pittman-Bland romance seemed to be on track and I was very happy for Molly.

Phil Pittman was flitting all over the place with his camera, getting pictures for the *Beacon* and for my scrapbook. Phil's smart, hardworking, and talented, and it isn't often he has to exert himself at all at running the *Beacon*. Today, though, he was enjoying hobnobbing with the out-of-town media. I was happy for him, too.

The weather was too forbidding for Mr. Pittman. He had gone straight to Kathi's Koffee Kup, where the after-party would be held, and was waiting there. His romance with Lou-Ella Purvis had withered. Phil said it withered when the Geezerettes once again put their swim party on indefinite hold and there was no need to butter up the *Beacon* for coverage. I think it withered when Mr. Pittman learned to play mah-jongg on the computer and didn't need to have a checkers partner. Neither Phil nor I think Mr. Pittman and Mrs. Purvis had an actual falling out, but even if they did, I was happy for Mr. Pittman.

The program wasn't long, but of course Ozzie Rhodes had to speak.

"As mayor of Ogeechee"—this must have been for foreign media, since the locals surely knew who he was— "I want to welcome you all to a truly historic moment in our town's history. Recent events have put Ogeechee in the limelight. I won't dwell on the more unpleasant events. Y'all know what I'm talking about, and our fine police department under Chief Henry Huckabee did a good job of taking care of that."—as though Hen did it all, and single-handed—"No, I won't dwell on that. I'll move instead to the cause for celebration, the unveiling of this unusual sculpture we're about to unveil here. But you've heard enough from me"—more than enough— "so let's hear from the man who made this monument, Mr. Oscar Jackson."

The Frog Pond group made themselves heard, but they were by no means the only ones who clapped enthusiastically at this point. The general level of applause might have made a more thoughtful man than our mayor wonder if it was pro-Jackson, anti-Rhodes, or merely an effort to warm up.

I knew Oscar hadn't wanted to talk at all but the ubiquitous and influential Calvin Simmons, supported by Brad, had persuaded him with a three-pronged attack: it was his due and a chance to correct the idea that Coreen was the sculptor; his friends would bask in his reflected glory; and he owed it to Lettie. Oscar had bowed to this pressure, but he hadn't gone so far as to hire a speechwriter.

He stood, booger stick in hand, and spoke. He didn't need notes for his few words, and it was obvious he meant what he said, no more and no less, and the presence or absence of cameras and reporters was apparently a matter of no interest to him. He certainly didn't kowtow.

"I don't talk much. Everybody knows that. If I did talk, nobody'd want to hear it. I'm up here now because I made this thing to show how I honor my sister, Lettie. Lettie says she likes it and I'm glad she does. If anybody else likes it, that's fine, but that isn't why I made it."

Then he climbed down off the dais and went to stand by his sister. Say what you will, simple sincerity will almost always be more compelling than glib hot air.

Somebody gave a signal and the people who had been stationed at the sculpture began pulling on ropes. The sides of the protective enclosure fell away, revealing "Lettie." She was huge. Goodness knows how many derelict cars had to be dismantled to produce the towering figures of what I took to be a woman and a child. The woman-figure stood almost twelve feet high, if you counted the wire coils that made up her hair, and she was, apparently, unclothed, not that it mattered. She was not, as we say in artistic circles, representational. From the engine block that comprised her torso dangled a number of symbolic items—an old flatiron, a treadle from a sewing machine like the one in my back room, a washboard, a cook pot—symbols of the life of an aging black woman.

I fought my way through the protective crowd around Lettie. As I approached, I could hear Oscar. "Lettie, I'm glad you're here today to see this. I'm glad everybody who goes through this town will see it."

And Lettie, softly. "You called it after me? I don't see the likeness, but it might be my glasses. It's pretty big, isn't it?"

"That's how big you are to me," Oscar said. "How strong, how powerful. That's how you look to me, Lettie. This is how I'm saying thank you."

I gave them another moment before I intruded. "I'm Trudy Roundtree, Mrs. DeLoach. I'm so glad you could be here for this and I could meet you in person. I might not have recognized you from your portrait here." She smiled up at me sweetly. "Congratulations to you both," I said. "I know you don't enjoy all this hoopla, Oscar, but you deserve it. Are you ready to go on over to Kathi's? You'll be warmer."

Oscar stood tall and looked away. "No. I don't think we'll want to go over there. Me and my friends got somewhere else to go."

In the past months I'd gotten used to his manner. Still, I was puzzled and a little miffed at his abrupt bad manners. I'd thought he had come to terms with being the center of attention for the day. Was he worried about Lettie overdoing, in spite of the fact that she seemed to be enjoying herself? He could have said so. Then I followed Oscar's glance to the big neon sign over Kathi's Koffee Kup. The mist and gloom of the day obscured almost everything about the sign but the huge capitals.

My sense of good feeling and accomplishment vanished as quickly as a puff of breath in the chilly air. Caught up in the occasion and all it stood for, I'd forgotten how different the community looks from different points of view. I couldn't think of anything to say. I nodded and moved away.

TWENTY-THREE

THE KOFFEE KUP WAS already crowded by the time Phil and I got there. I suspected that some of those who had come to the courthouse out of a sense of civic duty instead of an interest in sculpture had been attracted by Kathi's desserts, as a reward for enduring the ceremony at the courthouse.

Kathi had really put herself out. The lunch counter was lined with pie plates, the pieces sliced into slender wedges so that people could sample several without hurting themselves too much. Pumpkin, mincemeat, apple, peach, pecan, coconut cream, chocolate cream, banana cream, icebox lemon, lemon meringue—everybody's favorite was there somewhere and as soon as a pieplate emptied, an efficient Kathi, a sullen Becki, or a friendly volunteer replaced it with a full one.

Tables had been pushed together on the opposite side of the room to make a buffet for the salty things—boiled peanuts, salted pecans, cheese-and-sausage bites, biscuits with biscuit-sized slices of ham and sausage. At the back of the room stood a table with pitchers of iced tea, a bowl of sweet punch, and pots of coffee.

It was a bewildering array of food, but I always know where to start. Phil went for the coffee while I put two of the skinny slices of pecan pie on a plate for myself, took a piece of apple and a piece of lemon meringue for Phil, and made my way to where Mr. Pittman sat in his wheelchair working through a pile of boiled peanuts.

"Everybody in town must be here," he said, smiling broadly. He does love a party.

"Just about," I said, recognizing the overstatement for what it was and not wanting to point out a few conspicuous exceptions. As I scanned the room to see who was there, I noticed Tanner Whitcomb sidling in the door, attracted by the free food, no doubt, as well as a sense of ownership about the occasion. He and his hubcaps had, after all, been involved in the case from the discovery of the body right down to the end. He had with him the ever-present bag of who-knew-what. He put it under one of the biscuit tables, out of the way but where he could keep an eye on it, and then grabbed a plate and headed for the pies, all without meeting anybody's eye.

Dwight loomed above us with a plate loaded with ham and biscuits.

"Hey, Dwight." Phil had come into view with two cups of coffee.

"Thought you were one of these women thinks she's as good as a man," Dwight said, grinning at me. "But here you are having a man wait on you. I call that hypocritical, wantin' to have your cake and eat it, too."

Before I could decide if I wanted to waste a piece of good pecan pie by dropping it on Dwight's shoes, Phil said, apparently innocently, "Here's your coffee, Trudy. What kind of pie did you get me?"

It may have been too subtle for Dwight, but I appreciated it. I was suddenly hit by a debilitating wave of appreciation for Phil. I gave him my best smile along with his plate. I realized only then how tired and even let down I felt with the murder investigation behind me with all its ups and downs. My eyes misted over and I looked away.

I didn't want to have to try to explain to anybody what on earth I had to be crying about. Looking down and away, so that I wouldn't meet anybody's eye, my gaze happened to light on Tanner's bag. Was it a trick of my unshed tears, or was it moving? Was he still bearing a grudge about the hubcaps? Could he have smuggled some kind of an animal into the party with evil intent? I blinked hard and took a steadying bite of pie before I looked again. I still couldn't be sure, but it took my mind off my mood and offered a way to get rid of Dwight.

"Dwight?"

"Hmm?" he said around a mouthful of biscuit.

"Is Tanner's bag moving?"

He sucked a tooth while he studied the bag as well as he could through the shifting knots of people. Then he nodded, set his plate down on the table behind us, and made his way across the room toward the bag.

In spite of all the attention he'd been paying to the food, Tanner must have been keeping a close watch on his bag. He reached it about the same time Dwight did.

It was hard for me to make out what was happening, but I did hear Dwight: "Whatcha got in the bag?"

And Tanner: "Nothin'. Just my stuff."

And Dwight again: "We got health laws about what kind of stuff you can bring into a restaurant. I'm gonna hafta take a look."

Tanner's voice rose. "Police harassment. Police harassment."

"I'll show you police harassment, Tanner," Dwight said, then remembered where he was. "I just want to check his bag," he explained to whoever else was listening. Most everybody had inched away from the two men, leaving an open space like a stage around them.

In the silence that followed Dwight's explanation there

came the unmistakable cry of a cat. It was followed by the unmistakable cry of Delcie. "Paws!"

Teri elbowed her way to Delcie's side, on the edge of the circle around Tanner, Dwight, and the bag. She folded her daughter into her arms. "No, sweetheart. Paws is gone. If this is a cat, it's another cat."

The cry sounded again. Dwight looked triumphant. There was an animal in there! Tanner looked confused. Then he saw me and pointed.

"It's her cat," he said. After Dwight had talked to Tanner about my rash of flat tires and missing wheelcovers and that mischief stopped, I'd so thoroughly quit thinking about Tanner that I'd put the missing cat down to accident or some other mischief-maker. Maybe it had been Tanner. Maybe it was Paws in the bag. Maybe we really are going to have to do something about Tanner.

"Outside," Dwight ordered. "We're not opening a bag of wild animals in here."

He was right. There could have been anything from a rabid squirrel to a skunk in that bag. Dwight seemed to be enjoying himself. He made everybody stay inside while he took the bag outside and took his time about opening it.

For a moment there was nothing. Delcie, at the window, was jumping up and down with impatience. Then a black leg with a white paw snaked its way through the opening. Then another. Then a face. Dwight picked up the bag and emptied it onto the sidewalk. A cold, frightened cat hunkered down outside of Kathi's Koffee Kup. A cheer went up inside.

"Paws!" Delcie was through the door, with Teri right behind her. The cat was not so frightened or cold or nervous that she didn't recognize Delcie. The two came together like magnets.

I made my way to the reunited pair in time to hear Teri say, "We'll take her home, Delcie. I've got in mind a really good place for her."

"I thought you were allergic," I said. "I don't mind keeping her. I—"

"Pause," Hen said from somewhere behind me. I don't know how I knew he wasn't saying "Paws," but I knew and I paused to think. That's when I realized my trouble with Teri was rooted not so much in jealousy of Hen, but of Delcie.

"But I do have other cats," I finished.

This turn of events called for another piece of pie. Craig Bland was studying the array of pies when I reached the counter.

"Have you seen Oscar?" he asked.

"Not since the courthouse," I said. "He said he had somewhere else to go."

"Shoot! I thought I'd catch him over here. I wanted to let him know the school approved that internship program we talked about."

"The internship program? Great!" The pies were forgotten for the moment.

"Isn't it? Actually, it turned out that Mr. Wacker was more of an obstacle than the school district. He doesn't like the idea of Clint doing anything that doesn't seem to be directly related to job training, and he doesn't like the idea of him working with Oscar. Hen helped convince him," Craig said.

"Y'all quit hoggin' the pie," Hen said, having materialized behind me.

"I was telling Trudy about your talk with Mr. Wacker," Craig said, backing away from the counter.

Hen oozed in to take Craig's place. "I explained to the man how the police like to keep an eye on troublemakers and a good indication that a young'un is on the straight and narrow is if he's responsible enough to hold down a job. A job? Somehow Wacker had missed the part of the deal where Oscar would be paying Clint. Made a big difference.''

"Good," I said, watching to see how many pieces of pie Hen would be able to get on that little plate. "Good for Clint. Even if it does sound a little like you blackmailed his daddy.''

Hen looked at me with Delcie's innocent eyes and cross-stacked a piece of pecan pie on top of the rest of his collection. "Kathi's sure got a touch with pie crust," he said.

I merely took two pieces of cherry pie, one for me and one for Phil, and returned to Mr. Pittman, who had finished his peanuts.

"I've about had all the partying I can handle," he said, "but before I go home I want to ask you something, Trudy.''

"Ask away," I said.

"I've been reading everything about this murder case of yours in the *Beacon*, but that paper just doesn't have the investigative edge it used to have. It doesn't tell me everything my inquiring mind wanted to know.''

Phil tried to look insulted.

"What do you want to know?" I asked. "Ask me anything.'' Amazing. The appearance of a ball of fluff had turned me from tired, let-down, and misty-eyed to vivacious, powerful, and omniscient.

"This murder."

"I'm the expert on it," I said, knowing that Hen was across the room with Teri, Delcie, and Aunt Lulu, and

Dwight was off dealing with Tanner, so there was nobody handy to contradict me.

"Did that woman set out all along to murder her husband and frame somebody else?"

"I don't think so," I said. "I don't see how it could have been premeditated, not too far in advance. She probably took advantage of circumstances when he called her and they arranged for him to be waiting for her by the bridge."

"Why'd she want to kill him?" Mr. Pittman asked. "For runnin' around? Sounds like she was pretty free about that, herself."

"No, I don't think it was that. It might have been a part of it, but it turns out he was making deals behind her back, stealing from her like he was from Oscar and Lettie, and really was undermining the business that meant so much to her. She couldn't stand that."

"But she tried to make it look like Andrew had done it, didn't she?" Phil interjected. "Why did she want to frame Andrew? I thought they were, as Daddy would say, an item."

"They may have been an item of sorts, but I never got any sense that their connection went beyond the physical," I said.

"Unlike my attraction to Trudy, which is based almost entirely on her spiritual beauty," Phil said to his father.

Mr. Pittman and I both put down our forks and stared at him. Phil blinked at us.

I recovered first. "Uh. She may not have been especially trying to frame Andrew, as much as she was trying to give us somebody else to look at in case we needed suspects. Andrew didn't seem to be particularly hurt."

"A very forgiving nature," Mr. Pittman said.

"Or a sadly cynical one," I agreed. "The truth is, I

don't think Coreen really cared who we hung it on—Oscar Jackson, Brad Phipps, Andrew Lamotte, even Becki Harvey—as long as it wasn't her.''

"Where is old Brad, anyway?" Phil asked. "Didn't he come to the party?"

"No. He hopped in his mama's little Miata and headed back to Atlanta. He has bigger fish to fry now that he's done his part to promote Oscar. How did he put it? Oh yes. He's sure Oscar and 'Lettie' will do for Ogeechee what onions did for Vidalia."

"I didn't mean to change the subject," Phil said.

"You were talking about how she tried to frame Andrew," Mr. Pittman said.

"Well, she found that bandanna of Andrew's in the truck and I'm thinking she left it with the body, in case we needed a clue. It obviously had to have been planted."

"What do you mean?"

"The truck knocked Tariq off the bridge and he fell and rolled up against the pilings. How could the driver's bandanna have gotten down there, under him?"

We all shook our heads at the obvious impossibility.

"It's still hard to believe it was Coreen," Phil said.

"Yes. She was so good, so convincing, so cool. It must have taken iron self-control for her not to overplay it. She was willing to leave us alone and see where the investigation took us, as long as it wasn't in her direction. Any more questions?" I asked, enjoying my authoritarian status.

"No," they said.

It was getting late. Phil and I helped Molly and Craig bundle Mr. Pittman and his wheelchair into their car and went back inside to collect Phil's camera.

We walked back toward the courthouse where we had left our cars. "Lettie" loomed in the dark.

"It'll be interesting to see what she does for the town," I said.

"She'd be enough to make me behave," Phil said. "Maybe she'll reduce speeding through the intersection."

"She'll probably cause accidents because people will be gawking instead of watching where they're going. You know, Phil, there's something about her that reminds me of my grandmother."

"The spine of steel? The will of iron?"

I laughed. "Could be. She'll be here a while. Maybe I'll figure it out. In the meantime, I think you ought to know I've had enough of the art world and Atlanta for a while."

"No problem," he said, adjusting his glasses. "We'll just think of something else."

"Something that will allow me to display my spiritual beauty?" I asked.

"I was afraid you'd missed that," he said.

"I'm a trained investigator," I reminded him. "I don't miss much."

At least he didn't laugh.

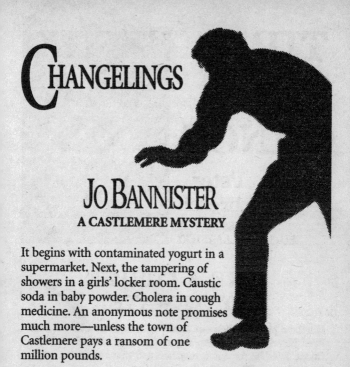

CHANGELINGS

JO BANNISTER
A CASTLEMERE MYSTERY

It begins with contaminated yogurt in a
supermarket. Next, the tampering of
showers in a girls' locker room. Caustic
soda in baby powder. Cholera in cough
medicine. An anonymous note promises
much more—unless the town of
Castlemere pays a ransom of one
million pounds.

Superintendent Frank Shapiro, recovering from a bullet
wound, has been cleared for desk duty. But with Sergeant
Cal Donovan on holiday cruising the Castlemere Canal,
he must rely on Inspector Liz Graham as hysteria rises.

The situation worsens when the detectives learn Donovan's
abandoned boat has been found—and that the volatile
sergeant is believed dead by the hand of the blackmailer....

Available February 2002 at your favorite retail outlet.

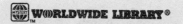

INTIMATE MOMENTS™

Where Texas society reigns supreme—and appearances are everything!

When a bomb rips through the historic Lone Star Country Club, a mystery begins in Mission Creek....

Available February 2002
ONCE A FATHER (IM #1132)
by Marie Ferrarella
A lonely firefighter and a warmhearted doctor fall in love while trying to help a five-year-old boy orphaned by the bombing.

Available March 2002
IN THE LINE OF FIRE (IM #1138)
by Beverly Bird
Can a lady cop on the bombing task force and a sexy ex-con stop fighting long enough to realize they're crazy about each other?

Available April 2002
MOMENT OF TRUTH (IM #1143)
by Maggie Price
A bomb tech returns home to Mission Creek and discovers that an old flame has been keeping a secret from him....

And be sure not to miss the Silhouette anthology

Lone Star Country Club: The Debutantes

Available in May 2002

Available at your favorite retail outlet.

CRIMES OF

Passion

Sometimes Cupid's aim can be deadly.

This Valentine's Day, Worldwide Mystery brings you
four stories of passionate betrayal and deadly crime
in one gripping anthology.

Crimes of Passion features FIRE AND ICE,
NIGHT FLAMES, ST. VALENTINE'S DIAMOND,
and THE LOVEBIRDS by favorite romance authors
Maggie Price and B.J. Daniels,
and top mystery authors Nancy Means Wright
and Jonathan Harrington.

Where red isn't just for roses.

Available January 2002 at your favorite retail outlet.

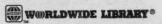

WCOP